Wild Card

Wild Card

A NOVEL BY

RAYMOND HAWKEY and ROGER BINGHAM

STEIN AND DAY/*Publishers*/New York

First published in 1974
Copyright © 1974 by Raymond Hawkey and Roger Bingham
Library of Congress Catalog Card No. 73-91858
All rights reserved
Designed by David Miller
Printed in the United States of America
Stein and Day/*Publishers*/Scarborough House, Briarcliff Manor, N.Y. 10510
ISBN 0-8128-1683-8

We would like to thank Dr. Richard B. Fisher for his contribution to the long debates from which the detailed plot of this novel finally emerged. It was reassuring to have the advice and guidance of someone so well acquainted with American affairs and, at the same time, fascinated by the world of science; he first noticed the research paper that sparked off the concept of memory molecules and suggested how it might be used as an element of the story.

But most important, perhaps, was his encouragement—often forcefully applied—during the period of writing.

R.H., R.B.

Be well advised, and think what danger 'tis
To receive a prince's secrets: they that do
Had need have their breasts hooped with adamant
To contain them. I pray thee yet be satisfied;
Examine thine own frailty; 'tis more easy
To tie knots, than unloose them: 'tis a secret
That, like a lingering poison, may chance lie
Spread in thy veins, and kill thee seven years
  hence.

> *The Duchess of Malfi*, Act **V**, Scene ii

Wild Card

1

THE SHOCK WAVE RATTLED the windows in the White House and set the chandelier in the President's bedroom tinkling. He stirred, and his eyelids began to flicker.

He was dreaming. Dreaming that it was Thanksgiving and he was a child once again, back in the old house. They were all there, his parents, brothers and sisters, uncles, aunts, and cousins—even his wife and children. Everyone, in fact, except Jack. And although in his dream he was no more than six, it was he who had prepared lunch. He didn't know why, except that it had something to do with the time: it was thirty-one minutes past eleven.

As he finished serving and took his place between his parents at the center of the oval mahogany table, he realized that the setting of the dream had changed. They were now all in the Cabinet Room of the White House.

The chatter subsided and he clasped his hands in front of him as his father began to say grace. Although no one, so far, had noticed that his brother was missing, he began to feel afraid. He turned his head and saw

9

that the meat on his mother's plate had begun to pulsate. Now very frightened, he watched as she slowly picked up her fork and began to probe the meat.

Suddenly, as though an artery had been severed, it began to bleed. Horrified, she dropped her fork and started back, her hands and face and the front of her white lace dress spattered with blood.

His father stopped speaking and, along with everyone else in the room, stared accusingly at him. He began to panic; he knew something terrible was about to be done to him. It was all so unfair, he thought bitterly. If he had not killed his brother and served the body to them, they would themselves have died . . .

Somewhere a bell had begun to ring. The President reached out, fumbling for the red telephone on his bedside table.

"I'm sorry to disturb you again, sir." It was the Situation Room duty officer, and it was the third time he'd had to wake the President that night. "But we've just had word that they've taken out the Lincoln Memorial."

The President heaved himself up onto his elbow, rubbing his eyes. "The *what?*"

"The Lincoln Memorial. It looks like they tunneled under the defenses."

"Was it a nuke?"

"I'm afraid so."

"Christ!" said the President, suddenly wide awake. "Was it clean?"

"We think so. It was planted deep down and was small—not more than one eighth of a kiloton according to the seismic signal. Just enough to prove they weren't kidding—"

"And without any real risk of a white backlash." The President groaned. "Exactly the way Nadelman said it would be."

There was a rap on the door and his valet entered the room carrying a tray. He laid it on the bedside table and crossed to pull aside the drapes. Mingling with the dawn chorus the President could hear the distant wail of police and ambulance sirens. "What about casualties?" he asked, shielding his eyes against the light.

"The guys in the tanks seem to be okay, but that's about it, I'm afraid."

The President watched as his valet poured coffee and shook out a napkin. "Listen, I'm leaving for Cleveland in"—he glanced at his watch—"just under two hours, and I want a full report before I do." He replaced the telephone, wondering whether he was about to be sick. It had been the threat of a "people's" bomb that had convinced him of the need to have a think tank examine the wave of civil disturbances within the United States. And it had been Dr. Richard Nadelman, his science adviser, he'd asked to head it.

They had met to discuss it at the end of January. It had been late at night and in the Yellow Oval Room, the President remembered. Waving his highball glass at the reams of internal security reports and memoranda that lay scattered across the yellow carpet, he'd said to Nadelman, "I want you to take a long, hard look at all this crap and tell me who—if anyone—I'm supposed to listen to.

"I don't want poetry, and I don't want a lot of shit about historical inevitabilities—just tell me what I'm supposed to *do!* Because the way things are going, pretty soon I'll have not just one, but all ten fingers in the dike!

"It's going to be an eyes-only operation, so if you think I've got a McNamara or a Bundy or a Rostow in my shop—say so!"

While he'd waited for Nadelman to reply, he'd fixed himself the third—or maybe the fourth—drink he'd had since Nadelman's arrival. With anyone else he'd have had to watch his step. It had been around then that the old joke about him being a computer with alcohol in his circuits had started up.

But with Nadelman it hadn't mattered; he wasn't a gossip, like so many on the Hill, *and* he was loyal. Not a sycophant—he would never have kissed his, or any other president's, ass in Macy's window at high noon, as Johnson had demanded. That was what made him so valuable; not only could he see the forest for the trees on almost any issue, but he was prepared to tell it like it was and damn the consequences.

"For the kind of operation you're talking about," Nadelman had said, "I'll need a sociologist, a cultural anthropologist, certainly a psychologist—there's a guy over at Walter Reed who'd be first-rate—a wargamer, a systems analyst, and an historian."

They had talked until the early hours of the morning. "One last thing," the President had said, as he walked with Nadelman to the elevator. "I don't want you, or any of the guys you convene, going to Interior or Defense for information. Anything you want, ask *me* for it. Type the report yourselves. No stenographers. No carbons. And for Chrissake don't let anyone near a Xerox machine!"

The study group had operated from within the National Security Agency's headquarters at Fort Meade, and had been given decision-critical facilities. It had taken a month to prepare the report, which had been handed to the President the previous evening.

As he had expected, the group's analysis of the factors which had led to the present crisis was brilliantly incisive. And although it had obviously been careful to avoid value judgments, he was gratified to find no suggestion that he, or any member of his administration, had been responsible for what had gone wrong.

But what had knocked him sideways was the appendix to the report. It had been prepared subsequently by Nadelman with the assistance of the psychologist from Walter Reed. Based on the study group's general conclusions, it had proposed an alternative plan—code-named Wild Card—for dealing with the crisis. He'd had to read it several times before he'd been able to convince himself that he wasn't imagining things. Outraged, he had dismissed it as the work of madmen and gone to bed, determined to bust Nadelman's ass the next day.

But had he dismissed it, he now asked himself? The dream seemed to suggest that he had not.

Alarmed, he swallowed two Libriums with a mouthful of the now tepid coffee and picked up his internal security adviser's overnight status report.

There had again been rioting in a number of major American cities, but the scene of the fiercest fighting was still St. Louis. Forty-eight hours earlier he had federalized the Missouri National Guard and authorized the use of Army paratroopers in the city. One of the decisions he would have to take before he left was whether or not to declare St. Louis a major disaster area, the thirteenth that month.

The report concluded: "Apart from the events detailed above, racially motivated, disruptive, and disorderly incidents continue throughout the Nation."

He threw the report to one side and, ignoring his daily news digest, reached for the pile of papers on the silver breakfast tray.

Today would be the first time he had left Washington in almost a year, and all of the papers—with the exception of the *St. Louis Post-Dispatch*—had led with the story. In spite of the massive security arrangements, he knew that rewrite men throughout the country would be making the final updates to countless stand-by versions of his obituary. In fact, several of the editorials—particularly those in the *Washington Post* and the *New York Times*—already read like obituaries.

The last paper in the pile, the *Denver Post*, carried a cartoon that attracted his attention. The President's tall, athletic body, handsome face, and warm, empathetic personality, made him a difficult man to caricature. Over the years a stereotype had been evolved depicting him as having a shock of unruly hair, an aggressively square jaw and eyes as lugubrious as a bloodhound's.

The *Post*'s cartoon showed him as the captain of a Mississippi sidewheeler that was breaking up in a choppy, shark-filled sea, the surface covered with stars and stripes. Huddled in the stern was the terrified crew—he recognized the faces of several of the more caricaturable members of his cabinet—and a number of passengers drawn to look like archetypal Middle Americans. He was shown leaning over the ship's gunnel, grinning inanely and dripping oil from a can labeled LEGISLATIVE PROGRAM. Written on the sides of the largest and most ferocious-looking sharks were the words KU KLUX KLAN, VIETNAM VETERANS, BLACK STATE, DE MAU MAU and COMMIES. The caption said simply: OIL ON TROUBLED WATER.

He flung the papers angrily to one side and got out of bed. When he had showered and dressed he crossed to the door of the First Lady's bedroom. Not sure whether she would be awake yet, he opened the door quietly, just wide enough to look into the room without disturbing her.

She was sitting up in bed drinking coffee and reading a letter. She took off her glasses and looked up. They kissed and he sat on the edge of her bed.

"And what time did *you* get to bed?" she asked, studying his deeply lined, tired face.

"Just after one. You've heard about the Lincoln Memorial?"

She nodded. "Darling," she said, in a manner calculated to ensure he'd pay serious attention to what was to follow. "I know I said I wouldn't mention Cleveland again . . ."

The President smiled. "But?"

13

She took his hand, anxious to seem neither scolding nor petulant. "If you have to go, couldn't you let me at least drive with you to Dulles? And why Dulles anyway? Wouldn't it be quicker and safer to take the chopper to Andrews?"

He sighed, and began picking at the rose-patterned bed hangings. "Not you too? I've already had a long lecture on victimology from the boys in the Secret Service detail."

She shook her head sadly. "I think you're crazy," she said. "Risking your life to open a water-purification plant!"

He shrugged, as if inclined to agree. "I just feel that anything I *can* do to make things look better than they are, I *must*—particularly after what happened this morning." He glanced down at his watch. "I guess I'd better make a move," he said reluctantly.

They kissed and he left. As he closed the bedroom door he knew that he had brought to an end, once and for all, the weeks of talk about whether or not it was safe for him to leave Washington.

It was a bright, beautiful morning, and as the President stepped out of the ground-floor elevator he decided he'd walk through the Rose Garden to his office in the West Wing. Taft had called the White House the loneliest place in the world, but for the President, one of the persistent irritations of the job was the difficulty he experienced in *ever* being alone. It had been bad enough at the start of his term, but since the fall riots the Secret Service detail had been doubled and the mansion's police force augmented by a company of Marines. Uncomfortably aware of the two Secret Service agents following him, he walked down the steps of the South Portico, then paused for a moment under the budding magnolias. He looked across at the fountains in the middle of the park. The sun, emerging from the low-lying mists over the Potomac, had created a rainbow in the spray being carried across the circular pool by a light southwesterly breeze. Except for the glacis and the moat that now surrounded the park, the watchtowers and the searchlights, the armed guards and the gun emplacements, it was a scene that would, it occurred to him, probably have delighted a nineteenth-century landscape painter.

Although the United States Weather Bureau had forecast a noon temperature in Washington that would be in the middle seventies

—eighteen degrees above the average for March—it had not yet warmed up, and the President was relieved when he at last entered the Oval Office.

He had outraged the White House Historical Association by removing from the room every trace of its traditional furnishings. Gone were the elephantine furniture, the blue oval carpet woven with the Great Seal of the United States, and Peale's portrait of George Washington that had dominated the room from above the white marble mantelpiece.

The President had argued that he could most easily hear what a predecessor had called "the quiet voices, the inner voices—the voices that speak through the silences" by surrounding himself with remnants of his country's rural and maritime past. The vigor and unembarrassed patriotism of its early folk art was, he liked to believe, what America was still fundamentally all about.

The white walls and ceiling of the Oval Office, the glowing wood-block floor and the well-chosen pieces of modern American furniture were a perfect foil for his magnificent collection of early tradesmen's signs and figures, scrimshaw, sternboard eagles, and weather vanes.

He stopped to admire his latest acquisition, a ship chandler's sign once common on the eastern seaboard, before crossing to his long white-plastic and stainless-steel desk.

He sat down and began to work his way through the letters and memoranda which had been transcribed and typed during the night. He was dismayed to find fifty letters of condolence to the next of kin of troops killed in counterinsurgency operations. A year ago he had made a point of writing such letters personally; now he had no alternative but to delegate the task. And he knew that if casualties continued to escalate, it wouldn't be long before even his signature would have to be written by an automatic stylus.

As he signed the letters a phrase in one of them caught his eye. ". . . a life cut short that was rich in achievement and promise . . ." He read the letter through from beginning to end—it was to the mother of a National Guardsman—and looked up the boy's background. He shook his head incredulously, struck out the line and scribbled in the corner of the sheet: tone down. With the best will in the world, you really could not say that about an apprentice butcher from Wichita Falls.

15

He put the letters to one side and switched on his dictating machine. He had almost worked his way through a pile of telegrams, diplomatic cables, and intelligence reports when his appointments secretary came through on the intercom. "Are you ready for Dr. Nadelman now, sir?" she asked.

The President frowned. "What the hell's he doing here?"

"You asked to see him, sir. His appointment was for seven-fifteen."

The President felt his hands begin to sweat. He had not only completely forgotten the appointment but, it occurred to him, he had probably unconsciously extended his dictating session so that there should be no time left in which *to* see Nadelman.

He glanced down at his watch and swore. "I'm due to leave in five minutes. Right?"

"Yes, sir. Would you like me to set up a meeting with Dr. Nadelman for a later date?"

The President hesitated, wanting to put the meeting off but, at the same time, wanting to get it over with.

"No," he said wearily. "I'd better talk to him. Would you let Security know he'll be traveling with me to the airport? I'm afraid they're going to have to do a bit of reshuffling. I want to talk to him alone."

"St. Louis?" she prompted.

"Of course, St. Louis! You'd better try to raise the governor. And then find out what the hell happened to the report on the Lincoln Memorial bombing I asked for!"

The President pushed his sunglasses tight against the bridge of his nose as he emerged from the shadow of the West Wing office colonnade and began walking down the path to the driveway. He was closely followed by the Signal Corps officer whose job it was to carry the thirty-pound metal case that accompanied the President at all times. It had been public knowledge for many years that the case contained the program for a nuclear retaliatory strike against a foreign aggressor. But what hadn't been known, until television commentator Douglas Wallcroft had revealed it six weeks earlier, was that the case now also contained codes and contingency plans to be used in the event of a revolution within the United States.

Ahead of the President, clustered around the waiting cars and buses, were the political advisers, military aides, press attachés, and personnel from the White House Communications Agency, secretarial pool, and Secret Service detail who would travel with him to Cleveland, as well as staffers from the West Wing office, there to see them off.

The President made his way through the crowd, smiling and waving, saying "Hello" and "Good morning," and climbed into his armor-plated Lincoln Continental.

It was several minutes before Nadelman appeared and climbed into the car. He slumped onto the seat next to the President, his knees apart and his belly rising and falling as he breathed. A quivering jowl hid the knot of his tie and much of the collar of his crumpled shirt. His eyes, nose, and mouth seemed small and absurdly close together. He peeled off a pair of steel-framed glasses which left livid indentations in his temples, and wiped his face with a handkerchief. "Well, I don't know where they're getting their plutonium from," he said, in a voice that was curiously thin for a man of his bulk, "but they sure as hell know how to use it!"

The President said nothing, watching Secret Service agent Hal Botha unfurl the small American and presidential flags mounted on the front fenders.

"You know what this means?" Nadelman continued, stroking the top of his almost hairless head. "It means that suddenly they can pack the punch of a trainload of TNT into something no bigger than that!" He nodded at the black leather attaché case that lay on the ledge in front of the President. "Think about *that* for a minute!"

Botha took his seat alongside the chauffeur and picked up the telephone. He looked around to reassure himself that all was in order and spoke briefly into the receiver. The police motorcycle escort moved into position and began revving up their powerful V-twin motors. Botha nodded to the chauffeur and the convoy moved slowly away.

The President returned his sunglasses to his jacket pocket and opened the case. Inside lay Nadelman's report, its white cover bearing the presidential seal and the words EYES ONLY THE PRESIDENT. He lifted it out and began flicking over the pages as though they were contaminated.

"I'll level with you, Dick," he began. "I've been badly frightened many times during my term in office, but this"—he slapped the report in a derisory manner with the back of his hand—"this *really* scared the hell out of me!"

"Mr. President, we're in trouble," said Nadelman. "We're seesawing into a civil war. The operation we've code-named Wild Card," he continued, pointing a thick finger at the report, "is the one thing that just might head it off."

The President stared at Nadelman, disbelief on his face. "You want me to authorize the premeditated murder of American civilians, and the best you can say is that it just *might* head it off?"

Nadelman breathed on his glasses and cleaned them with the corner of his jacket.

"If it's to be convincing," he said. "We make that point in Summary and Conclusions. Page two twenty-eight."

The President found the page and folded the report back on itself. Holding it in one hand, he began to read aloud in a voice that made the sentences sound faintly ridiculous. "It is the opinion of this committee that the reunification of the United States can best be achieved, in a manner that is politically and economically viable . . . ." The President looked up. "What the hell is a Wild Card, anyway?"

The science adviser turned to look out of the window. "It's a term used by wargamers to describe an unpredictable event likely to have far-reaching effects on the outcome of a game."

They were now on Pennsylvania Avenue, and the cars had slowed to three miles an hour as they bumped over the first set of antigetaway ramps. Overhead a gunship waited for the convoy to pick up speed again, its doorgunners anxiously scanning the roofs below for snipers.

Nadelman stared out at the bullet-pocked buildings—now painted black up to second-floor level to make it harder for gunmen to pick off Army patrols at night—and the boarded-up windows, the aerosol slogans, the barbed wire and the stacked sandbags, the signs warning that unattended cars would be blown up by the security forces. He stared and wondered what *would* convince the President that something more than a road show was needed to save a country dying of self-inflicted wounds.

The President turned back to the report and began reading again. "While it is to be regretted that credibility can only be given to the alternative enemy gambit by the premeditated and random destruction of American citizens, the casualty figures envisaged would be only a fraction of those incurred during a large-scale armed insurrection." He paused and looked up at Nadelman. "Incidentally, this is page two twenty-eight and there're no figures mentioned."

"I didn't say there were!" snapped Nadelman. "I said they'd have to be *convincing*. The figures are on two thirty."

The President gave up. "But," he said incredulously, "you're asking me to kill Americans!"

"To *save* Americans. Isn't that what wars are all about?"

The President tossed the report contemptuously back at Nadelman. "And another thing, it would cost too much."

"This country sacrificed fifty thousand American lives in Vietnam," snorted Nadelman, "and one hundred and eight billion dollars in the pathetic belief that—"

The President cut in. "Christ, Dick," he said. "You could have come up with a better precedent than Vietnam!"

"I'm not putting Vietnam forward as a precedent," he protested. "There were no precedents to help Truman decide whether or not to drop the bomb, and none to help Jack when Russia put her missiles up in Cuba."

"There's one good precedent for *not* going ahead—'Watergate!' "

Nadelman waved away the objection. "Amateur night! I'm talking about—"

"All right, all right," said the President irritably. "Supposing we did go ahead—can you be sure of coming up with a package that'll stand examination by an international team of scientists? Because we'd have to let the U.N. in on it if we want it to look kosher. And just what's it going to cost? There's a limit to how much I can load the supplementary appropriations. And if—*if*—we went ahead, what about security—who would I use? If word of this ever got out I'd be drawn and quartered on the floor of the Senate!"

"Security," Nadelman conceded, "*is* a problem, but it's not insurmountable. And as far as funding is concerned, the money can be obtained openly through the cover project."

Nadelman looked quizzically at the President and handed him back the report. "Just how much of this *have* you read?" he asked. "Both these points are dealt with fully on pages two ninety-six through three seventeen.

"You ask whether or not it'll stand up to expert examination. I'm confident that it will. It's worth remembering that it took scientists nearly forty years to discover that the Piltdown Man was a fabrication. And the guys who pulled that one, Mr. President, didn't have anything like our resources!"

The police motorcycle escort switched on their sirens. Ahead, sparkling in the sun, were the traffic tower and glass-fronted terminal building of Dulles International Airport.

The President tossed the report back into his case and snapped the lid shut. "Dick," he said sadly, flicking the wheels of the case's two brass combination locks, "it's clever. Damned clever. But I can't do it. I just *can't*!"

As the convoy came to a standstill beside Gate 25 on the heavily guarded emplaning ramp, the President suddenly stiffened. "Christ," he said to Hal Botha, "you boys sure weren't taking any chances! Closing the access roads and overpasses I can understand, but this . . . !" He nodded angrily toward the vast public parking lot, deserted now except for a handful of Army personnel carriers. "I'm in enough trouble already without having everyone using Dulles this morning hating my guts!"

The crowd behind the police lines at the far end of the building greeted the President's appearance with a slow, derisory handclap.

The presidential party began to file aboard the mobile lounge that was to take them on the mile-long journey to the parking apron. Preceded by two Secret Service agents, the President and Nadelman walked through the lounge and sat down on a bench directly behind the driver's cabin, a position which placed them away from the windows and as near as possible to the emergency stairs.

If his proposal had been rejected, why, Nadelman asked himself, had he been asked to ride out to Air Force One? It must mean, he decided, that the President was still open to persuasion. The lounge was now full and the engine had begun to tick over. The doors at the terminal end were closed, and a moment later the lounge began to move.

"Mr. President," he said, "I'm sorry. Believe me, I really am sorry." He spoke quietly, choosing his words with care, so that even if he was overheard it would not matter. "I can do no more than present you with our diagnosis and recommend surgical procedures. You're the patient's legal guardian, and you have to decide whether you want us to attempt a heart transplant or carry on with the leeches."

The President nodded, his face grave, but said nothing. Nadelman waited for a moment, then turned and looked out the window. They were now, he guessed, more than halfway to the jet parking apron.

Suddenly the air brakes hissed and the lounge began to decelerate. The two men, puzzled, stared blankly at one another. Hal Botha, the Secret Service agent standing nearest the President, tensed and someone at the rear of the lounge yelled, "What the hell . . . ?" From inside the driver's cabin came a crackle of instructions over the control tower loudspeaker. Although no one in the lounge could make out what was being said, there was no mistaking the panic in the speaker's voice. Botha, alarmed, started to turn toward the cabin door. He froze. Another mobile lounge, traveling in the opposite direction, appeared alongside.

Immediately, several men dressed in white TWA overalls and carrying automatic rifles appeared at the windows of the second lounge, smashed the glass, and opened fire. The noise was deafening. One cluster of bullets thudded into the driver's cabin and the engine, another tore the tires on the right-hand wheels to shreds. The presidential lounge heeled over, throwing its passengers violently to the floor, one on top of the other, and began to fill with smoke. People shouted and screamed as another burst of fire showered them with broken glass. One of the bullets struck a window stanchion on the opposite side of the lounge and was deflected, with a high-pitched whine, back inside. Misshapen and with much of its force spent, it smashed Hal Botha back against the door of the driver's cabin, tearing away his entire lower jaw.

The President, pinned between Nadelman and the side of the lounge, looked up and saw, to his horror, that the wound had exposed all of Botha's upper teeth. They were white and even and, except for two right molars which—he remembered—had troubled Botha only a month earlier, free from fillings.

Botha began sliding slowly down the door, finally splashing into a pool of his own blood, his head lolling forward and his legs splayed out in front of him. The only indication that he was still alive was a pulsing cluster of blood bubbles where his mouth had been.

The Secret Service agents began to disentangle themselves from the mounds of struggling bodies. "The M-16s!" one of them began shouting above the noise. "Where the fuck are the M-16s?"

Two more Secret Service agents had begun scrambling over the bodies in the aisles, treading on hands and faces in their frantic attempt to get to the emergency exit. "Down!" screamed one of them, dragging the President out from under Nadelman and onto the floor, while the other smashed the glass in front of the door-and-stairs locking release. The two Secret Service agents dropped to the ground, slipping and sliding in the oil pouring from the vehicle's broken fuel lines, and took up positions at either end of the lounge. Using the shot-up wheels as cover, they lay flat on the ground, holding their Colt Pythons in a double-handed grasp. Each cocked the hammer, took careful aim, and squeezed the trigger twice in rapid succession. Two of the men at the windows of the lounge opposite disappeared as though they had been struck by a jackhammer.

There was a moment's lull as the men's companions ducked out of sight. One of the Secret Service agents scrambled to his feet and began running toward the commandeered lounge. He had covered less than half the distance between the two vehicles when a Negro holding a grenade launcher appeared at one of the windows. The agent lying on the ground fired and the black face exploded in a cloud of red vapor.

Immediately, two more men—one black, the other white—appeared at the windows at either end of the lounge.

Both agents fired at the white man. The man under the lounge was the first, by a fraction of a second, to realize what had happened. He spun around, aimed at the Negro, and squeezed the trigger. Nothing

22

happened. His revolver was empty, and with no time to reload, all he could do was yell a warning at his companion.

The man in the middle hesitated, recollections flashing through his mind of the day he had been confronted by the same situation electronically simulated at the firing range of the FBI Academy at Quantico. And on that occasion the adjudicator had pronounced him dead.

The Negro aimed his AK-47 and fired. The 7.62-millimeter bullets ripped through the agent's chest, sending him spinning backward, his arms outstretched, as though playing blindman's buff. He collapsed a moment later, blood gushing from a gaping exit wound in his back, as his killer was cut down by a fusillade of shots from the presidential lounge.

The tires of the assassins' lounge blew out and it rolled over like a dying elephant, blood dripping from bullet holes punched into its side at floor level.

More Secret Service agents were now racing toward it, and a voice, amplified by a loudspeaker, called to the assassins to come out with their hands above their heads. There was no response.

Without waiting for the order to be repeated, one of the agents pulled the firing pin from a CS gas grenade and lobbed it through a window.

There was a muffled bang, and the white gas began to billow through the windows and the bullet holes in the vehicle's side. Someone inside began to retch.

By the time the President, limping from a sprained ankle, was allowed out onto the roadway, the two mobile lounges were surrounded by police cars and Army personnel carriers, fire engines and ambulances. Nearby, medics finished threading an endotracheal tube into Hal Botha's lungs before rushing him away in an ambulance.

Now that he was outside, the President noticed several small white splinters embedded in his jacket. Puzzled, he picked one of them off and began rolling it between his finger and thumb. It was a fragment of bone from Botha's jaw.

Picking his way through the broken glass and the shell cases, his eyes red from CS gas, he began looking for Nadelman. He found him several minutes later sitting forlornly in the shadow of the ambushed lounge, his back resting against one of the wheels. He had been sick down the front of his jacket and, unable to find his handkerchief, was attempting to wipe off his vomit with his bare hands.

"Are you okay?" asked the President, handing him his own handkerchief.

Nadelman, his face ashen, nodded.

The President reached into his pocket for his sunglasses, but the unfamiliar shape he encountered told him there was no point in taking them out. He looked around, shielding his eyes from the sun with his hand. "You know," he said, "I'm beginning to think we *may* have to do something pretty damned drastic . . . ."

2

Douglas Wallcroft—described by *Time* as "the greatest virtuoso of the electronic front page since Walter Cronkite"—was tall, broad-shouldered, and possessed the rugged good looks a model agency would have categorized as "middle-aged man of distinction."

He had just finished breakfast on the terrace of his Long Island home when he heard what sounded like a tray full of china crash to the floor inside the house. He groaned. Breakfast always seemed to be the occasion for a domestic crisis and he waited for the inevitable raising of voices. He was not disappointed.

"Mr. Wallcroft. Oh, my God, Mr. Wallcroft!" It was the maid calling from the kitchen. "Mr. Wallcroft!" she shrieked. "They've killed the President!"

Why he thought she meant the president of the television network that carried his daily news background program, *Countdown*, was later to be a subject for prolonged discussion with his analyst. Even before he had started to run toward the house, he had begun to compile a list of possible successors, subdividing them into "barracudas" and "good guys.'' The barracudas were the men who would, in the interests of economy and even higher ratings, try to give him a bad time; good guys were the ones who would leave him alone rather than risk rocking the boat.

Wallcroft delivered an audience of twenty-four million every night, five nights a week. But his was a tough business and nobody, he believed, was ever so big that he couldn't be screwed by barracudas who got into the higher echelons of management. He had been through all that a long time ago when WABC-TV had dreamed up the format for *Eyewitness News*. Almost overnight, authority-figure anchormen like himself were out. In their place came a new breed of what had been called ''journalistic japesters'': teams of young, informally dressed newscasters who projected a happy-go-lucky, just-folks image and read lines on a TelePrompTer in a way that made them sound like ad libs. It had not been Wallcroft's scene at all, and he'd had to eat a lot of dirt to stay in the business through its *Laugh-in* phase.

But one by one, the happy-talking high-fliers of the early seventies had burned out as events, too somber to be treated as a laughing matter, forced them back to earth. And week by week, news beat by news beat, Wallcroft had reestablished his reputation until once again he had been able to function as a journalist.

Wallcroft threw open the kitchen door just as his four-year-old daughter switched channels on the television set. The picture now on the tiny, color-saturated screen was of a dancing carton of cornflakes.

He turned to the maid. She was trembling and staring at the television set as though she expected it to explode.

''Debby!'' he yelled. ''What the hell's going on here?'' She immediately burst into tears. Pressing her apron to her face, she stumbled into the garden sobbing hysterically.

Wallcroft started after her, but stopped when he heard a man's voice say: ''We interrupt this program to bring you an important news flash.''

Kicking aside his wife's breakfast tray, he grabbed at the television set—but not quickly enough to stop his daughter from once again switching channels.

Ignoring her screams of rage, he turned up the volume and switched back to the channel transmitting the news flash.

The newscaster was reading what Wallcroft recognized as rip-and-read copy—a story that had just come up on an agency teletype machine that the news editor rated too big to hold while it was rewritten.

". . . a mobile lounge carrying the President and members of the White House staff was fired on within the last half hour as it was transporting the presidential party from the terminal building of Dulles International Airport to the jet waiting to fly them to Cleveland.

"The President, together with Prime Minister Pelling of Canada, was due to open the controversial nuclear-powered water-purification plant on the shores of Lake Erie later today.

"Eyewitness reports from Dulles confirm that there *have* been a number of casualties but it is not yet known whether any members of the presidential party were among them."

Stunned, Wallcroft tried to remember whether anyone from *Countdown* had been sent to cover the President's departure. Probably not, he decided. Cleveland was where he had believed an attempt on the President's life might be made, and Cleveland was where most of his camera crews and reporters now were.

He snatched the receiver from the wall-mounted telephone and inserted the repetory dialing card for his office. All he got was a curious pulsing sound. He tried again. While he was waiting for something to happen, his wife came running into the kitchen.

"Douglas! Will you please tell me what on *earth* you think you're doing?" she demanded, picking their daughter up in her arms. Between sobs, the child began to give her side of the story.

Wallcroft pressed his hand to his ear and strained to identify the unusual noise coming from the telephone. He suddenly realized that it was a slow dial tone caused by a massive overload at the exchange. He had encountered it only once before, the day that Jack Kennedy had been assassinated.

"You have upset Rosemary and God knows what you've done to Debby!" his wife was saying. "In case you've forgotten, your parents are coming to dinner tonight, and if Debby walks out on me now *you're* the one who'll have to do the explaining!"

"Shut up!" Wallcroft shouted. He thrust the telephone at his wife. "Here—stay with this until you get a line, call my office, and *don't* let them hang up on you. I'm going to try to get them on the car telephone."

He returned to the house several minutes later, having failed to get through from his car, and hurriedly dressed.

Making no attempt to tell his wife he was leaving, he ran back to the car, climbed in, and turned the ignition key. With a great roar, the Lamborghini Uracio GTX shot forward, its rear wheels throwing up a shower of gravel. Cursing himself for having left it in gear, he spun the steering wheel but was unable to avoid plowing a furrow through the circular shrubbery in front of the house.

As he shot past the electronic scanner that opened the gates at the end of the driveway he remembered—too late—that it was about now that King's Point was due for a four-hour-long power cut. He was still furiously pumping the brake pedal when the car hit the heavy wrought-iron gates.

Immediately, the air bag in the steering-wheel housing inflated with a noise like a shotgun blast. That, thought Wallcroft as he struggled with the billowing plastic, is all I needed.

Any advantage he had gained by his sixty-mile-an-hour drive out of Kings Point was—in spite of gas rationing—soon eroded by the density of the traffic he encountered on the Long Island Expressway. The car telephone was still not working, despite a thirty-dollar repair the previous day, and he was not yet within radio transmission range of his office in Rockefeller Plaza.

Stuck in traffic near the Van Wyck cloverleaf, he lowered the passenger-side window and leaned across to ask the driver of a cab standing alongside if he had heard the latest from Dulles. But he changed his mind when he saw the man's hand slide toward the sawed-off shotgun lying on the seat beside him.

As he waited, ID card in hand, to pass through the Queensboro Bridge checkpoint, the wind blowing down the East River was rank with the smells of untreated sewage, rotting garbage, and smoke. Particles of soot, carried across the river from fires still burning in Harlem, began to settle on the windshield.

He reached into the glove compartment for a rag, opened the door and began to climb out. His foot had barely touched the ground when a National Guardsman, armed with an automatic rifle and a bullhorn, shouted, "Get your ass back into that heap, mister!"

A line from a song in a movie he had seen as a boy came into his head, something about New York being a wonderful town. That might have been true once, he thought, as he sat looking across at the skyline of midtown Manhattan rising triumphantly from the smoke haze. But strikes, bombings, rioting, and looting had long since turned New York into a stinking, dangerous jungle.

That morning he had read of yet another baby being bitten to death by rats less than five minutes from his office. And the number of typhoid cases in the city had risen alarmingly during the weekend.

The police officers who searched Wallcroft's car before allowing him through the toll gate did so with the cold eyes and laconic manner of a pit crew at a Grand Prix circuit assessing a rival entry. Satisfied that it contained no illegal firearms, explosives, or subversive literature, they spent several minutes discussing the Lamborghini as though Wallcroft were not present. After agreeing that it was overrated and not worth the money, they allowed him back into the car and waved him through.

Wallcroft drove up to the toll gate, tossed three quarters into the basket, and accelerated onto the bridge.

Now at last within transmission range of his office, he lifted the transceiver microphone off its hook, switched on the set, and called in.

Wallcroft's dayside assignment editor, Russell Gorman, replied.

Wallcroft adjusted the volume and put the microphone to his mouth.

"Russ, this is D.W." Wallcroft's wife was the only person who called him by his first name. "What the hell's happening?"

"You tell *me!* Where are you?"

"On the Queensboro. What's the story?"

"Right now it's anybody's guess. We've just heard Wall Street has shut up shop, but there's nothing coming out of Dulles."

"Have we got a crew there?"

"There's one on its way. Hold it a minute . . ."

Christ! thought Wallcroft. What's the point of sending a crew *now*? He turned up the volume and tried to filter something meaningful from the background clutter. He heard Gorman yell at somebody, "Will you get out of the way, for Chrissake!"

Wallcroft blasted a warning at the driver of a Mustang who was trying to pull in front of him, made a heel-and-toe gear change, and roared down the ramp. But a moment later he was forced to reduce his speed drastically as he was bounced around by a section of road badly pitted by tank tracks during the night.

"D.W., it's Russ again. WCBS has just put out footage of the

President leaving Dulles. He seems to be walking with a limp, but the word is that he's okay.''

"Is that supposed to be good news or bad?''

Gorman laughed. "It's just come through that the Cleveland game has been rained out.''

Wallcroft thought for a moment. "You know what, Russ,'' he said. "Maybe today *is* the day—God damn it—to let the general see what we've gotten hold of!''

3

It had been a terrible day. An editorial in the *Washington Evening Star* had, the President knew, summed up the situation all too accurately when it described him as having "tried—disastrously—to prove that he had tamed the tiger by putting his head in its mouth."

He got up from behind his desk in the Oval Office, poured himself a bourbon, and took it across to one of the sofas beside the fireplace. It was nearly seven, and he switched on his four television sets to watch the evening news shows.

It was as though he had opened an electronic Pandora's box. Channel 4 was transmitting the eight-millimeter film of the two mobile lounges—lying alongside each other like ships of the line exchanging broadsides—that by now, he guessed, must have earned a fortune for the amateur cameraman who'd shot it.

Channel 7 was showing film of a paratrooper splattered with blazing napalm.

On Channel 26 troops wearing antiradiation suits were picking over the ruins of the Lincoln Memorial.

And on Channel 9 Douglas Wallcroft was mouthing silently in front of a screen on which was projected a photograph of the Statue of Liberty, its head and upraised arm shattered by a terrorist's bomb.

The President was about to switch the sound to Channel 9 when Wallcroft was replaced by the program's titles. Instead, he switched to Channel 4 and a voice behind the Dulles film began to say: ". . . a member of the White House Communications Agency and the five heavily armed attackers—all believed to be members of the Revolutionary Alliance—died in the seven-minute-long gun battle.

"The question being asked tonight is: How and when did the gunmen gain admission to the heavily guarded—"

That's a good question! thought the President, flicking the sound through to Channel 7 as a photograph of a dollar bill riddled with bullet holes appeared behind the newscaster. "As the first rumors of this morning's nuclear bombing percolated through onto the floor of the New York Stock Exchange," the newscaster was saying, "a deluge of panic selling tumbled prices to their lowest level this year."

The film on Channel 26 had been replaced by a newscaster whose face was unfamiliar to the President. Curious, he cut away from the Wall Street story. "And in Pittsburgh," the woman was saying, "steel mills began shutting down furnaces in anticipation of the threatened strike by the United Steelworkers Union. Meanwhile, East and Gulf Coast longshoremen were today told to prepare for new strike action as union leaders flew to Washington for last-ditch efforts to—"

The President shook his head sadly and switched the sound back to Channel 7 as a photograph of him appeared on the screen. "A Gallup poll published today," the newscaster was saying, "shows the President's popularity to be at an all-time low. Eight out of ten Americans now believe—"

The burning soldier was back on the other screen, trying to beat out the flames with his bare hands, and the President once again switched the sound. "Army paratroopers were today rushed into riot-stricken St. Louis at the request of the governor and mayor. This brings the number of troops now in the city to twelve thousand." A film of helicopters disgorging flak-jacketed paratroopers was replaced by shots of a blazing tenement building sinking into a cloud of dust and sparks. "The scene of the heaviest fighting," continued the newscaster, "is still the racially tense Chase Park area of the city."

Hoping for a moment's respite from the torrent of depressing news, the President switched to the film of a wedding reception that had come up on Channel 4. "An eighteen-year-old stenographer who lost both legs and an arm in a Baltimore dance hall blast last fall was today married in—"

Sickened, he cut back to Channel 26. "A weekly newsletter published by the Democratic Congressional Committee," said the woman, "attacked the President today for what it calls 'the astounding incompetence with which he is handling the crisis in the U.S. economy.' The report went on to say—"

Wallcroft had now reappeared, and the President switched off all the sets except the one carrying *Countdown*.

"Tonight," Wallcroft began, "*Countdown* presents a special report examining the events leading up to today's nuclear bombing of the Lincoln Memorial and the attempt on the life of the President. Events which have confronted the United States with the most serious internal crisis since Confederate troops fired on Fort Sumter in eighteen sixty-one."

The President sat up, suddenly alert, as a photograph of the Chairman of the Joint Chiefs of Staff appeared on the screen behind Wallcroft. "But first," Wallcroft said, "the big story in a day that's had more than its share of big stories.

"Highly placed sources in Washington are tonight predicting the imminent resignation of Chairman of the Joint Chiefs of Staff General James P. Hinshaw.

"What lies behind the fifty-eight-year-old general's decision is not yet known, but it is believed to be connected with the tapping of his telephone, together with those of a number of other high-ranking Army and Air Force officers, by an as yet unnamed government agency during the fall of last year.

"Since nineteen seventy-two, it has been necessary for the government to obtain a court order before it can tap the wires of persons it believes to be a threat to the internal security of the—"

Cursing, the President snatched the receiver from the telephone console beside him and jabbed the button that would connect him with his press secretary. "Where the hell did Wallcroft get the story about Hinshaw resigning?" he snapped.

"Probably from Hinshaw," suggested his press secretary. "Somebody leaks the story of the wiretap to Wallcroft, and Wallcroft gives it to Hinshaw on the understanding that Countdown gets first bite at it—"

"What wire tap?" demanded the President. "Nobody told me about any wiretap!"

"They didn't?" His press secretary sounded suddenly very flustered. "But I thought the Attorney General—"

The President broke the connection and, without replacing the receiver, glanced back at the screen. Wallcroft was still on camera and saying: "General Hinshaw has made no secret of his growing dissatisfaction with what he regards as the President's dovish handling of the internal-security situation. It was in response to the general's demands that Congress should be asked to declare the existence of a state of insurrection within the United States that the President, in a coast-to-coast TV appearance last month, said"—a section of the video tape of the broadcast appeared on the screen—" 'Let there be no doubt in the mind of anyone—we are *not* fighting a war, but endeavoring to cure a disease. A disease of democracy. And the choice I have had to make was not, as some would have you believe, a choice between idealism and realism, but between good medicine and bad.

" 'I am therefore resolute in my determination to allow no more force to be employed than is absolutely necessary to assure the maintenance of law and the enactment of this administration's legislative program. To do otherwise would be to infringe on those very rights that I, as your president, am sworn to uphold and defend.'

"Whether or not the general will decide to throw his cap into the ring as a presidential candidate," Wallcroft concluded, "the fact remains that his decision to resign, and his reasons for doing so, will be a grave embarrassment to an already severely embarrassed administration.

"We'll take a short break now. *Countdown* returns in just a moment with this evening's special report: *Anatomy of a Crisis*."

Angrily the President turned back to the telephone console as a government-sponsored commercial selling the advantages of law and order appeared on the screen, and buzzed the Attorney General's office.

"Is he there?" he demanded. "Well, find him and have him call me back."

He slammed down the telephone and, trembling with rage, sat staring at the screen. As the pictures flashed by, the old, familiar phrases oozed out. Phrases which plotted the steady rise on the national fever chart—freedom ride, civil rights sit-in, antiwar demo . . .

Inevitably, the film shot by Abe Zapruder outside the Texas Book Depository appeared on the screen, and the President turned away, busying himself by mixing another drink.

By the time he had finished, pictures of armed guards and citizen patrols were on the screen, intercut with newspaper ads for hand-held sirens, tear-gas pens, and signs reading "No cash kept in this office," "This house electronically protected," "Operator does not make change."

"And as street crime continued to escalate," Wallcroft was saying, "so did the trend toward citizens banding together for self-protection. Urban planners began talking about 'defensible space', the media about 'Fortress America.' "

A light on the telephone console had begun to flash, and the President picked up the receiver.

"I have the Attorney General on the line for you, sir," said his secretary.

"Put him on," he replied. "Then hold all interruptions for ten minutes."

There was a brief pause and the Attorney General, sounding shaken, was on the line.

"Where are you calling from?" asked the President.

"Bethesda Hospital. My wife's—"

"I know, I know. Have you heard the news? Well, get your ass over here on the double. Use the west basement entrance," the President added. "I don't want anyone thinking that sonofabitch has us on the run." He was about to hang up when he heard the Attorney General call his name. "What is it?" he growled.

"Mr. President," the Attorney General said, "I swear to you this was done without my knowledge or consent. The parties concerned were severely reprimanded—"

"Save it for the grand jury," the President replied grimly. "I know we've been friends for a long time. But if you've gotten me into another Watergate I'm going to have your head.''

The President put down the telephone as pictures of himself shot during the primaries appeared on the screen. Without taking his eyes from the screen, the President bent over to massage his aching ankle and found himself thinking again about the conversation he'd had with Nadelman that morning. The unlawful tapping of the chairman of the JCS's telephone was bad enough, but that he should have even *discussed* the plans for an operation like Wild Card would, he knew, be a catastrophe of Wagnerian proportions were it ever to become known.

The screen had filled with shots of him taking the oath of office on the steps of the Capitol, while Wallcroft—off camera—listed the bills which had been passed during his first year in office.

"Activists," continued Wallcroft, as the cheering, flag-waving crowds were replaced by rioting mobs, "impatient with what they considered compromise reforms, were quick to instigate situations which led to an upsurge of violence surpassing anything experienced during the sixties and early seventies. The haves, bewildered by the have-nots' violent rejection of what they had for so long apparently demanding, finally themselves became angry.

"Increasing polarization within the political spectrum finally caused what so many had feared for so long—the coalescence into huge paramilitary organizations of what had been, until then, a myriad of isolated cadres, each determined to impose its ideologies by force.

"Sabotage, terrorist attacks, and economic depression widened still further the fissures dividing black from white, left from right, young from old, rich from poor, and accelerated the slide toward anarchy.''

The President reached for the TV remote-control panel and switched off the set. A picture of bodies being dug out of the ruins of the bomb-blasted Yankee Stadium shrank into a bright pinpoint of light and disappeared.

He rested his head against the back of the sofa and closed his eyes. Something Wallcroft had said, half heard by the President while he'd been talking to the Attorney General, had brought to life an old, dark memory. A memory of a night, many years ago, when he had been brought face to face with himself and had found himself wanting. Against all the odds he had somehow managed to survive the humiliation that followed. Now, it seemed, fate was calling him to account. Would he, he wondered, turn from the challenge of Wild Card and run, as he had done then?

Not to run, insisted one part of his mind, would on this occasion be unthinkable. But if he did run, another more insidious voice told him, it would be in response to the same weakness which had betrayed him during that earlier crisis.

The thought was unbearable. He sat up, suddenly alert once again, and picked up the telephone. "Get me Dr. Nadelman," he said.

4

THE BREAK IN THE hot weather made its first tentative appearance during the late afternoon. A troop of wispy cirrus clouds passed through on a scouting mission and by six o'clock they had summoned reinforcements. Feeding on the ground heat and high humidity, towering clouds began to mass threateningly.

The first drops of rain began to fall as Dr. Simon Chesterton swung his gleaming Mercedes SSK onto the tree-lined gravel path leading to Nadelman's house in Chevy Chase. With a sound like an enormous steel whip being cracked, lightning flickered across the sky. For what seemed like several seconds, he was able to see every detail of the ivy-covered neo-Gothic building ahead of him. Stained-glass windows, ogee arches, castellations, crockets, and gargoyles—all were clearly discernible in the three-billion-watt flash.

Although Chesterton had known Nadelman for nearly ten years, this was the first time he had ever been invited to what the Washington scientific community had dubbed the House of Usher. That he should at last have seen the house in such theatrical circumstances was, he decided, compensation enough for having been summoned late at night and at such short notice. His only regret was that he did not, at that moment, have his *Götterdämmerung* tape playing in the car's stereo unit.

Simon Chesterton was the senior psychiatric consultant at the Walter Reed Army Medical Center and a special adviser to various branches of the administration and the judiciary. Aged forty-eight and a bachelor, he was the apotheosis of charm and urbanity. Everything about him, and everything he'd gathered about him, was in the best possible taste. His face was as pale, smooth, and symmetrical as the faces of the Dresden figurines he collected, and he carried his tall, slender body with an ease verging on the languorous. He spoke and dressed like an English gentleman and conducted his affairs—both professional and private —with the guile and reticence of an English gentleman. Born Alexis Dobanozov, the only child of a Pittsburgh steelworker, he had absorbed his adopted life-style so successfully that he sometimes gave the impression that he was trying to conceal an aristocratic rather than a proletarian background.

He stopped the car in front of the steps leading up to the front door of the house. The rain was now torrential. He turned up the collar of his London-tailored tweed suit (Chevy Chase was the country as far as Chesterton was concerned, and he'd dressed accordingly) and, flashlight in hand, opened the car door. Taking care not to splash his hand-sewn brogues, he ran up the steps and tugged at the antique bell pull. From somewhere within the unlit, rambling house came a sound like chains being rattled in a dungeon.

It was several minutes before the entryphone crackled and Nadelman's voice said, "Who is it?"

"Count Dracula!"

"Very funny!" Nadelman did not sound at all amused.

Chesterton waited, huddled against the driving rain. "For God's sake, Dick!" he yelled. "Hurry up. It's Simon. I'm getting soaked!"

The door gave a loud click and swung back into a hall that was as dark, and smelled as damp, as a cave. Chesterton slowly stepped inside and swung his flashlight around. The walls were covered with a trellis-and-vine-leaf paper, some of it peeling, and hung with large framed engravings of mournful-looking cattle standing beneath moonlit skies.

To his right was a huge staircase; on the balustrade stood a bronze figure of Pan supporting an unlit candelabrum. Facing him, a door encrusted with linen-fold paneling was guarded by a pair of chairs made from deer antlers.

"Dick?" he called uncertainly. There was no reply.

He had begun to move toward the door when he felt something brush against his legs. He shined the light down at his feet. Two cats, their backs arched, their yellow eyes blazing, stared back at him. That would have been bad enough—Chesterton hated cats—but to his disgust he saw that both of the animals' heads had been covered with what looked like dental cement.

The bulbs in the candelabrum suddenly lit up. "Ah! There they are!" said Nadelman cheerfully, from the top of the stairs. He was holding what appeared to be a small radio transmitter of the type used to control model aircraft. He began to twiddle the dials on the front of the apparatus. First the tortoise-shell and then the black cat rolled over, purring loudly. He turned the dials again and the cats bounded across to one of the chairs, curled up, and immediately fell into a deep sleep.

"Brain implants," he explained. "Easier to look after than Alsatians, and just as dangerous when their aggression centers are fully stimulated. Alpha—that's the black one—almost blinded a prowler last week!" He turned and began to walk away. "Come on up," he called, almost as an afterthought.

Chesterton followed him up the stairs and along a dimly lit passage stacked with books, bric-à-brac, and oddments of furniture. They eventually entered what Chesterton guessed had once been a ballroom but now looked like a warehouse. It was filled with furniture—all late Victorian and much of it broken—unhung pictures, stuffed birds and animals, a great deal of scientific apparatus, and books. Tens of thousands of books. Books everywhere, piled one above the other on the bare floorboards, the furniture, the mantelpiece, and the window ledges.

Nadelman removed a set of *Wood's Natural History* from a leather davenport, blew the dust off the seat, and indicated that that was where Chesterton was to sit. He walked across the room, rummaged around in a pile of papers and EEG printouts, and returned with two glasses and a bottle of brandy. He filled the glasses and passed one to Chesterton.

"Simon," he said, "we're going ahead with Wild Card!"

Chesterton set his glass down carefully on the table between them. "What on earth do you mean, we're going ahead with Wild Card?" he demanded.

"The President's given it his okay!" Nadelman answered gleefully. "We're to get Wild Card rolling immediately!"

Chesterton stared hard at Nadelman, wondering whether overwork and loneliness had finally unbalanced him. "Dick," he said, "if you've dragged me out on a night like this . . ." He drained his glass and stood up, hoping to shock Nadelman into more rational behavior. To his dismay, Nadelman stared back as though *he* were mad.

He sat down again. Nadelman refilled his glass and passed it to him.

"But, Dick, the study group was just a"—Chesterton paused to wave away a basket of pretzels Nadelman had thrust at him—"an *academic* . . . a *theoretical* exercise! Government departments play politico-military games all the time! Surely, there was never any question of anyone actually going *through* with it? And anyway"—he chuckled at the absurdity of the notion—"where would you find scientists prepared to work on something like Wild Card?"

Nadelman took a handful of the pretzels and pushed the basket to one side. "Well," he replied, his mouth full, "they didn't have too much trouble persuading scientists to cook up the fission bomb, for example." He began brushing crumbs from the front of his cardigan. "And who were the wonderful folks who gave us nerve gas, made weapons out of anthrax, brucellosis, encephalomyelitis, plague, psittacosis, Q fever, Rift Valley fever, Rocky Mountain spotted fever," he spluttered. "Soda jerks?"

Chesterton took a handkerchief from his pocket and, with exaggerated care, wiped away a fragment of damp pretzel that had landed on his cream mohair-and-wool tie. "My dear fellow," he said, without warmth, "when they came up with the atomic bomb this country was at war!"

Nadelman leaned over and, from under a saucer of cat food, picked up a copy of the previous day's *Washington Post* and tossed it across to Chesterton. The headline read: 200 DIE IN DC SUPERMARKET BOMBING. "*This* isn't war? You sat on the study group and you saw the evidence. God damn it, Simon, intelligence reports prove we're on the verge of revolution!"

Chesterton was not impressed. "Just try recruiting a team of scientists to work on something as bizarre as Wild Card," he said, still trying to save his tie. "They'll have you certified—when they've finished laughing!"

Nadelman took a deep, weary breath. "Fieser, the guy who came up with napalm," he explained patiently, "had teams working at Harvard, MIT, and the University of California for two years during World War Two to equip bats—yes, *bats*—with miniature incendiary bombs. The little bastards even managed to burn down a two-million-dollar hangar in New Mexico before disenchantment set in!"

Chesterton put away his handkerchief, resigned to the fact that his tie was ruined. "All this is totally irrelevant!" he snapped. "Working on a project to equip bats with incendiary bombs may have stretched credulity, but it's unlikely to have posed much in the way of an ethical dilemma! Even working on the atomic bomb would have been easy, compared to Wild Card. For God's sake, don't you see the difference? All those people were working *within* the laws of the United States, with the *approval* of the United States, against a clearly defined *enemy* of the United States!"

"So okay, it won't be easy!" Nadelman was now becoming irritated. "But that's not to say it'll be impossible, for Christ's sake!"

Chesterton shook his head. Of course, he thought, anything's possible. The fact that Nadelman had apparently persuaded the President, no less, to partner him in this monstrous *folie à deux* was evidence of that. "Dick, you're crazy," he said. "I just hope to God you're not expecting me to become involved in this scheme."

Nadelman bristled. "You became involved when you took fifty thousand dollars for sitting in on the study group! What we expect you to do now is tell us which of the scientists on the short list I've compiled are psychologically capable of working on Wild Card."

Chesterton took a deep breath. "How in the name of God do you expect me to do that?"

"By evaluating their motivations. We've had checks run on the usual things—family, friends, faculty, banks, and credit companies —and these people seem to fit the bill."

Nadelman pulled a pile of blue folders out from under his seat and handed them to Chesterton. Each was marked: TOP SECRET/EXCLUSIVE

43

DISTRIBUTION. Chesterton began flicking through the closely typed sheets. "Just what have they been told?" he asked, without looking up.

Nadelman refilled their glasses. "That they'll be working on an unspecified internal-defense project, requiring them to be confined under top-security conditions for about eight months. They also know that they'll be very well paid, and that we'll be keeping an eye on their families while they're away."

Chesterton raised his eyebrows. "And they've all agreed? Even the superstars?"

"Yes."

Chesterton sighed and handed the folders back to Nadelman. "They must be mad," he said. "Stark, staring mad!"

Nadelman shrugged, as though that was a matter of little consequence.

"How long do I have?" Chesterton asked. "Even those head cases," he nodded contemptuously at the pile of blue folders, "are unlikely to walk in and spread their unconsciouses on the table like an Army-kit inspection."

"Two weeks."

Chesterton threw his head back and laughed aloud. "Now I *know* you're joking! Even if I canceled all of my other appointments, it couldn't be done."

"I'm not joking," Nadelman replied grimly, "and it *must* be done. I'm not interested in their masturbation fantasies. All I need to know is whether or not we can rely on the bastards!"

5

DR. PAUL McELROY, THE first scientist on Nadelman's list, was fifty minutes late for his appointment. Chesterton was not surprised. Confronted with roadblocks, checkpoints, areas cordoned off by the police and the National Guard, and wildcat strikes, people frequently fell behind schedule. Although the Army staff car bringing McElroy from Andrews Field to Walter Reed had traffic priority, it had been turned back at Sixteenth and Monroe by a bomb disposal team. Unable to drive through Petworth because of rioting, the driver had telephoned to say that he would have to approach the hospital from the west.

Chesterton used the time to dictate a report of his examination of Louis Chavez, the Commander in Chief of the Revolutionary Alliance and the man thought to have planned the attempted assassination of the President at Dulles seventy-two hours earlier. Chesterton had come away from the examination convinced that if there had been a conspiracy Chavez, at least, was not in on it. Behind the man's invective there had seemed to be genuine resentment that his authority had been superseded. Chesterton concluded his report by advising against harsher methods of interrogation in this instance, then switched off the dictating machine.

He glanced down at his gold Jaeger-LeCoultre watch; McElroy was not due for another ten minutes. He took out the scientist's dossier and looked again at the closely typed pages headed TOP SECRET.

Although he was now Chairman of the Biochemistry Department at the Massachusetts Institute of Technology, McElroy had graduated from Harvard as a physicist. His immediate postgraduate years had been devoted to the production of a thesis on aerofoils which had won him a sabbatical year at the Cavendish Laboratory in Cambridge, England. There, he had developed a keen interest in the biological applications of his training. On his return to the United States he had taken up a postdoctoral fellowship at MIT and had begun work in the field of biophysics. Eighteen months later, he had been invited to join the Defense Department's study group JASON.

That, Chesterton assumed, would be where he had first met Nadelman. It was probably Nadelman who had been responsible for his subsequent appointment as a consultant to the National Aeronautics and Space Administration.

McElroy had turned more and more toward the biological sciences, finally devoting his energies to the relatively unexplored field of memory research. Chesterton remembered reading a paper in which McElroy had speculated about storing memories in long-chain molecules. Although McElroy took too mechanistic a view of these matters for Chesterton's taste, he nevertheless recalled that he had been impressed. McElroy had seemed to be onto something very big. There was no doubt that he was one of the most brilliant and successful members of the scientific community.

He looked again at the section in the dossier dealing with Margaret Ann McElroy, *née* Cohen. Aged thirty, the daughter of Jewish parents, she had left Radcliffe after her freshman year and borne McElroy two children—a boy and a girl—within the first two years of their marriage. Her photograph showed her to be attractive—but not remarkably so. She was wearing jeans, a Snoopy-shirt and a head scarf. The picture had been taken—apparently through a telephoto lens—while she had been working in the front garden of their ranch-style home in Cambridge, Massachusetts. In the background a small boy, wearing a baseball fielder's glove, was playing near a sprinkler. It could have been a still from a TV commercial.

He turned back to the report. The marriage had been categorized as stable. Why on earth, he wondered peevishly, do these damned FBI fellows insist on using the word *stable* when all they mean is that they have failed to uncover evidence of infidelity by either party?

Chesterton was about to dictate a memo complaining about value judgments in security clearances when his secretary announced the arrival of the biochemist.

McElroy was much taller than his photograph led Chesterton to expect. He had a strong face, with a broad, square jaw and a straight nose. A scar on his upper lip—so small that Chesterton thought he probably wouldn't have noticed it had McElroy not been deeply tanned—turned his smile into an appealing, slightly lopsided grin.

Judging by the way he was dressed, he was not plagued by the great American fear of aging. Unlike many men on the threshold of forty who engaged in sedentary occupations, he could have worn clothes intended for a man half his age without looking ridiculous. Yet he had chosen a gray suit that had been cut to reflect no more than a distant echo of what men younger than himself currently considered fashionable.

His handshake was unostentatiously firm, his manner relaxed and friendly. Chesterton motioned him toward an easy chair and took a seat opposite. He knew that it was not going to be easy to penetrate McElroy's defenses. His work in the field of brain function would have equipped him with considerable knowledge of the rules of the game of personality evaluation.

Chesterton made the first move, using a gambit designed to uncover political attitudes.

"I'm sorry you had such a trying time getting here," he began.

Apart from the difficulties he had encountered in the city itself, a strike of airline pilots protesting against the recent spate of hijackings had required that McElroy be flown to Washington in a military aircraft.

McElroy shrugged. "I'd fly USAF all the time if I could, short of enlisting. At least you're sure you're not going to end up cutting cane in Cuba!"

"What have things been like in Boston?" Chesterton asked. "I have the impression you've been less hard hit than a lot of cities."

McElroy looked doubtful. "I suppose so," he finally acknowledged. "Certainly less than you have here in Washington. Downtown has been pretty badly roughed up, but for some reason terrorists have left the older parts of the city alone. On Beacon Hill, for instance, I don't think there's been a single shot fired."

Chesterton noted his use of the word *terrorist*, rather than the more neutral *guerrilla*. "How interesting. Why do you think that is?" he asked.

"It's hard to say. I can't believe it's out of respect for history."

Chesterton smiled encouragingly and waited to see if McElroy would continue. Many people would have used his question as a soapbox from which to deliver an impassioned political dissertation. McElroy did not.

Chesterton tried again.

"Where do you think it's all going to end?" he asked.

McElroy shook his head sadly.

"I've no idea. Probably in a bloody, senseless massacre."

A good start, thought Chesterton. He did not want people who believed in a political solution, even if they were pro-administration. Such people, once they learned what was required of them, could well prove as dangerous as if they had been violently anti-administration.

"Well," Chesterton said, as though reluctant to conclude an agreeable conversation, "I suppose we really ought to get down to work."

McElroy settled back in his chair and crossed one leg over the other, waiting attentively.

"You know about the somewhat unusual conditions attached to this post?"

McElroy nodded. "Yes, I do."

An exceptionally secure man, Chesterton decided. Anyone less secure would have seized the opportunity to ask for more details.

"And you know that the project is one which has a defense application?"

McElroy replied in the same matter-of-fact tone, "Yes, I do."

"Do you realize, though, that this so-called defense application is specific to the nation's *internal* security?"

This was as far as Chesterton dared go in hinting at the true purpose of Wild Card.

48

McElroy shifted uneasily in his seat.

"I think it was Edmund Burke," he began hesitantly, "who said the only thing necessary for evil to triumph is for good men to do nothing."

Chesterton cleared his throat, unsure which of them was the more embarrassed. "I understand," he replied, as if disposing of a rather tiresome matter that should not have been raised between one gentleman and another. "How do you feel about being away from your wife and children for so long?"

"I didn't think there was much point in raising it until I knew whether or not I was wanted."

Chesterton guessed that McElroy was less—probably a lot less —dependent on his wife than she was on him. The blandness of his reply also suggested that he felt in no way imprisoned by his wife's dependence.

"I suppose you have known Dr. Nadelman for a long time?"

"Since we were on JASON together."

"You obviously have great respect for his integrity."

McElroy raised his eyebrows. "Obviously!" It was, Chesterton knew, a polite way of saying, What the hell would I be doing here if I didn't! "He is a logician of exceptional ability," McElroy added, as a peace offering.

Chesterton gave him another high score. The fact that he associated skill as a logician with integrity would contribute greatly to his ability to work on Wild Card. Nevertheless, Chesterton waited a full minute before speaking. He knew that if McElroy harbored any unconscious fears concerning Nadelman's integrity he would, unless he was playing a *very* skillful game of counterbluff, have attempted to suppress such fears by going on to praise Nadelman's virtues further. But he said nothing; it was the psychiatrist's move and McElroy was sufficiently self-assured to wait patiently for him to make it.

Chesterton settled back into his chair and took off his spectacles, smiling affably. It was a gesture intended to convey the idea that there was to be an intermission.

"I'm told you're an excellent glider pilot."

McElroy laughed. "I glide once in a while."

McElroy's dossier said he had hundreds of flying hours to his credit. Two years earlier, in California, he had come within fifteen hundred feet of breaking the world's glider altitude record. Why, then, Chesterton wondered, had McElroy sought to minimize—not so much his skill, but the amount of time he allocated to his hobby?

"It must be a very thrilling sport."

McElroy shrugged, as if that aspect were of little interest to him. "It's certainly the most relaxing one I know," he replied.

Chesterton had caught the scent of something very interesting. This man's superego disapproves of a pastime that is *thrilling*, he told himself, but tolerates one that is *relaxing*. Why?

"It's very important—relaxing, I mean," said Chesterton. "When I was much younger and living in Chicago, I did a great deal of sailing for that reason." Chesterton had visited Chicago, but never lived there. Only once had he been on a ship smaller than a liner. He had lied to put McElroy off his guard. "But that was all a very long time ago," he added quickly, in case he was asked a question about either the city or the sport. "Don't you find gliding rather lonely?"

"No more than sailing."

"But I always had at least one friend aboard. You're absolutely alone up there."

"I've never thought of it as lonely," McElroy insisted. "My wife says it's a selfish—" He stopped abruptly, aware that he had somehow put himself in check.

Chesterton pressed home his advantage. "Because it takes you away from her and the children for long periods?"

"I guess so." McElroy sounded deflated. "That and the fact that it's so damned expensive!"

So that's it, thought Chesterton. That's the reason for the guilt. Or, at least, the reason that *conceals* the reason for the guilt.

McElroy's father, a distinguished USAF fighter pilot, had been killed in Korea. The son's choice of engineless—and therefore less potent—aircraft might, Chesterton suspected, be an unconscious attempt to lessen anxieties created by the feeling that he was competing with his father. He didn't doubt that McElroy was in awe of father figures. His almost reverential attitude to Nadelman was evidence of that. It would be interesting to see how much he unconsciously blamed his mother—or himself—for the death of his father.

Chesterton decided that McElroy was sufficiently promising a subject to be questioned under narcohypnosis. During the session, Chesterton would regress him and explore more thoroughly his patterns of response and feeling. Not all of them; there simply wasn't time. But enough for Chesterton to form an opinion of McElroy's suitability for a role in Wild Card.

Chesterton smiled. "Well, Dr. McElroy," he said briskly, "if you're ready, perhaps we should proceed to the main item on the agenda."

He rose and led McElroy across to a black leather couch in the corner of the room. Two pillows, covered by a paper towel, lay at one end. Mounted in the burlap-covered wall at the opposite end was a flashlight bulb. On a table nearby were two tape recorders, a loudspeaker, a pushbutton control and a mysterious-looking black box.

Chesterton switched on the tiny bulb. "You're no doubt familiar with all this," he said.

McElroy leaned forward and examined the instruments mounted on the front of the black box. "An autohypnosis kit?"

Chesterton nodded. "Used in conjunction with a low dose of sodium amytal, it simply makes it easier for you to answer questions without, shall we say, undue equivocation!"

McElroy grinned, took off his jacket and began rolling up the left sleeve of his shirt. Chesterton carried the jacket across to a closet and hung it up. He dimmed the light and crossed to a Sheraton cabinet behind his writing table. While he filled a syringe with sodium amytal, McElroy, who was now lying on the couch, questioned him about the uses, and effectiveness, of narcohypnosis.

"Its application is limited," Chesterton conceded. "Many patients just aren't sufficiently suggestible. But if the potential for hypnosis exists, there's no doubt it can be most quickly realized by this method."

Chesterton returned with a stainless-steel instrument dish and sat down beside the couch.

"Just relax," he said softly. "Look at the light and relax." He rubbed McElroy's upper arm with an ether pad, compressed the flesh gently between his finger and thumb, and eased in the needle. He returned the syringe to the tray, placed the pushbutton control in McElroy's right hand and flicked a switch on the black box. A recording of Chesterton's voice, soft yet insistent, floated out of the loudspeaker.

"I want you to look at the light," it said. "Concentrate completely on the light . . . do not allow your eyes to wander away from the light . . ."

Chesterton turned down the volume fractionally. "This and subsequent phrases will be repeated until you feel ready to move on to the next stage. When you do, please press the button in your hand. Take your time—there's absolutely no hurry."

The machine gave a slight click and repeated the instruction to look at the light. McElroy listened for several minutes before pressing the button. The machine clicked again and a new set of instructions issued from the loudspeaker. "You will discover that looking at the light is very tiring . . . very, very tiring . . . your eyes will soon become very, very tired."

After eight minutes, Chesterton decided to test the depth of his subject's hypnotic trance. He switched off the instruction tape and gently lifted the pushbutton control from between McElroy's limp fingers, telling him, as he did so, that he would now be unable to open his eyes. The greater the effort he made to open his eyes, Chesterton told him, the more firmly would his eyes be closed.

"Now try to open your eyes."

McElroy strained to carry out the order but failed.

Chesterton switched on the tape that would record the examination and leaned forward, his elbows resting on his knees and his hands clasped in front of him. "Now, Paul," he said quietly, "I want you to think back to when you were six . . ."

Chesterton was now almost at the end of his task. During the previous ten days, he had selected twelve of the thirteen section heads required for Wild Card. On the evening of the eleventh day he lit the hurricane lamps in his blacked-out office, said good night to his secretary and settled down to crack the problem of what to do about Dr. Mary Anderson.

Nadelman's insight into the personalities of the scientists who were final candidates had been even better than Chesterton had expected. Any one of the three biochemists would have been acceptable, and it was only Paul McElroy's neurotic need to earn the approval of those he regarded as father figures that had given him a slight edge on the other candidates.

But Chesterton had run into serious trouble with the last group to be examined—the geneticists. His first appointment had been with Dr. Anderson. But the day before she should have flown to Washington, she had been injured by a car bomb which had exploded outside her laboratory at the University of California in Berkeley.

Chesterton had not been unduly worried. He had expected one if not both of the other geneticists to pass muster. But against all the odds, he'd had to reject one for conventional security reasons—a married man who had somehow managed to conceal his homosexuality from the FBI investigators—and the other because she was on the verge of a schizophrenic illness.

Nadelman had immediately asked for security checks to be made on two more geneticists. Only one had been cleared by the FBI, and when Nadelman approached him, he had declined.

Dr. Anderson was at last well enough to travel, and Chesterton had talked to her the previous day. Although her injuries were minor—a fracture of the left collar bone and lacerations—she had been badly traumatized by the experience. Five of her students had been killed in the explosion and a number of others injured.

On the face of it, Mary Anderson was the most highly motivated of all the scientists invited to work on Wild Card, for she had experienced the tragic consequences of violent protest not just once, but twice. A year earlier both of her parents had been killed by snipers while driving home from a movie. Because of her most recent experience, Chesterton had though it unsafe to use narcohypnosis on her. There was still, therefore, a great deal he did not know about her.

He poured some coffee from the flask his secretary had left for him and ran over the facts—such as they were—once again. Dr. Anderson had put her work before all else. This had resulted in an emotional life that was surprisingly barren for someone so young and attractive. She had lived at home until she was twenty-four and had moved into an apartment of her own only because, as she said, "living with my parents was just too easy."

There had been a number of men in her life, but each, it seemed, had finally come to resent the fact that she was so work-oriented.

Chesterton rewound his battery-powered tape recorder to where he had asked her why she had agreed to work on Wild Card and listened, again, to her reply.

"I wish I could say that it was out of a sense of patriotism. But I'm afraid the truth is that I was simply immensely flattered to have been asked!"

Chesterton was still deep in thought when the telephone rang. It was Nadelman. He switched on the scrambler and carried the phone over to an easy chair beside the window.

A cluster of flares suddenly lit the overcast sky to the south and began to drift languorously in the night breeze, flooding the blacked-out city below with phosphorescent light.

He asked Nadelman to hold on for a moment. Behind the familiar paper-thin crackle of distant rifle fire he could hear a new, more ominous thudding.

Chesterton put the phone back to his ear. "Has the Army started using mortars in Brightwood?" he asked.

"Probably," Nadelman replied. "The President was under a lot of pressure to okay it when I was with him earlier. I think he was hoping to starve the bastards out," he added.

Chesterton rested his head against the back of the chair and closed his eyes. "I suppose you're calling about Dr. Anderson," he said.

"That, and the fact I've decided we will, after all, need a couple of virologists. I'm bringing in Pedlar and Zelinski."

Chesterton sat up, startled. "You're what?" he said. "If the West Germans realize we've lifted an ex-Treblinka doctor from Paraguay —let alone have him working for us—they'll slap an extradition order on us so fast—"

"Exactly!" said Nadelman, interrupting him. "And that's why he won't be giving us anything but his full cooperation!"

"And Pedlar!" Chesterton said.

"So he shoots a little heroin occasionally—"

"Shoots a *little* heroin *occasionally*? Pedlar's been on a tenth of a gram a day since his tour with the Army Chemical Corps in Vietnam!"

"He's still a good operator."

"I'm at a loss to understand," said Chesterton. "We reject Cantrell because of his homosexuality, yet let through a heroin addict and an ex-Nazi! It makes nonsense of everything I've been doing for the past ten days."

"Pedlar and Zelinski are special cases," replied Nadelman, "and I shall be making myself personally responsible for the pair of them. Now let's move onto Mary Anderson—what's the hang-up with her?''

"There's no hang-up," said Chesterton, still deeply offended that Nadelman should have overridden him on Pedlar and Zelinski. "If you want her, have her! I would advise against it, but I'm sure you won't allow that to influence your decision.''

"What have you got against her?" he asked, ignoring Chesterton's jibe.

Chesterton took off his glasses and began to rub his eyes. He could feel the beginnings of a migraine. "She's still very much an unknown quantity,'' he replied, now only wanting to settle the matter quickly, so that he could go home to bed. "As you know, I wasn't able to use narcohypnosis on her. But it's patently obvious that she is a totally work-oriented young woman who consistently sets herself goals that are barely within her reach. The fact that she always appears to achieve these goals is a tribute—if one can use such a word in this context—to an ability to sublimate very powerful aggressive forces.''

"I would've thought that was to her credit," said Nadelman.

"Up to a point it is, but like all these things, it's a matter of degree. I'm worried about what would happen if she were ever to *fail* to achieve a goal. My guess—and it is only a guess—is that it would precipitate a slide into a psychotic depression. But before her aggression turns inward, so to speak, and causes a depression, it might well do a great deal of damage to those around her.''

"What *exactly* are you saying?" demanded Nadelman.

Chesterton was silent for a moment. "I'm not sure," he replied, "and it's because I'm not sure that I think we should wait until I can complete her testing.''

"Does she still want to come on board?''

"Very much so.''

"Well, that settles it, then!" Nadelman sounded resentful that Chesterton should have wasted so much of his time. "We give her a try.''

Chesterton was about to say that Wild Card was not a project they could possibly try people out on when he realized they had been disconnected. There was, he decided, little point in waiting for Nadelman to call him back. He extinguished the hurricane lamps and left.

6

McElroy was halfway through clearing the snow from the driveway when his wife appeared at the door. "Paul!" she called. "Telephone!"

He brought the snowblower to a standstill, and without getting out of the seat called over his shoulder, "Who is it?"

"They didn't say. And, dear, don't let the boys play with the blower," she added, before closing the door.

McElroy switched off the engine. He could hear his son and the kid from next door arguing loudly in the garage. "Johnny!" he yelled. There was no reply. He was about to call again but changed his mind. He stood a better chance of them not tampering with the blower, he decided, if they remained ignorant of the fact that it would be unguarded.

He hurried inside the house and picked up the telephone in the hall. "McElroy," he said.

"Dr. *Paul* McElroy?" a man asked.

"Yes?"

"I have a call from Mr. Matt Whitaker, if you'll hold the line a moment, sir."

McElroy frowned, trying to place the name. His wife had taken the call on the kitchen extension, and he could hear her moving about as she prepared dinner. It was the housekeeper's day off, and Margy had promised to fix the children an "indoor picnic" as a special treat.

"I've got it, honey!" he shouted, covering the mouthpiece with his hand. There was a click as she replaced the handset and, a moment later, Whitaker came on the line. "Dr. McElroy? Whitaker, FBI Boston. I've been asked to call to let you know you've been cleared for your project. I hope it's in order for me to congratulate you, sir."

For a moment McElroy could think of nothing to say. He hadn't expected to hear anything for at least another week, and then to have heard from Nadelman, either by telegram or letter.

"Hello?" said Whitaker, thinking he had been cut off.

"I'm still here."

"Dr. McElroy, would it be convenient if a colleague and I were to call on you sometime this evening?"

"This evening?" McElroy lowered his voice a tone. "Couldn't we make it tomorrow, maybe on the campus?"

"Ummm . . ." Whitaker sounded reluctant. "The problem is time. If you have dinner guests, we could come after they've gone."

McElroy heard his wife calling their son in to supper and covered his ear with his hand. "It isn't that, Mr. Whitaker," he explained. "it's just that I—well, frankly, I haven't gotten around to telling my wife yet . . ."

"You mean she knows nothing?"

"Nothing at all," McElroy replied, suddenly feeling very foolish.

"But, Dr. McElroy!" Whitaker's tone had become almost scolding. "There's the question of insurance, installing security equipment and so on. If we're going to look after things while you're away—"

McElroy interrupted him. "I know, I know," he said irritably. "And if you say it has to be tonight, I guess it *has* to be tonight." He glanced at his watch. "Can you make it as late as possible? Say around ten-thirty?"

"Okay, ten-thirty it is. And, Dr. McElroy," the FBI man added wearily, "tell her before we get there, huh?"

McElroy did not attempt to tell his wife until after the children had finally been driven, protesting, to bed.

She returned to the living room and dropped onto the sofa, exhausted. No sooner had she done so than the boy began calling for a glass of water. She looked despairingly at McElroy and braced herself to·get up again.

"If that kid doesn't quiet down," said McElroy, "I'll—"

His wife looked alarmed. "Paul, you'll only make him even more insecure than he already is."

"Insecure, my ass!" snapped McElroy. "*We're* the ones who're insecure! And, Christ, don't they know how to take advantage of it!"

His wife ignored him. "Mommy'll bring you a glass of water in a minute," she called.

McElroy shook his head and got up to pour himself a brandy. "Do you want one?" he asked.

"Paul, you've got your head in the clouds all day. I sometimes wonder if you've any idea what it's like running a home and bringing up two children the way things are."

McElroy sloshed some brandy in a glass and thrust it at her. "Okay, okay. Here, drink this."

She took the glass, but refused to be placated. "And Johnny's been just impossible lately. If only we could afford to send him to that special counselor his teacher recommended . . ."

McElroy saw his opportunity and jumped in with both feet. "As a matter of fact, I think we soon might!"

"Darling!" She opened her eyes wide and sat up, suddenly bright and alert. "You've gotten a raise?"

"A new job!"

Some of the radiance went out of her expression. "We won't have to leave here?" she asked anxiously.

He shook his head. "*I'll* probably have to go away for a while . . ."

"Go away?" Suddenly she was on the brink of tears.

He put down his glass and returned to the sofa. "Margy," he said, gently taking her hand. "It won't be for long. A month or two at the most."

"A month or two! You're leaving us for a month or two at a time like this?"

"It'll be all right, honey. It's a Defense Department job, and part of the deal is that the families of the guys on the project'll get around-the-clock police protection. They'll be putting shatterproof glass in all the windows, electronic sensors in the yard—"

"When do you have to go?"

"Soon. Hey, maybe your mother could come and stay for a while. She'd be better than a squad of cops any day."

"*How* soon?" she asked, not amused.

McElroy shrugged. "In a day or so, I guess."

"A *day* or so!" She pulled her hand away. "How long have you known about this?" she asked suspiciously.

"The call just before supper was to say I'd got the job."

"When did you first *apply* for it?"

"About a week ago."

"Paul, you're lying!"

"Okay, so it was ten days—"

"Why didn't you mention any of this before?" she demanded.

"I wanted it to be a surprise."

"Some surprise!" She blew her nose gently. "Where will you be working?"

"I don't know yet—someplace near Washington, I think."

She brightened. "Then you'll be able to get back for weekends?"

McElroy shifted uneasily. "That's the one hangup—it's a maximum-effort, top-security operation. Part of the deal's that we stay put until we're through doing whatever it is they've got lined up for us."

"It's not dangerous, is it?" she asked. "Paul, you haven't done anything silly?"

He took her head in his hands and kissed her wet cheeks. "The most dangerous thing I'll be doing is shaving in the morning." He began to unbutton her blouse.

"Be serious," she said, trying not to smile.

"I *am* being serious!"

She entwined her arms around his neck. "What am I going to do, with you away for two whole months?"

McElroy twisted his head around so he could see the carriage clock above the fireplace. "Listen, Margy," he said, "I've got a couple of guys coming to see me at ten-thirty . . ."

60

She let one hand drop and began unfastening his belt. "What's the time now?"

Between kisses he replied, "Nearly ten."

"Well," she whispered, "we'll just have to be quick then."

Suddenly there was an uproar from the direction of the children's bedrooms. She froze, then drew away, fumbling with the buttons of her blouse. "Damn!" she cried, and rushed out of the room.

McElroy groaned, and refilled his brandy glass.

7

BILL BARRINGER MOVED his shoulder holster to a more comfortable position and slid from behind the steering wheel of the black Plymouth parked outside of the terminal building of Dulles International Airport. He was a big, heavily muscled man who took as much pride in his powers of observation as he did in his strength and the speed of his reflexes.

He crossed the road and began easing his way through the crowds. Barringer saw that the young woman he had been sent to meet was tall, well dressed, and exceptionally attractive. As an ex-police officer he categorized her as height five-ten to five-eleven; weight one thirty to one thirty-five; build slender; hair brown; eyes hazel; complexion medium; race white. Her cream trouser suit was impeccably cut and, like her tan silk blouse and amber beads, almost certainly expensive. He recognized the matching luggage on the porter's trolley beside her as having come from Gucci.

"Dr. Anderson?" he asked. There had been some talk earlier about using passwords, but nothing had ever been done about it because it was thought that not many of the scientists could be relied upon to remember them.

She took off her tortoise-shell sunglasses and nodded cautiously. Instinctively, Barringer superimposed a mental Photo-Fit grid over her face and, starting with Basic Outline 1/3 (broad, tapering to pointed chin), began laying in the facial feature cards. Large, widely spaced eyes; high, prominent cheekbones; straight, slender nose; wide mouth with full underlip.

Although he knew the perfume she was wearing contained sandalwood, it annoyed him that he couldn't with any certainty put a brand name to it.

He smiled what he hoped was a reassuring smile and touched the brim of his hat. "Barringer, ma'am," he said. "I'm sorry I wasn't inside to meet you, but I got snarled up in the demos downtown. What was your trip like?"

She shrugged, as if to say it could have been worse. "Mr. Barringer, where are you taking me?" she asked, taking care that the porter would not be able to hear her.

Barringer glanced back at the no-unattended-parking sign above his car. "I'll fill you in when we get rolling," he replied. "They're pretty quick to call in the bomb-disposal squad around here."

Followed by the porter, he hurried her across the road and into the front passenger seat of his car. He returned a moment later, having helped stow her luggage in the trunk, got in, and started the engine.

"Mr. Barringer," she said, watching him closely. "You still haven't answered my question."

He flicked down the left-turn indicator and twisted around in his seat, waiting for a break in the slow-moving stream of traffic. It did not occur. He shook his head sadly and reached for a switch on the dash. From behind the front fender came the paralyzing rasp of the police klaxon. Immediately, the traffic behind him came to an abrupt halt. He released the switch and swung out into the gap. As he straightened up he lifted the radio telephone and began speaking into it. "Valkyrie to Valhalla. Car Twelve and pickup proceeding to destination. Message timed at"—he glanced at his watch—"seventeen-thirty. Over and out."

Mary Anderson couldn't help laughing. "That, if I may say so, Mr. Barringer, is a most unfortunately phrased message!"

He put down the telephone and smiled, but said nothing.

"And you still haven't told me where we're going," she added.

He waited until he was on the access road and gaining speed before replying.

"Fort Detrick," he said flatly.

She turned and stared disbelievingly at him.

"Fort Detrick?" she asked. "Are you sure?"

"Quite sure, ma'am!" he replied, as though he wished he'd been able to give her better news.

She turned away, trying to remember everything she had ever heard or read about Fort Detrick. She knew that for twenty-five years it had been the Army's center for research into biological warfare. It had been at Detrick that scientists had first isolated botulinus toxin, four ounces of which could, it was said, wipe out the entire population of the U.S. And she remembered reading a paper published in the mid-sixties which had listed the diseases caught by researchers at Detrick. They included tularemia, brucellosis, Q fever, anthrax, psittacosis, and viral equine encephalitis. The fact that the fort had become a cancer research center in 1971 in no way exorcised the sinister associations it had for her.

For the remainder of the forty-mile journey she remained silent, staring out at the ravaged, litter-filled capital and—later—the defoliated countryside, wondering what on earth she had let herself in for.

A watery sun was sinking behind the cloud bank on the horizon by the time they arrived at the twelve-foot-high chain-link fence encircling Fort Detrick. Floodlit notices warned that the inner perimeter fence was electrified and that the flat expanse of balding scrub grass behind it was patrolled by guard dogs. In the distance, entangled in a spider's web of overhead telephone wires, Mary Anderson could see a motley collection of unlit buildings, electricity pylons, and water towers. It looked, she thought, more like an abandoned mining town than a fort.

Barringer pulled up alongside the glass-fronted sentry booth that stood guard over the entrance to the Fort and lowered the car window.

An immaculately uniformed military policeman came out and peered through the window.

"Good evening, ma'am," he said, his breath smoking in the cold evening air. "May I see your identification?"

She opened her handbag and passed him her ID card and letter of authorization. The policeman studied them carefully, comparing her with the photograph, and wrote something on a clipboard.

"Thank you, Dr. Anderson," he said, handing her papers back to her. "And welcome to Fort Detrick. I hope you'll enjoy your stay with us."

The red- and white-striped barrier spanning the road ahead of them swung up and he waved them forward.

The buildings turned out to be much farther away than she had imagined. It took them several minutes to reach the first, a long, single-story hut with a pitched roof below which hung the sign U.S. ARMY FORT DETRICK HEADQUARTERS. Like the rest of the buildings, it looked deserted and was badly in need of a fresh coat of paint. The stunted cherry trees and tubs of wind-blighted geraniums in the forecourt did nothing to relieve the feeling of desolation.

"This," said Barringer, "is the reception center." It was the first time he had spoken since they had left Dulles.

He switched off the engine and the headlights, and together they got out of the car. By the time they arrived at the door of the hut, it had been opened for them by another military policeman.

The room into which he led them was startlingly different from the dismal exterior of the building. It was warm and softly lit and looked like the reception area of a Madison Avenue advertising agency. White deep-piled carpet covered the floor and the tan walls were hung with abstract paintings. The air smelled of fresh paint and brand-new uphol-stery. Sitting behind a large marble-topped reception desk flanked by two bay trees was an attractive, immaculately groomed young woman.

"Dr. Anderson!" she exclaimed, as though delighted by the unex-pected arrival of a close friend. "Welcome to Fort Detrick."

Now totally bewildered, Mary Anderson could only nod at the smiling girl.

"It would save time," Barringer said, "if you'd let me have the keys to your suitcases now. I could be having them checked while you're—"

"Why do you want to check my suitcases?" she demanded.

The receptionist, still smiling, cut in ahead of Barringer. "It's only a formality," she explained. "And if you'd prefer it you can, of course, be present during the search."

"But just what do you expect to find?"

The receptionist smiled patiently. "How do we know until we've looked?" she replied, not unkindly.

Mary Anderson sighed and handed Barringer her keys.

The receptionist stood up and turned to take a coat hanger from the closet behind her desk. "I'm sure you must be exhausted after your journey, Dr. Anderson, but I'm afraid there are certain formalities to go through before personnel can be admitted to the top-security zone. I do hope you understand. And now," she said, holding out her hand, "if you'll let me have your jacket, we'll make a start!"

The receptionist led her into what looked and smelled like the examination room of an expensive clinic. An elderly man wearing a white physician's tunic came forward and shook Mary Anderson warmly by the hand. "Let me say straight off that if there were any way of avoiding these rather tiresome formalities, I for one would be delighted. As it is," he shrugged apologetically, "we must persevere."

"But just what *are* these formalities everyone keeps talking about?" she asked.

"Fingerprints, voiceprint, tissue typing—that sort of thing."

She looked puzzled. "But I went through all of that when I was accepted for the project. Why do I have to go through it again?" She turned, hoping for support from the receptionist, but she had left the room.

"How can I best put it?" he said, leading her slowly toward an examination table. "I hope you won't be offended, but, you know, on a top-security project such as this, it is absolutely essential that we reassure ourselves beyond any shadow of a doubt that you *are* who you *appear* to be. And the only way we can do that is by comparing the data acquired during your earlier examination with the one we will undertake now. It may seem far-fetched, but let me assure you that it is not unknown for a person such as yourself to be abducted by—shall we say—an interested party, and a substitution made. Although I've no idea of the nature of the work you and your colleagues will be engaged upon,

I'm sure that none of you would want such a—such a misunderstanding to occur!''

At the end of the examination, Mary Anderson dressed and was shown back to the reception area. The girl behind the desk smiled her stewardess smile and helped the geneticist on with her jacket. Then she opened a drawer and took out a clip-on ID card, a bleeper, and a silver-jacketed folder with the title *Fort Detrick Orientation Manual* printed on the front cover. ''Your card key will not be ready until the morning,'' she explained, ''but you can take these with you now.'' She slid forward a sheet of paper and a pen. ''Perhaps I could ask you to sign for them''—she pointed to a dotted line flanked by two pencil crosses—''right there!'' While Mary Anderson wrote her name, the girl held her breath as though watching a trick requiring a high degree of skill and nerve. ''Thank you so much,'' she beamed.

Barringer put down the copy of *Playboy* he had been reading and stood up.

''Mr. Barringer will now take you to your apartment,'' said the girl. ''You'll find a snack waiting for you in the refrigerator. I'm afraid we're running a *little* behind schedule''—she glanced enquiringly at him—''but I don't suppose it'll matter if Dr. Anderson is a *teeny* bit late arriving at the reception?''

Barringer shook his head. ''As long as I get her there before the briefing, it'll be okay,'' he replied.

Barringer unlocked the door of the apartment that had been assigned to Mary Anderson and switched on the light. Although the living room he led her into was bigger than the one in her Los Angeles apartment, it had been furnished and decorated in an almost identical manner. A much more expensive version of her own Victorian buttoned-back chesterfield stood in front of the same Mies van der Rohe glass-topped table she had at home. The walls had been painted an identical shade of cornflower blue and hung with magnificent examples of the same nineteenth-century American primitive paintings that she collected.

''How on earth—'' she began, turning to Barringer. But he had disappeared into one of the adjoining rooms with her luggage.

''Is anything wrong, ma'am?'' he called.

She shook her head and walked, as though in a daze, over to an inlaid marble chess table on which stood thirty-two exquisitely carved ivory pieces. The table alone, she guessed, must have cost anything up to three thousand dollars. Whoever had furnished the apartment not only knew what she had at home but also seemed to know what she would like to have had if only she'd been able to afford it.

It was raining when Barringer returned, at nine-thirty, to drive Mary Anderson to the briefing. The Reception Center turned out to be a bleak, barracks-like building less than two hundred yards from her apartment. Barringer parked the car and, shielding her with an umbrella, hurried her up the steps into the foyer.

The room he took her to was large, softly lit, and comfortably furnished. Standing in the middle of it, sipping drinks and talking in hushed voices, were a dozen or so men and a plump, middle-aged woman wearing diamanté spectacles. They seemed ill at ease and faintly embarrassed, like people waiting for the start of a blue movie.

As soon as they caught sight of Mary Anderson they stopped talking and turned, tense and unsmiling, to stare at her. Four of the men she recognized. Standing next to Simon Chesterton was a tall, lean young man with a freckled face and fair, crew-cut hair: Mark Weiner. An aerospace scientist, Weiner had received a great deal of publicity a year earlier for his part in bringing back a crippled space shuttle.

To his right, looking like a small-town haberdasher in his black alpaca jacket and rimless pince-nez, was the cytologist, Dr. Daniel Johnson.

Next to Johnson was the Cal Tech materials scientist, Dr. Philip Benedict, his black bushy eyebrows contrasting oddly with his white hair. He was looking far less self-assured than when she had last seen him on a TV talk show.

Chesterton put down his drink and strode across to greet her. "How nice to see you again," he beamed. "Let's get you a drink, and then we'll introduce you to your colleagues."

A young man carrying a tray of drinks appeared at Mary Anderson's side and she took a glass of champagne. Then, careful not to spill any on the white carpet, she allowed Chesterton to guide her across to the waiting group.

"Dr. Paxton . . . gentlemen," he began, glancing at the clock above the door. "May I introduce you—very quickly, I'm afraid—to the last member of our little team, Dr. Mary Anderson. Dr. Anderson is a geneticist from Berkeley."

No one spoke or moved. The strain of keeping a forced smile on his face for so long had set a nerve twitching beside Chesterton's mouth. "Come and meet Dr. Paul McElroy, one of the gentlemen with whom you'll be working particularly closely during the coming months."

They shook hands and Chesterton introduced her to Weiner and Johnson and to a very old man with sad watery eyes and an almost hairless head speckled with liver spots. Chesterton had to explain twice—in a mixture of English and German—who Mary Anderson was and where she had come from before the old man nodded. After explaining that Dr. Zelinski was a virologist, Chesterton lowered his voice a tone, adding, "Unfortunately, the old gentleman has become a little hard of hearing lately."

Standing next to Zelinski was a man with a pale, sharply pointed face and thinning, straw-colored hair. He was wearing a pair of rose-tinted spectacles that made him look curiously like a sick albino ferret. Judging by the fit of his white mohair and silk suit, Mary guessed that he must have lost a great deal of weight recently. His handshake was soft and damp.

"Dr. Pedlar—who, I should have explained is also a virologist —has an advantage over the rest of us in that he has worked here before," said Chesterton, moving her quickly on to a man with a full red beard. "Dr. Kavanagh—Dr. Anderson." Kavanagh put the pipe he'd been smoking into the pocket of his Norfolk jacket and shook Mary's hand enthusiastically.

"As you probably know, Dr. Kavanagh is associate professor of molecular biology at the Rockefeller Institute. And the gentleman next to him, Dr. Peter Kochalski, is a neurologist from Cornell."

She shook hands with a stocky man with a mop of black, curly hair and a face like a delinquent cherub.

"First a biochemist, then an aerospace scientist, a cytologist, two virologists, a molecular biologist, and now a *neurologist*?" she asked incredulously.

Kochalski shrugged. "I don't get it either," he said.

70

"All in good time," said Chesterton. "All in good time." He was in the middle of introducing her to Philip Benedict when the door was thrown open and Nadelman hurried in. He was followed by two other men: one looking like a retired defensive back who was doing well in the real-estate business, the other like his attorney.

The man who had been serving drinks left the room, locking the door behind him.

"Good!" said Chesterton, looking questioningly at Nadelman. "Well . . . if we're all ready?"

Nadelman nodded curtly and Chesterton began shepherding the bewildered scientists toward three rows of chairs at the far end of the room. A table and a large screen faced the chairs. Nadelman and the two men with whom he'd entered sat down behind the table. Chesterton made sure everyone was seated before joining the others at the table. He, however, remained standing, nervously fingering the gold watch chain that hung from his vest pockets. He cleared his throat and looked down at the big man on his left. "Let me first introduce you to Mr. Frank Napier and"—he leaned forward to catch a glimpse of the man to the right of Nadelman—"Mr. Henry Jerome.

"Mr. Napier is chief security officer and Mr. Jerome chief administration officer of the project." Chesterton's smile flickered on again for a moment. "If you want an appropriation for more equipment," he added, "I suggest you see Mr. Jerome. If your equipment keeps disappearing, Frank Napier's your man."

Nadelman blew his nose loudly and several of the scientists shifted uneasily in their seats. No one laughed.

Chesterton pressed a remote-control switch. A beam of light from the projection booth at the opposite end of the room cut through a cloud of smoke from Dr. Kavanagh's pipe, illuminating the screen behind the table.

Chesterton began, as he put it, at the beginning, explaining how the study group had been convened, its composition, the duties with which it had been charged and the procedures by which it had discharged them. From time to time illustrations from the group's report—maps, photographs, diagrams and charts—were projected on to the screen. Although it was only a summary of their findings and conclusions, it still took Chesterton fifty-five minutes to complete his background briefing.

He paused to take a sip of water. "We have seen," he continued, looking intently at his audience "that conflict creates, in the protagonists, a profound sense of group unity, a willingness to endure deprivation and discomfort, and, most important of all, a willingness to submit to a common discipline.

"After the most searching evaluation of the various scenarios adduced from the evidence I have set before you," he concluded, "it was the unanimous opinion of the study group that the United States has become divided into so many opposing factions that the restoration of social cohesion is now wholly dependent on the appearance of an overwhelming alternative enemy. An enemy that will represent a threat to each and every one of us, irrespective of creed, color, or political persuasion."

Chesterton sat down. The only sound that could be heard was an almost imperceptible buzz from above the screen. Only the men at the table knew that it came from the concealed cameras recording the scientists' MMEs—the micromomentary expressions—that would later help Chesterton evaluate their reactions to what they were about to be told.

Nadelman looked along the rows of bewildered faces. "Ladies and gentlemen," he began, "it has fallen to *us* to produce that overwhelming, alternative enemy." He spoke slowly, his voice grave.

"Our job, during the next eight months, will be to fabricate evidence that this planet generally, and the United States in particular, is threatened by an aggressive, technologically advanced civilization from outer space." Ignoring the flurry of whispered exchanges, he went on at the same measured pace.

"We will construct a spacecraft, crew it, arm it with a nonlethal pathogen, and transport it to Los Angeles, where it will be made to appear to have crashed during a reconnaissance mission.

"In order to introduce the all-important element of threat, it will be necessary to expose a minimum of ten thousand people to the effects of the pathogen."

8

"AS DR. BENEDICT SHOULD know, I am not in the habit of making jokes," said Nadelman as soon as he could make himself heard above the uproar that had just greeted his opening statement. "Neither, as Dr. Weiner suggests, have I taken leave of my senses!"

"Well, someone has," said the man next to Mary Anderson. Although his hair was white, he was lean and tall and looked extremely fit. "If we so much as began work on a project like this, they could throw the goddamn book at us! Just who the hell has authorized it?"

Nadelman waited impassively until the fresh wave of chatter triggered by the man's remark had subsided. "The answer to Colonel Lawrence's question is the President of the United States."

Several people laughed derisively, and someone said, "We've heard that one before!"

Nadelman smiled. "We have indeed, Dr. Conrad," he said. "But on this occasion it happens to be true."

"You talk about a *nonlethal* pathogen . . ." began Paul McElroy.

Nadelman nodded. "One that will incapacitate for a short period of time, but not kill."

"But surely," McElroy continued, "you're asking for the impossible." He turned to Pedlar, expecting support, but the virologist remained silent.

"I think I understand the point Dr. McElroy is making," said Nadelman, grateful for having at last been asked a question that was not hectoring in tone. "I'm not going to pretend that if, for instance, the pathogen chosen were to be specific to the bronchial tree and lungs, it mightn't—in some cases—prove fatal to patients suffering from diseases of those organs.

"However, one of Dr. Paxton's first tasks will be to compile a statistical analysis of the diseases prevalent in the area under consideration and the number of persons likely to be affected at any one time within each category. It will then be for Dr. Pedlar, and Dr. Zelinski, to concentrate the search for a pathogen within those categories where the risk of fatal exacerbation of existing symptoms is minimal."

A plump young man with a shock of brown hair and the open, unlined face of a schoolboy stood up. "Even if only *one* person were to die fr-fr-from the effects of the pathogen," he stammered, "we'd all face—at best—charges of conspiracy to murder if we were ever to be f-f-found out."

"Perhaps Dr. Nadelman has executive clemency in mind!"

Nadelman ignored Kochalski's interjection and the laughter that followed. "Dr. Darrow," he replied, "the risks you are being asked to take are infinitely less than those taken by the average infantryman assigned to counterinsurgency duty, and the rewards immeasurably higher."

"Well, I want no part of it," said Weiner, pushing past the others toward the door.

Nadelman took no notice. "I didn't for a moment imagine I could force anyone to work against his will," he continued blandly, "but I can—and shall—prevent them from leaving the compound."

Weiner hesitated.

"I understand your anxieties perfectly well," Nadelman continued pleasantly. "Although I do not intend to deal with that aspect now, I will say this much: you will be safer *here* than anywhere else in the United States." His manner hardened. "And you will *not*, repeat *not*, find yourselves involved in a Watergate-type fiasco."

74

Weiner returned sheepishly to his chair, while Nadelman polished his spectacles, waiting for total silence. "Detrick may not be as pretty as Woods Hole or Cold Spring Harbor, but it has two great things going for it. The equipment you'll be working with is the best money can buy —and the thinking you can go in for is unlimited."

This, Chesterton knew, was the moment of truth, and he watched anxiously for a reaction. McElroy was the first to look interested, then Benedict, and then Darrow, Kochalski, and Kavanagh. Weiner leaned forward to rest his elbows on the chair in front of him, and Pedlar clasped his hands behind his head. Several of the others settled back in their seats, their arms folded.

Nadelman had won: they were hooked.

"Okay," he said at last, "let's begin. I want to get one thing out of the way at the start: although what we build here will inevitably be described by the media as a 'flying saucer,' no useful purpose will be served by studying the history of this phenomenon, so bedeviled is it with irreconcilable factors. Is that understood?

"Some of the astronomical data will be familiar to the ex-NASA people here, but I'd like them to bear with me nevertheless." He pressed the remote-control projector switch and an equation—headed "Greenbank Probability Formulae (after Drake, von Hoerner)"—appeared on the screen.

"We are residents on one planet in the solar system of an average star of spectral class G2—the sun—which, together with a hundred billion other stars, makes up our immediate galaxy, the Milky Way. Since there are at least one billion other galaxies, to suppose that we are the only technologically proficient civilization verges, as the formulae suggest, on the ridiculous."

Nadelman went on to explain the formulae in detail, dealing with rates of star formation, planetary environments in which intelligent life forms might arise, and the lifetimes of the various star types.

"This last factor," he continued, "is critical. All stars spend a relatively stable period of their life-cycle on what is called the main sequence. Our sun entered the main sequence some four and a half billion years ago and we've already had ample time to evolve into an intelligent species through a process of mutation and natural selection.

"Now, it's reasonable to assume that a speeding-up of the evolution-

75

ary tempo might result in even more highly developed life forms. Up to a point, a warmer environment than ours should accelerate metabolic processes, produce more mutations, and eliminate unsuitable life forms more quickly. The resulting species could make us look like intellectual ants.

"But there's a hitch to these hotter stars—the F class." A Hertzsprung-Russel diagram of star types appeared on the screen. "As you can see, they veer off the main sequence earlier than stars like the sun. So we have two conflicting effects: the possibility of a more rapid development of intelligence, but less time before the star swells into a giant and cooks its surrounding planets.

"Other systems—G or K classes—could, of course, develop intelligent civilizations, but if they did it's likely that their space flights would be for research and exploration. They have time on their side. But in F systems, interstellar travel becomes a question of survival rather than scientific curiosity. They have to find another home or perish—and that could mean an aggressive program of colonization, starting with a reconnaissance flight . . ."

Nadelman paced up and down. "So far, so good," he said, the light from the projector glinting on his steel-framed spectacles. "Now for the difficult part—the fabrication of a spacecraft and crew. Let's start with the biochemical arguments. As you're probably aware, several distinguished scientists have suggested that, in different environments, our carbon-based biochemistry would have been a nonstarter. For example, silicon might be more suitable in low-temperature, nonaqueous, high-ultraviolet flux conditions. Liquid ammonia and F_2O have been suggested as substitutes for water. I don't doubt that life forms based on these alternative biochemistries may exist, but for this project—forget them!

" Carbon, hydrogen, oxygen, and nitrogen are among the most abundant elements in the cosmos. An alternative biochemistry, I suggest, would be the exception rather than the rule. Carbon-based life combines a flexibility, stability, and survival factors that far outstrip the other possibilities."

He paused to pour a glass of water. To Chesterton's relief the audience remained impassive. When discussing the presentation with Nadelman, he had stressed the importance of moving as quickly—and

76

as forcefully as possible—from a statement of the project's aim into an analysis of the scientific problems. "Give their minds something to catch hold of," he'd advised. "Try, as far as you can, to create the atmosphere of a military briefing rather than an academic seminar."

"But this basic elemental makeup," Nadelman continued, "is capable of a vast number of permutations. You only have to look at the dissimilarities between the creatures on this planet. We have two eyes with limited peripheral vision, the snail is sensitive to X rays, and the bat employs a form of radar, and so on.

"The key, the underlying link factor, in all forms of life is that they are *highly organized*. Even the most modest bacterium manages to pack into a space of one thousandth of a millimeter a genetic message that would fill several volumes of Webster's.

"What I'm asking you to come up with is a highly organized, hyperintelligent, carbon-based life form. I'm confident that it can be achieved, *provided* you avoid the trap of chasing little green men up blind alleys. This task," he said, squinting up at the names displayed on the screen, "will be the responsibility of the molecular-biology team, headed by Dr. McElroy and comprising Drs. Anderson, Johnson, Kavanagh, and Kochalski.

"Let's move on to the hardware," Nadelman said. "Dr. Benedict, I would like you, Dr. Weiner, Dr. Conrad, and Dr. Darrow to produce a spacecraft for the extraterrestrial crew—but first, let me define 'spacecraft' by completing the scenario I mentioned earlier. I've already suggested that you should regard the extraterrestrials as having originated from a planet in the solar system of a dying F star. Right? The planet is similar in some respects to earth. The inhabitants launch an interstellar mother ship, containing at least one reconnaissance craft and crew. The mother ship enters our atmosphere and releases the reconnaissance vehicle, which then suffers power loss above Los Angeles, crashes, and explodes.

"Question. What happens to the mother ship at this point?" He shrugged. "We don't know. Maybe it has other craft aboard and stays in the atmosphere, intending to send out a follow-up sortie. Maybe it carries on to other planets, 'seeding' the galaxy with its occupants. The important thing is this—for the purpose of your planning, Dr. Benedict, the mother ship exists. You can save yourselves a hell of a lot of problems by assuming that the bulk of the expedition's supplies and heavy-duty equipment are on board it. What I want from you is a modestly sized, limited-mission vehicle.

"Dr. Weiner, you and Dr. Darrow have both worked with NASA. So have I. We know what kind of hardware gets onto the launch pad. And that is precisely the kind we have to avoid on the project. If there's any suggestion of this ship having an earthly origin, we've lost the ball game. Now," he went on quickly, "that doesn't mean you have to start from scratch. As with the crewmen, I believe there are a number of techniques and properties that you can legitimately use. I shall call these cosmic primes. We know from the spectra of distant stars that the chemical elements, for example, occur throughout the galaxies. Any advanced civilization would therefore have access to these same materials. The elements constitute one cosmic prime, electromagnetic radiation another.

"That leads me on naturally to the question of measurement. One of the ground rules I shall lay down is that you'll have to use a completely new system. As you know, the meter originated as the length of one ten millionth part of the earth's meridional quadrant, and the foot—well, that's obvious. For this operation, they're out! Nor can we use the decimal system. I suggest you use another cosmic prime as your unit of measurement—the wavelength of the radio emission line of neutral hydrogen.

"Dr. Pedlar and Dr. Zelinski will concentrate on the production of a suitable pathogen. As you might expect, the facilities here are exceptionally good. The cancer people had little use for the aerosol test chambers, but they've been kept in perfect condition. In fact, I think you'll find there have been several improvements since you last worked here, Dr. Pedlar." Nadelman turned back to the screen, and called up a new diagram.

"The type of agent finally created is entirely up to you," he said. "But, as you can see from this list, I am anxious for it to meet the following specifications. It must incapacitate without killing, it must be airborne, it must be stable within a wide range of physical parameters, it must become harmless after a three-hour exposure to air, and it must *not* be of a type already known to medicine.

78

"Dr. Paxton, you will be available for consultation with all team members requiring computer assistance.

"The area that's been chosen for the crash and subsequent explosion of the spacecraft borders on Hawthorne and Gardena." A large-scale map of Los Angeles appeared on the screen. "Several houses have been earmarked as possible crash sites," Nadelman continued. "The final selection will be your responsibility, Colonel Lawrence.

"You will also have the job of transporting the completed craft and crew to Los Angeles, and installing them on site. Although they can't be with us at the moment, you'll be assisted by a squad of three men who possess skills similar to your own. Obviously, you'll be liaising closely with Dr. Benedict's team over the coming months.

"We have two points left to cover. First, I naturally don't expect you here to do much in the way of spadework. We have, therefore, brought together a full support staff able to perform all the routine procedures —amino acid analysis, tissue culture and so on. Anything, in fact, that you can delegate without arousing suspicion. Let me stress this point —the support staff do *not* know about your project. Nor will they. As well as giving indirect assistance via the interlab conveyor system, they will provide you with cover by working on a program to investigate the most effective means of maximizing natural resources on a global scale. Part of their work will involve breeding hybrid foodstuffs; part will concentrate on the production of alternatives in materials science. This information will be for public release. However, they will also be investigating techniques for maximizing human potential—correction of genetic abnormalities, for example. The support staff are aware of the sensitivity of such programs and will not be surprised to find that the area we will occupy is subject to top-security restrictions.

"Second—scheduling. As you can see from the screen, I've constructed a network analysis that allows for a total project life of thirty-three weeks. The figure was arrived at by balancing the study group's estimate of the urgency of the situation against the time-consuming nature of your work here. I know you'd probably like much longer, but it can't be done. You'll just have to pull out all the stops.

"The simulated crash will take place on or about December third. You begin on-site work six weeks before that, Colonel. Each of you will be supplied with the critical path data, and we'll be meeting regularly to assess progress." Nadelman used the remote-control switch to cut the projector beam and raise the room lighting. "I think that about covers it. Thank you for your attention. If there are any questions, I'll be glad to answer them."

McElroy was the first to speak. "I'd like an assurance that if things improve, this project of ours will be aborted."

"I can gladly give you such an assurance," said Nadelman. "The President intends to continue to run a program of conventional methods of containment in parallel with Wild Card in the hope of avoiding final committal."

Kochalski asked the next question. "Why was Los Angeles picked as the crash site?"

"Two reasons. We wanted to avoid any ethnic bias in the group hit by the pathogen. We can't afford to have interracial tensions exacerbated in the period between the explosion and the realization that the threat is from an extraterrestrial civilization—and that could easily have happened if we hadn't selected a mixed area like L.A. The second reason is the climate. For our use of the pathogenic agent to be as controlled as possible, we require stable climatic conditions with minimal air movement. Los Angeles' inversion effect fits the bill exactly." He studied Kochalski intently for a moment, as if expecting a further question, then said, "Were you perhaps thinking about your friends, the Littmanns?"

Kochalski was obviously taken by surprise. "Well, yes, as a matter of fact I was."

Nadelman smiled. "Let me set your mind at rest. *None* of you have friends or relations living within, or anywhere near, the maximum exposure zone of the pathogen . . . Yes, Dr. Kavanagh?"

"It occurs to me," he said, cautiously, "that the investigators might not be satisfied when they fail to discover any witnesses to this mythical crash of ours. Surely a falling spacecraft would be plainly visible?"

"I could postulate a number of scenarios to answer that point," Nadelman replied. "For example, the explosion will occur at dead of night, the streets are deserted, and the craft is carrying no lights. I could go on from there to suggest that it escapes radar detection by purposely descending through the cone of silence until it's low enough to fly unobserved." He gave an impatient wave of his hand. "What we do know, from a study of ufology, is that as soon as there is the slightest suggestion of an extraterrestrial crash, the police and the media will be inundated with reports from people willing to swear they saw the ship over Texas, Idaho, Arizona—you name it!"

Lawrence got up next. "I want to clarify a couple of points about the security arrangements," he said. "I've had a little experience in this field, and there's no doubt that your induction procedures have been pretty impressive. But on a project like this, *everything* must be absolutely watertight." He paused, then asked his question slowly, weighing the words. "When it's all over, just *how* do you intend to keep us quiet?"

"I think this is one for you, Frank," Nadelman said.

Napier nodded gravely and stood up. He put one foot on the seat of his chair and leaned forward, hands together with one elbow resting on his knee. "Let me first talk about security in general," he began. He spoke slowly, as though chewing a straw, with a southern accent. "I think it's evident that if as much as a whisper gets out about this operation—whether it achieves reunification or not—none of our lives are going to be worth a plugged nickel. So we're going to have to ask you to tolerate restrictions of your liberty that would be unthinkable in any other situation.

"No outside telephone calls may be made or received. No one may leave the fort—apart from the crew responsible for the L.A. end of the operation—until the project has been completed. Compassionate leave might be granted"—he shrugged, as if the chances of its happening were almost nil—"in exceptional circumstances. Should that be the case, officers from the security detail will accompany the subject at all times. You'll see from your orientation manuals"—he held up one of the silver-jacketed folders—"that all outgoing mail will be censored. Incoming mail will reach you via the box number quoted on page ten. Surveillance equipment is installed for your protection in all laboratories and recreational areas.

"What happens if one of us wants to opt out?" Napier shook a cigarette from the crumpled pack in front of him. "The straight answer is—we can't. Having come this far, we're here for the duration, like it or not." He lit the cigarette. "How do we keep the lid on when it's all over? Well, this was a tough one, but I think we came up with a Jim Dandy answer. A phony psychiatric history has been compiled for each member of the team—Dr. Nadelman and myself included—that shows us to have been confined to various mental institutions from April through December this year. So"—he paused to pick a shred of tobacco from his lip—"if one of us should get the notion, for example, to write a book about the project in five years' time, such action could be made to appear symptomatic of a return of the mental illness which necessitated the original prolonged hospitalization." It sounded as if he might have been quoting the last few phrases from the concluding paragraph of an official report. "Who would believe such a story coming from a sane man or woman," he added, smiling, "let alone a head case?"

It had been made very clear at the start of the briefing that, for the team to work effectively, it had to be free of the fear of exposure. Chesterton, by devising the false case histories, had hoped to provide such reassurance, but now he waited uneasily, wondering if he'd gone perhaps too far.

Apparently he had not, for from that point on the questions became progressively more scientifically oriented. McElroy stood up again and asked why it was necessary for the spacecraft to be manned at all. Perhaps crew it with robots, he suggested.

Nadelman shook his head. "No," he said firmly, "that wouldn't do at all. The whole purpose of this exercise is to build up such a complex network of items of supportive evidence that the investigating authorities will be forced to conclude that the craft is not terrestrial in origin. Ergo, it must be *extra*terrestrial. An unmanned craft doesn't fit in with the aggressive colonization scenario. We're building a jigsaw here—all the pieces have to fit. As for robots, they've become far too earthly in connotation." Nadelman smiled, pleased with the paradox.

Benedict followed with a query about materials, which quickly developed into a closed debate among the members of his own team about the relative merits of beryllium and titanium as the basis for alloys.

Finally, at 11:30, Nadelman brought the meeting to a close. By then, the smoke-filled room had taken on a different character. Chairs had been shunted around into groups, ashtrays were spilling over, and the floor was littered with note-covered scraps of paper.

Frank Napier waited until the others had left the room, then went around picking up all the paper and the coasters and putting them into a burn bag. He returned to the security-detail block, dumped the bag into the incinerator terminal, and went through to the surveillance room. The night-duty security officer was sitting at a console listening to the radio and monitoring the banks of screens. Napier waited, without speaking, until he saw the last red light flash on, signifying that all of the scientists had entered their quarters. Only then did he go to bed.

9

ONCE BACK IN HIS quarters in the residential block, Paul McElroy went straight to bed. But no matter how hard he tried to lull himself to sleep, recollections of Nadelman's briefing kept insinuating themselves into his mind.

He plumped up his pillows and tried again, tuning in the various memories that formed his favorite fantasy until, at last, he was totally enveloped by them. The warmth from the summer afternoon sun through the sailplane's plexiglass canopy; the noise of wind streaming over its aerodynamic body; the faint perfume of rubber and leather. Above floated the white cumulus clouds, cool and moist, that waited to enfold him; below, dappled with their shadows, the flat scrubland burned brown as the hands on the controls in front of him. In his imagination he glanced at the instrumentation panel—the airspeed and turn and bank indicators, the altimeter, and the variometer. What he read in their mat black faces looked good: a long, inviolate afternoon lay ahead, cool and empty as a snowfield.

He awoke at 6 A.M. from a deep, dreamless sleep. Putting on the blue and white polka-dot robe his wife had given him for Christmas, he crossed the room and opened the venetian blinds. A thin sheet of pink cirrocumulus clouds promised a period of fine, settled weather.

He exercised for ten minutes in front of the open window, showered, and, for the first time, examined the layout and contents of the tiny, galleylike kitchen. He made coffee and carried it and a bowl of wheat germ into the lounge. He'd liked this room as soon as he had walked into it the previous day, but it was only now that he fully realized why. It was as clean and functional as a glider—quite unlike his cluttered, split-level home, with its chintzes, phony antique furniture, and plastic floral wallpapers.

He switched on the TV set and sat, the breakfast tray on his knees, in one of the two black leather and rosewood reclining chairs—the kind of furniture that he had always wanted but his wife had never liked.

The picture which appeared on the screen was of a vast area of turbulent brown floodwater, the tops of telegraph poles marking what had once been roads. As he ate, he learned that saboteurs—thought to be members of the American People's Liberation Party—had somehow infiltrated the heavily guarded Grand Coulee Dam and blown a hole in it. The newscaster was talking about "damage estimated to be in the region of three hundred million dollars and a final death toll which some sources believe could go as high as fifteen hundred."

He switched off the TV set and opened his copy of the orientation manual, turning to the section headed "Postal Services." He read through it quickly, reached for a pen and paper, and began writing.

When he had finished he folded the letter and, without reading it through, put it in an envelope on which he wrote his wife's name and address. This, in turn, he placed in a large cardboard wallet, on the outside of which was printed "Mail Censoring Department. DO NOT SEAL ADDRESSEE'S ENVELOPE."

Before setting out, he clipped his ID card to his lapel, pocketed a bleeper and an automatic entry and exit card key, and spent several minutes studying the map of Fort Detrick in the orientation manual.

The Molecular Biology Laboratory was less than half a mile away, and McElroy decided he would walk rather than drive one of the small electrically powered cars that were parked outside the residential block. He turned onto Boyles Street, passing the stable and feed bins, the corral, and the miniature village of experimental-animal buildings—the Animal Farm Division, the manual had called it.

Across the road from Animal Farm was the two-story Leroy D. Fothergill Laboratory, where Pedlar and Zelinski would be working. The Molecular Biology Laboratory turned out to be just around the corner, a long, low building on Chandler Street. The gray box mounted on the wall beside the steel door in the foyer reminded him of a laundromat slot machine. Attached to the box was a notice headed "Security Procedure."

"Personnel are cleared for entry to top-security wings," it read, "by means of voiceprints. Place your card key in the slot indicated. When the RED light is activated, please state your name, department, and job function clearly and in that order. If you are authorized for entry the RED light will be replaced by a GREEN light and the door will automatically open. Scanning monitors are installed to ensure that unauthorized persons are not given access under cover of an authorized person."

McElroy's office was bright, clean, and spacious, with a conference table and six chairs, a couch, and a desk. As he had begun to expect, the equipment and furnishings had been chosen with taste and without regard to cost. Bookshelves over the desk held a full selection of advanced biochemical texts and scientific journals, including *Science*, *Nature*, *Virology*, and the *Journal of Molecular Biology*. He glanced briefly at Luce and Stassik's latest paper on memory models to reassure himself that they had in no way preempted him, then settled down to study the laboratory manifest that was lying on his desk. McElroy was accustomed to working with the best equipment that foundation grants could buy, but he had never before had access to such a concentration of analytical and preparative apparatus. It was obvious that Wild Card's dowry was more than adequate. He shut the manifest and set out to explore the laboratories.

He passed a small alcove, which housed an emergency eyewash basin and chain-pull shower, and turned into the first laboratory. Its appearance contrasted sharply with the friendly disarray of his lab at MIT. There were no half-empty boxes of medical wipes lying on the ultracentrifuge; no grease-pencil messages scrawled on the gleaming white enamel door of the tall refrigerator; no product catalogs propped against the environmental growth chambers. Regimented rows of media and reagent bottles lined the shelves, and packets of disposable medical gloves and micropipets were stacked neatly in a glass-fronted cupboard. McElroy thought of the transformation that the presence of five busy scientists would bring. Researchers rarely had time to worry about the minutiae of their laboratory environment; it was of more consequence that the apparatus should perform, and perform well. He continued his examination of the other facilities and, twenty minutes later, returned to his office to await his team.

Kavanagh, Johnson, and Kochalski arrived three minutes later.

While they waited for Mary Anderson, McElroy—like a proud parent showing off his children—took them on a tour of the laboratories. Kochalski summarized their reaction perfectly when he described the facilities as being like a "research biologist's dream of Christmas morning."

Mary Anderson arrived, pale and apologetic, at eight-fifty. She had slept fitfully, she explained, until it was almost time to get up and had then fallen into a deep sleep.

As they strolled back through the laboratories to McElroy's office, they discussed their impressions of Detrick and their reaction to the previous night's briefing. "I think we should just turn Nadelman loose in the streets of L.A.," Kochalski said. "That ugly sonofabitch would sure scare the crap out of me if I ran into him on a dark night!"

McElroy, laughing, motioned them through to his office. "The only thing they seem to have forgotten," he said, pointing to the bookshelves, "is a subscription to *Astounding Science Fiction.*"

"We may have to put in for it yet," replied Kochalski. "I have a hunch it could turn out to be more useful than a truckload of the *Journal of Molecular Biology.*"

"Well," said McElroy, taking off his wristwatch and propping it up in front of him, "where in the name of God do we begin?"

"Where indeed?" Mary Anderson murmured.

Kochalski rubbed his hands briskly together. "The best SF movie I ever saw," he began, "and I speak now, you understand, as a guy who's seen a lot of active service at drive-in movies, was about these heavy-duty ants that—"

"No good!" said McElroy firmly. "We'd have too fast a turnover in lab technicians.'' He paused to switch on the tape recorder. "Before we can begin to draw up the blueprints for the extraterrestrials, we need to refine the design brief. So far, we know we're aiming for a life form that's hyperintelligent—or at least looks that way—and is based on carbon biochemistry. I guess for practical purposes we have to accept that constraint.

"Okay, just for starters, what's our working definition of life going to be? Can we identify any factors in terrestrial life forms that we can reasonably assume to be common to an alien species?''

Kochalski looked doubtful. "I was going to suggest organization as the principal factor,'' he said, "but I suppose you could say that a salt crystal is pretty well organized . . .''

"Symmetrically structured would be more accurate,'' Kavanagh said. "Organization implies a dynamic situation, the ability to interact with the environment. By the way''—he held up his pipe—"does anyone mind if I smoke this?''

No one did.

"I'd define life,'' said Johnson, choosing his words with care, "as a system which has the basic ability to maintain, evolve, and repair itself.''

"But what about the ability to reproduce, grow, digest?'' asked Kavanagh.

"Strictly relevant only to terrestrial life, so far as we know,'' Johnson replied, squinting through the smoke from Kavanagh's pipe. He smiled. "And it would be bad science to generalize from one specific case. Anyway, what do you mean by reproduce? Suppose you have a computer capable of building an exact replica of itself—is that reproduction?''

"I think Dr. Kavanagh means that the system has to have some method of transmitting information from one generation to the next, and of translating it into chemical structures,'' McElroy interjected, "just as we use DNA, RNA, and protein. Otherwise, it loses its identity and mutates to a nonviable form.''

Kavanagh poured himself a glass of water from one of the carafes on the table. "All this gets infinitely more complicated,'' he said, "when you add the requirement for intelligence.''

McElroy shook his head. "Not necessarily. Let's do this in steps based on the systems definition of life—and see how far it takes us.'' He looked around the table. "Is there any way, for example, of using our carbon-based biochemistry, and reshuffling the basic building blocks to get a similar *system* but a different life form? Don't get me wrong," he added quickly. "I'm not suggesting we try to brew up something entirely new from primordial soup and UV light. Let's stay on the molecular level."

"We're accustomed to amino acids that rotate light waves to the left," said Kavanagh, prodding a pipeful of glowing tobacco with the end of a burned match. "Suppose we went after an organism whose amino acids all rotated light to the *right* . . ."

"It's too risky," said Johnson, "and anyway, I wouldn't like to take on the lab work the idea involves."

"It certainly would be a mind bender," Kavanagh admitted. "Okay—then how about synthesizing some kind of helical polymer to replace DNA? A new information molecule!"

McElroy put down the pencil he had been toying with and leaned back in his chair. "We'll be here for the next fifty years if we get into that."

"I vote we move up to the cellular level," Johnson suggested. "Hybridization, maybe?"

Kochalski tore a sheet of paper from the pad in front of him and folded it carefully in half, then in half again. "That's not such a bad line to take," he said, looking across at Johnson. "Which method?"

Johnson began polishing his pince-nez. "I was thinking of cell fusion with lysolecithin or inactivated Sendai virus as possible mediators. We could take two lines of mammalian cell—human and bat, say, and produce—"

"Anyone suggesting Batman," said McElroy, looking at Kochalski, "is in big trouble!"

The neurologist looked hurt. "As if I would! It's a nice gimmick, though—radar instead of eyes." He began to tear off the corners of the paper he had been folding. "Of course," he continued, "the other approach to hybridization would be to mutate a human cell with a transducing virus."

McElroy nodded. "It would certainly give us more scope. We could hitch up a train of genes to a virus and send it into the cell. Any of the existing genes we didn't want could be surgically removed by laser—"

90

"Then transplant the mutated cell into an enucleated ovum," Kochalski said, "and bingo!" He pulled apart the tightly folded wedge of paper to reveal a chain of anthropomorphic figures. "Produce a clone!"

"The trouble is that work in this field more or less stopped after the NAS came out against fooling around with genetic intervention," Kavanagh said.

"Isn't that an advantage from our point of view?" McElroy asked. "I mean, the fact that no one—so far—has actually succeeded in growing a man-animal hybrid to term."

Mary Anderson reached down beside her for her handbag and took out a packet of aspirin. "Thank God for that," she said.

McElroy took a glass and half filled it with water for her. "Aren't you feeling well?" he asked.

She put one of the tablets into her mouth and swallowed it with a sip of water. "Just a headache," she replied. "Do you think there might be anything as mundane as a coffee machine among all that gleaming hardware out there?"

McElroy switched off the tape recorder and stood up. "Now that's what I call a *good* question. If there is, how would you like it?" he asked, looking around the table.

He returned a couple of minutes later with a tray, five containers of coffee, and a doughnut for Kochalski. "It's in an alcove," he said, "just inside the main entrance." He passed out the coffee and they began again.

The five scientists broke for lunch at 1:20 and, with Kochalski as navigator (he was the only one who had remembered to bring a copy of the orientation manual with him), made their way along Chandler Street to the Recreation Center.

They spent ten minutes exploring the reading room, the lounge, a number of games rooms, a sauna, and a swimming pool before wandering into the restaurant—to discover that they were the first to arrive.

Like the other rooms in the building, the restaurant appeared to be completely devoid of staff. The north wall of the long, windowless room had been divided into booths by panels of smoked glass. Each booth contained a circular white dining table and six chairs. Set into the wall of each of the booths was a serving hatch, beneath which was a row of pushbuttons inscribed with the word SERVICE, the letters A, B, and C, and numerals from 1 to 9.

They settled themselves at the table farthest from the door and studied the shiny white menu cards that were resting on blue paper napkins on each of their side plates. Six appetizers were listed and three main dishes. The caloric value of each dish appeared beneath its name. There was a choice of six cooked vegetables and seven salads. A note, printed in red at the bottom of the card, asked that "menu cards and napkins which have been used for making notes should be disposed of in the shredder before leaving the restaurant."

While Kochalski waited for the others to make up their minds, he helped himself to a boutonniere from the bowl of white chrysanthemums standing in the middle of the circular table. He took their orders and following the instructions set out at the top of the menu card, pressed button number 2, then A, followed by the code for Vichyssoise. He followed the same procedure to order two roast shrimp in garlic butter and one avocado vinaigrette; two escallope of veal stuffed with Alaskan crab, one porterhouse steak—medium rare—and two red snapper amandine.

Kavanagh returned from the bar carrying a tray of bottled beer, as the bulb in the SERVICE button lit up, indicating that their food had arrived. Mary, who was sitting closest, opened the door of the service elevator and passed out the dishes.

When they had finished their first course, she replaced the empty dishes on the shelves of the elevator and returned it to the kitchens below.

Their main course arrived two minutes later, as the other members of the team began to trickle into the room.

Paul McElroy got up from the conference table and put his hand reassuringly on Kochalski's shoulder as he passed behind him.

"It's clever, Pete, very clever. But as Mary said, it just *won't* work."

He strolled back to his place at the table and picked up his wristwatch. It was six-fifteen. They had been at it for nine hours.

"How are you all feeling?" he asked.

Mary Anderson closed her eyes and pressed the tips of her fingers against her temples. "Tired," she replied. "If you don't mind, Paul, I think I'd like to stop soon."

"Sure," said McElroy. "How are the rest of you bearing up?"

Kochalski wiped his hands and the back of his neck with a handkerchief and looked for reactions from the other men. "If we can get some booze sent across," he replied. "I'm game to push on for a while longer."

"I'm not sure if they'll do that," said McElroy. "We must remember to bring some in with us tomorrow."

Mary Anderson picked up her bag from the floor. "Would you like me to try to get some for you at the place we had lunch?" she asked.

McElroy jumped in quickly before anyone had a chance to accept her offer. "We wouldn't dream of it," he said, walking across to open the office door for her. "I hope you sleep better tonight." He grinned.

She shook her head and smiled sadly back at him. "I'm afraid I've been too tired to be of much use today."

McElroy walked her part way down the corridor and returned with four bottles of iced Coke. "This'll have to do until we can get something stronger."

He made a space for Kochalski's drink in the litter of folded paper constructions that lay in front of him. "When did you get into this scene?" he asked, picking up a perfectly folded geodesic dome.

"When I stopped smoking, I guess. At least it gives me something to do with my hands." He sipped his drink in silence. "Paul," he said, suddenly brightening, "suppose we prevented the growth of the epidermis and substituted an inorganic membrane?"

McElroy shook his head emphatically and reached for one of Johnson's menthol cigarettes. "Heart? Lungs? Skeleton? What about them?" He borrowed Kavanagh's matches to light the cigarette. "No, I'm certain it's a mistake to think in terms of a complete working model; you provide too much information that way. Nobody says we have to grow something that can *walk* to Los Angeles, for Chrissake! As I see it, we are simply"—he laughed humorlessly—"*simply* expected to come up with what amounts to a damn good conjuring trick!" He looked across at the uncomprehending faces. "Don't you see? We've only got to make it *look* as though we've sawed a woman in half—we don't have to actually *perform* the goddamn operation!"

He studied his cigarette with an expression of acute distaste. "I don't know how you can smoke these things," he said, dropping it into the dregs of his Coke. "Tell me," he demanded, leaning forward, "what distinguishes man from all other forms of life?"

"A large brain," Kavanagh replied.

McElroy looked at the other men.

"Intelligence . . .?" offered Kochalski.

Johnson coughed gently. "You mean," he said, "the capacity for abstract thought? For complex language? For planning?"

"I think we all know what Pete's implying," McElroy cut in impatiently. "And intelligence," he said, looking at Kavanagh, "is *not* determined by brain size alone. If it were, whales would have declared a moratorium on hunting *us*! Even when you examine the ratio of brain weight to body weight, man comes off worse than mice. No, his gimmick is a highly developed cerebral cortex. A large brain coupled with an incredibly rich intercellular communications network.

"We were worrying about the organs of metabolism, skeleton, and so on. There's no need. Dispense with them," he said airily, tossing the box of matches back to Kavanagh. "I suggest, gentlemen, that all that needs to remain after the explosion is brain tissue, together with some sort of a protective shell and a life-support system. In fact—the ideal astronaut!"

"Right," said Kochalski. "We can call it a 'cerebroid'—you know, 'brain-like.' "

"Okay," said McElroy, rolling down his shirt sleeves.

"Now hold it a minute," said Kavanagh, looking puzzled. "You're *way* ahead of me."

"What I think he's suggesting," said Kochalski, watching McElroy warily, "is that we use the cell-transplantation techniques we were talking about earlier to produce a clone of mutants with abnormally large, highly developed cerebral hemispheres. Then we remove the brains from the mutants and rehouse them in mechanical bodies. Right?"

McElroy shook his head. "Not quite. I think we can go further than that. There's no sense in growing the creatures to term and *then* dissecting out the cerebral hemispheres. It's going to be far more effective if we take the brain explants much earlier at neural tube stage.

94

That'll give us our starting material: a mass of immature brain cells that we can culture on a three-dimensional matrix.''

Kavanagh scratched his head. "For all this to be worthwhile, the investigative team has to be able to identify the tissue as brain," he said. "If the cerebroids are to be blown up along with the spacecraft, we'll have to find some way of protecting them from charring, for example."

"That's one for Benedict," Johnson suggested. "If he builds a cryogenic tank into the spacecraft, it'll rupture on explosion, spray the tissue with liquid nitrogen, snap-freeze it, and provide perfect histological specimens for the investigators."

"The important point," said McElroy, "is that they'll find *only* brain cells in the debris—and that should *really* give them something to think about!" He stood up and lifted his jacket off the back of his chair. "But we're still left with one sonofabitch of a problem. Before we can get down to lab work, we still have to find some way of proving to the investigators' satisfaction that our cerebroids aren't man-made!"

10

MARY ANDERSON, KAVANAGH, AND Kochalski had gone straight to the common room as soon as they came off duty. The softly lit lounge had been empty, and for half an hour or so they'd sat drinking coffee and talking over the events of the day. McElroy had wandered in at eleven-thirty, just as they were leaving. Kavanagh and Kochalski had been complaining of feeling tired, and Mary had been the one who offered to stay behind to keep Paul McElroy company.

"How's it going?" she asked him as soon as they were alone. She picked up her cup with both hands and, watching him closely, sipped the steaming coffee.

"Terrible!" he replied, breaking open the pack of Camels he'd brought back from the vending machines together with the coffee.

He offered her a cigarette, but she shook her head. "Do you always smoke so much, Paul?" she said softly. He shrugged, as if that were the least of his problems. Was it only fifteen days since they'd all first met, she wondered? It felt more like fifteen months. The enormity of the task they had been ordered to undertake, their isolation from the support team, let alone the world beyond the compound, and the terrible risk each of them ran by working on Wild Card had fostered a sense of unity that would have been unthinkable in a normal situation. There were no cliques and no rivalries, only a profound sense of mission and total dedication to the task they had been asked to perform.

One of the films they had been shown during the briefing was of an experiment Konrad Lorenz had carried out at the Max Planck Institute. A stuffed hawk, suspended on a wire, had been "flown" over a flock of geese. The instant it had appeared the geese had abandoned their rigidly maintained social hierarchy and their fiercely guarded territories and had clustered together, their wings outstretched to protect their goslings, unified by a common danger.

Mary wondered, again, if all of the scientists realized that they themselves had now become participants in a similar experiment, an experiment that supported—in the most seductive manner possible—the thesis upon which Wild Card had been predicated.

"Do you want to talk about it?" she asked.

Paul McElroy looked puzzled. "About my smoking too much?"

"No, silly! About what Nadelman calls the Unanswerable Factor. That's what's bothering you, isn't it?"

"There's not much to talk about—that's the hangup."

She reached across and took a cigarette from the pack.

"I've finally gotten it into my head that you don't smoke," he said, lighting it for her, "and suddenly you start!"

She blew a plume of smoke at the ceiling, and laughed. "Only in a crisis."

Paul looked surprised. "I thought I was the only one around here having a crisis. What's your problem?"

Mary shrugged. "It's just that by the end of the week we're going to have gotten as far as we can—"

"Until I provide you with the Unanswerable Factor." Paul stared down at his cup and began stirring the coffee obsessively. He looked drawn and tired. The tan he'd had when he arrived had faded, and though she knew it couldn't be so, there now seemed to be many more gray hairs among the brown at his temples. She felt an upsurge of the resentment she had experienced when she had first learned what was expected of them—this time, to her surprise, mingled with what seemed like maternalistic concern for him. She wondered how much these feelings had to do with the fact that the cerebroids were to be grown from cells that had been taken two days earlier from Paul's body and her own.

"Paul," she said quietly, "this Unanswerable Factor you've been asked to come up with—it's nonsense. You know that, don't you? It has to be! How can there be a way of *proving*"—she used the word contemptuously—"that the cerebroids haven't been man-made, when they *will* have been man-made? Like the song says, 'Only God can make a tree,' and he's not playing on our team. The devil maybe—"

"Thank *you*!" he said, without enthusiasm. "So what are you suggesting?"

"Well," she began, then stopped, aware that she was in at the deep end more quickly than she had intended. "I think that you should go to Nadelman and tell him it was a great idea, but it just won't stand up. That we all want to do something to help, but think our time would be better spent as volunteer ambulance drivers or something."

"But it will stand up!" he protested. "You and Pete already know how you're going to culture the cells, Kavanagh and Johnson have cracked most of the problems associated with the matrix and the growth chambers, and Phil's boys have completed a mathematical model of the mechanical parts of the cerebroids *and* the goddamn spacecraft! I know those weirdos in virology are supposed to be having problems with the pathogen, but they'll crack it."

"So?" she said. He had in no way dented her conviction that the project would sooner or later have to be aborted. "You probably know the critical path on Wild Card better than any of us. Every branch of the network has to pass through the Unanswerable Factor box before arriving at Goal Achieved. And that's not going to happen because there isn't—and never can be—an Unanswerable Factor!"

"I don't believe it!"

"You don't *want* to believe it!" she said, not unkindly. "Don't you see that? You're all enjoying yourselves too much to—"

"Enjoying ourselves?" said Paul, stubbing out his cigarette with more force than was necessary. "You've got to be kidding! I interrupted the most important research program of my career, one I'd been working on for five years, to come here!"

Mary sipped her coffee. "Tell me about your project," she said.

"Something to do with memory research, wasn't it? Or shouldn't I ask?"

"I don't mind talking about it," Paul said, "if you don't mind me not going into too much detail. Have you heard of the work of Thompson and McConnell?"

Mary frowned, trying to remember. "Weren't they the ones who trained flatworms to curl up whenever a light was shined on them?"

"There was more to it than that. Having trained one group of worms, they minced them and fed them to untrained samples—"

"Which seemed to remember the light avoidance response learned by the original group," Mary interrupted. "It seemed to suggest that memory could be stored in specific molecules, rather like morse code, right?"

Paul nodded. "It was Georges Ungar's work with peptides that really turned me on. To make a long story short, I've figured out—or I think I have—the relationship between learning experiences and the chemical structure of the proteins that record them! I can even synthesize complete sequences. If I do that, and inject them into your brain, I can short-circuit the whole learning process and give you a memory of something you have never actually experienced."

Mary looked horrified. "My God," she said, "I didn't realize you'd gotten that far."

"Another six months of clinical tests and I'll be able to prove it," Paul said, looking at his watch.

"You want to be going," Mary said, getting up.

"No, stay a while, it isn't midnight yet. The night is young."

Reassured, she sat down again and waited while he fetched more coffee. She accepted another of his cigarettes, and he took one himself.

"With a line like 'The night is young,' " she said, leaning forward as he flicked the wheel of his lighter, "you should really be lighting both cigarettes simultaneously, then handing me mine."

"Huh?"

"That's what Paul Henried did for Bette Davis in *Now Voyager*," she explained. "It became one of the great romantic clichés—like the line 'The night is young.' "

"*Now Voyager*. Christ, at your age you should be quoting from *Easy Rider*."

Mary smiled. "I'm a late-night movie freak."

"What's an attractive girl like you doing—"

"Working in a place like this?" Mary raised her cup in a toast. "Here's lookin' at you, kid," she said with a Humphrey Bogart lisp.

"I was going to say, 'What's an attractive girl like you doing watching late-night movies?' Or is the answer to both questions the same?"

"I guess it is, at that," she replied, suddenly preoccupied with arranging the cigarette butts in the ashtray in neat rows.

"Those blue-green algae sure do have a helluva lot to answer for!" he said, gently.

She smiled. Blue-green algae were the first creatures on earth to reproduce themselves sexually. "I guess coming here was my equivalent of joining the French Foreign Legion. Although it wasn't just an unhappy love affair I was escaping from—it was myself, as much as anything. Anyway," she said, "it's all *very* boring. Tell me about you. You're married, aren't you?"

He nodded.

"Children?"

"One of each. Johnny's eight, Kathy's ten."

"What about your wife, does she work?"

"If she could overhear us, I'd have to be very careful how I answered that. She used to want to teach English when she was at Radcliffe—we met, would you believe it, at a Harvard-Yale Boat Race dance—but she stopped when we got married."

"Wanting to teach English or dancing?" Mary asked.

"Both!"

"Oh, I see," she said, suddenly sorry she had teased him. "Do you have a photograph of the kids?"

"Do I look like the kind of guy who carries around pictures of his family?"

"Most married men do. They're usually color Polaroids, and they keep them in their billfolds next to their credit cards."

He nodded gravely, as though he'd discovered a clue of great importance. "That explains it," he said.

"Explains what?"

"The blue-green alga you ran away from was married!"

She laughed, but said nothing.

"Do you want to talk about it?" he asked. "I'm a good listener."

"I'm sure you are, but if you don't mind I'll take a rain check. Right now, I'd rather hear about you. What about the sailplane bit? That all sounds madly glamorous."

"Who told you about that?"

"Pete, the other day at lunch."

"We've made a deal. When we get out of here, he's going to teach me surfing, and I'm going to teach him to fly."

"I didn't know you were interested in surfing," she said. "It's been a passion of mine for—well, I'm not saying how long—but for a long time. Hey, that's really great!"

"Well, maybe you'd teach me. That might be more fun than having Kochalski as an instructor."

"Do you think your wife would approve?" she asked, laughing.

Paul looked unconcerned. "At least she couldn't complain that I spend all my money on my glider."

"I'm sorry," she said, embarrassed that she had led him into making such an admission.

"Relax. I'm not about to launch into a my-wife-doesn't-understand-me routine."

"It must be getting awfully late," she said, pushing back the cuff of his shirt to look at his watch. "My God, is it *really* that time?"

They stood up.

"I hope you're not intending to go back to work now," she said, as they started toward the door.

"I thought I might try playing a little golf. I've got a hunch that there's something stirring at the back of my mind, and half an hour with a number two iron might just be what's needed to induce labor. But I'll walk you back to your apartment first."

She slipped her arm through his. "Try not to stay up too late. And since this must be one of the last places left in America where there's absolutely no risk of my being mugged, I can—thank you all the same—perfectly well see myself home."

11

MCELROY TRIED TO REACH the fourth green of the Oahu Country Club, Hawaii, with a rather optimistic two iron. His tendency to hook the ball was well under control, if not entirely eradicated, and he was putting better than he had the previous day on the West Course at Wentworth.

As the trajectory of the ball was superimposed on the computer-linked simulator screen of Fort Detrick's recreation center, and the picture changed to a view of the fairway, McElroy ground out his cigarette on the artificial green between the tee and the screen and studied his last stroke—an uphill lie.

He was well into his backswing when a curious thought occurred to him. He lowered his club and stared at the screen. McElroy had played on the Oahu course many times when he had been vacationing with his wife in Hawaii and there was no doubt that this was the same place. And yet the picture facing him was not of the fairway as it had been when he last played on it, he told himself, but as it was *on the morning it had been photographed*. One moment in the life of the fairway, recorded by the camera and transported forward in time. But there was another way of looking at it. By playing on the simulator now, he was, in effect, making a trip *back* in time . . .

Time . . . McElroy became transfixed as his unconscious delivered the conceptual jackpot that had eluded him for so long!

"Radiocarbon dating!" exclaimed McElroy. "It's so simple I could kick myself for not having thought of it before. By giving our cerebroids an unusually *low* carbon 14 content, we can artificially age them so that they'll appear to have undertaken an interplanetary flight lasting a thousand years. It's the final clincher—the Unanswerable Factor! Even if the investigative team starts out thinking that they're dealing with a Russian or Chinese experimental space capsule that's fouled up, how're they going to explain away the fact that it would have had to be launched in the tenth century? For Chrissake, even *gunpowder* hadn't been invented then!"

Benedict took a bottle of caffeine tablets from the pocket of his bathrobe, and swallowed two with a mouthful of black coffee. "I know I'm not exactly at my best at four-thirty in the morning," he said, "but how, for the love of God, are we going to use radiocarbon dating in our project? We're not on an archeological dig."

"As you know," McElroy said, "Libby first used it in the early forties for dating organic remains."

Kochalski yawned and turned to Benedict. "All living matter has a fixed proportion of carbon 14 in its structure," he said, rubbing his eyes, "which remains constant throughout the life of the organism. But when it dies—"

"Or if it were to enter a state of suspended animation—" added McElroy.

"No new carbon 14 can be taken in and the existing stock begins to decay."

"It's a kind of atomic clock," McElroy continued. "For example, after five thousand, five hundred and sixty-eight years, plus or minus thirty years, half the carbon 14 would have decayed and the number of radioactive pulses recorded on a Geiger counter would be exactly *half* that found in a living organism." He looked across at Benedict. "I tell you, man, it's foolproof!"

Nadelman got up, pulled aside the curtains, and began walking around switching off lights. He was the only person in the room, other than McElroy, who was wearing day clothes. "What I like about it," he said, "is that it'll almost certainly be the last thing the investigative team discovers—simply because it won't occur to them to look until late in the game. This will stamp it with the hallmark of many other great scientific discoveries—serendipity!

"The first thing we have to do," he continued, looking around the crowded common room, "is see what repercussions Paul's carbon 14 notion will have—if any—on the work already in progress. Dr. Weiner?"

At the mention of his name, the aerospace scientist looked up from the slide rule he had been studying and cleared his throat. "It all looks A-OK to me," he said. "We already planned to put in electromagnetic deflection shielding to minimize the effects of cosmic ray strikes on the crew quarters. But what you'll have to bear in mind," he added, turning to McElroy, "is that bombardment during the spacecraft's quote flight unquote will have the effect of *decreasing* the age of the crew—if you follow me?"

McElroy nodded. "What you're saying is that if the investigative team's date tests indicate an age of—I don't know—say fifteen hundred years, they'll regard that as being a *minimum* estimate."

"Right. However, we'll have to decide pretty quickly just what age we *are* going for. I'll have to know this, for example, before I can produce convincing ray tracks in the spacecraft's hull." He swung his legs over the arm of his chair and turned back to Nadelman. "It may seem a bit late in the countdown to ask this, but where the hell is this mission supposed to have originated from anyway?"

Nadelman brushed aside the question. "It doesn't matter," he replied. "The age of the spacecraft could only be determined by the speed of flight in relation to the distance traveled—two factors the investigative team will have no way of determining. I suggest we use the figure Dr. McElroy mentioned, fifteen hundred years. That would indicate that the crew set out shortly after the death of Attila the Hun!"

"I'd like to ask Paul how he intends lowering the c-c-carbon 14 content in the cerebroids' tissues," stammered Darrow.

"Simply by including the prescribed amount in their feeds. You are—as they used to say—what you eat!"

"B-b-but how do you actually *do* it?"

"The theory is simple enough. Isotopes have different zero-point energies and we can separate out all of the carbon 14 from the constituents of the feeds. If we stay with the idea that our crew should be fifteen hundred years old, the amount of carbon 14 we put *back* would give an activity less than living tissue by . . . help me, somebody . . ."

"Sixteen point seven per cent," said Charlotte Paxton.

McElroy smiled. "Does that answer your question?"

"I wish it were as easy as you make it sound," Mary Anderson said forlornly. "You realize we'll have to go through the same procedure with *all* the isotopic elements in the nutrient medium—just in case the investigators check them as well as the carbon."

McElroy leaned forward, looking across at the critical path analysis diagram that Nadelman had brought with him.

"Well, you've got until week two," he said, smiling at her, "before the proportions become significant."

"Great!" she replied, but there was no levity in her voice. She understood Paul's excitement because, as a scientist, she recognized the pleasure that comes with solving a tough, recalcitrant problem. But how, she asked herself, could someone as brilliant as he not see that Wild Card was as dangerous—and as pointless—as Russian roulette? It seemed clear that, brilliant though they were, the rest of the scientists were completely caught up in this mad scheme. She would never be able to convince even Paul against it. Her mind was made up. She would have to go and convince Nadelman herself.

"Dr. Nadelman," she said, as they were leaving. "Could I talk to you for a few minutes?"

Nadelman nodded, waiting for her to begin.

"I'd like it to be in private," she said, embarrassed to see that Charlotte Paxton and Benedict had also hung back, wanting to speak to him.

"Is it urgent?" he asked.

"I would like it to be as soon as possible, please."

He sighed, as though this were one task too many, and glanced at his watch. "Okay," he said, without enthusiasm, "then you'd better come across to my office in fifteen minutes."

Mary let herself into Nadelman's comfortably furnished outer office just before nine A.M. Originally planned to house a secretary, it was used only as a reception area because he thought it more secure to type his own memoranda and reports. Scientists who arrived and found the red bulb above Nadelman's door alight would sit there reading magazines or talking until they were summoned.

The red light was on and the door to his office slightly ajar. She could see him reflected in one of the partially open windows. He was standing looking out at the cherry trees, now heavy with ripening fruit, his jacket off and his red scrambler telephone pressed to his ear.

She coughed to let him know she had arrived, but if he heard he gave no sign. She coughed again, this time louder, but still he did not turn around. Feeling somewhat foolish, she was about to leave—intending to wait in the corridor until it was exactly nine and then knock—when she heard him say, in an irritable voice, "But, Dr. Pedlar, you still haven't answered my question! Does any of this affect what you're *actually* doing, not what the others think you're doing?"

Mary smiled to herself. Pedlar's loquaciousness had become something of a joke, with Nadelman suffering it less patiently than most. She was halfway through the door when Nadelman spoke again. "Okay, okay! That's enough about that. Now what do you intend doing to potentiate the virus's cytolytic properties? How they die is going to be as important as how many die, if Wild Card's to succeed."

Mary stopped, rooted to the spot. That meant a virus that *kills*, and, having killed, causes rapid cellular disintegration. Was this what they intended to arm the spacecraft with on the night? The question was answered for her a moment later.

"That doesn't interest me, Dr. Pedlar. Let me repeat, the destruction over the entire area must be *absolute*!"

She would tell Nadelman later that she hadn't needed to speak to him, after all. Stepping into the corridor, she closed the door silently behind her.

12

SHORTLY AFTER ARRIVING IN the molecular biology laboratory on the morning of April 10, Kochalski and Johnson—wearing sterile gowns, gloves, and masks—went through the UV irradiation barrier and airlock into the aseptic room and began work. While Kochalski swabbed down the stainless-steel working surfaces with alcohol, Johnson made a visual examination of the cultures in the hot room next door through an observation box set into one wall. The temperature in the room was maintained at 37° centigrade—body temperature and therefore ideal for cell growth—and it was here that the starting material for the cerebroids had been nurtured over the past few days.

Mary Anderson had collected the original cells by taking buccal smears—a scraping of oral epithelium off the inside of the cheek—from herself and McElroy. The smears had then been dissociated into cell suspensions and transferred to a series of petri dishes, each containing a nutrient medium. In this way, the team had obtained male and female cells without resorting to easily identifiable laboratory cell lines.

At regular intervals, the growing sheets of cells had been redigested with trypsin and inoculated into a fresh medium. After several passages to ensure that there were no cytopathic effects, Johnson had selected the purest subcultures—one cell strain derived from Paul McElroy and one from Mary Anderson.

Now, Kochalski and Johnson were carrying out the next phase of the program. Using a complex optical system that produced a laser microbeam, Kochalski irradiated a batch of six unfertilized ova, destroying their nuclei. Johnson removed the cultures from the hot room, sucked the nuclei of three cells from each of the strains into individual micropipets, and transplanted them into the vacant spaces in the host ova. It was a sophisticated piece of intercellular trickery. The ova reacted as though they had been normally fertilized and began to cleave into the ball of cells—the blastula—that eventually develops into a fetus. Only two of the blastulae would be needed for the subsequent stages of the experiment; the others were insurance.

Four days later, cloning began. One cell from the most successful Anderson-strain blastula and one from the McElroy-strain were transferred to separate culture dishes. It was like taking cuttings from a plant. Each of the cells possessed all the genetic information necessary for development into a mature organism. Every day for the next nine days a new pair of cells was put into culture. The result was two clones, each consisting of ten genetically identical embryos. The last pair were ten days younger than the first.

By May 9, the oldest pair of embryos—now about five millimeters long—had reached the neural tube stage and the cerebral hemispheres were visible under a dissecting microscope. Using remotely controlled instruments, McElroy and Kochalski removed the hemispheres and dissociated the tissues into suspension. The remains of the embryos they discarded. As each pair reached the same stage of maturity, the procedure was repeated.

This was the team's busiest period. As each dissection was complete, the two cell suspensions—one from a McElroy-strain embryo and one from an Anderson-strain—were cultured together in the presence of an inactivated virus. The two cell types fused—"a wedding in a petri dish," Kochalski called it.

For McElroy, this cell fusion was an important facet of the extraterrestrial deception. The fused neuroblasts were genetic mosaics of male and female strains and would develop into giant brain cells, containing an unusual number of chromosomes—many more than the normal human complement of forty-six. Paradoxically, although they would have stood no chance of developing into a viable adult human, such giant cells with their abnormal chromosome set would thrive when grown in culture.

By the end of May, the fused cells had been seeded onto three-dimensional matrices. For the next six months they would be nurtured in growth chambers and subjected to continuous intensive treatment with nutrients, nerve-growth factor, and electrical stimulation. At the end of the program, the number of cells would have increased a millionfold. The cerebroids would be mature.

13

PAUL MCELROY WAS FIFTEEN minutes early arriving at Mary Anderson's apartment. Although they had come to know one another very well, this was—for some unaccountable reason—the first time either had visited the other.

From within the room came the muted sounds of chamber music. Paul pressed the bell. He was beginning to wonder if Mary had heard when she appeared at the door. She was wearing a short white robe, and was still wet from the shower.

"I'm sorry," he said. "Do you want me to come back?"

"Don't be silly," she smiled. "Come in." She stepped back and, as he passed, he noticed the smell of clean, damp hair, freshly laundered towels, and talcum powder.

He turned after looking around the mellow, welcoming room, and nodded approvingly. She was standing, her head inclined to one side, rubbing her hair briskly with a towel. "What happened?" she asked.

"Dick had to go to the White House tonight—I guess to give the President a progress report. He should have left about now, but the

Weather Bureau came out with a storm warning. Our meeting was cut so he could fly in ahead of it.''

"I thought he always went by car?''

"Haven't you heard? Washington's solid with demonstrators. The latest estimate puts the figure at three hundred thousand!''

Mary whistled. "I guess if there's going to be a break in the weather, it couldn't have happened at a better time.'' She pointed to a white cabinet, on which stood an enormous bowl of daisies. "The drinks are in there,'' she said. "Help yourself.''

While she returned to the bedroom to dress, leaving the door between them open, Paul examined the bottles in the cabinet.

"What would you like?'' he called.

"Huh?''

He turned down the volume on the cassette unit and repeated the question.

"I think I'd like''—she hesitated for a moment—"a Cinzano Bianco. There's ice—and lemon if you want it—in the kitchen. When's he due back?'' she called, as McElroy returned to the living room.

"Who?''

"Dick!''

"The day after tomorrow,'' he replied, pouring Cinzano into two tumblers half filled with ice. "He has to appear before a housing subcommittee on the Urban Renewal Act in the afternoon. I think he's expecting trouble; the antiscience lobby is feeling pretty cocksure these days.''

"Maybe I'm becoming cynical, but I find myself increasingly unable to summon up much interest in the pros and cons of a nuclear-powered national grid system. We ought to be thinking about more fundamental issues.''

"Such as?''

"Well, we could start by toying with the idea of declaring a moratorium on all further scientific research, for instance.''

Paul chuckled. "I've poured your drink. Do you want it in there?''

"It's okay, I'll be right out. You think I'm joking—about the moratorium, I mean.''

"I know science has been having a bad press again recently,'' he said, "a lot of it, incidentally, originating from guys who wouldn't be alive to sound off were it *not* for science. But what are you suggesting as an alternative?" He carried the drinks across to the button-back chesterfield and sat down.

"We could start by giving up our obsession with progress," continued Mary. "We could even try taking a few steps *backward* for a change—although right now I'd settle for leaving things alone for a while. Man is so goddamned *meddlesome*!"

"Huh?"

"And before you say anything else—"

"I didn't *say* anything!"

"I'm not advocating the return of the Dark Ages. Quite the contrary. I'm talking about the internalization of more meaningful, life-enhancing values—not the imposition of repressive dogma."

"They have the nasty habit of becoming indistinguishable. But, okay, when you talk about internalization of more meaningful—what was it?—life-enhancing values—"

She laughed. "Don't be so damned smug!"

"What exactly do you have in mind? Genetic intervention?"

"No, I do *not*!" She sounded outraged. "I'm talking about education. Teaching people that cooperation can sometimes achieve more than competition."

"It's a beautiful idea," he said. "I also wish I still believed in Santa Claus! I just can't convince myself that we're ever going to be able to change man's basic destructive urge—and let's face it, that's what we're talking about—by anything other than genetic engineering. Even if we were to go to the lengths Skinner proposed."

"Skinner's a lot of shit!"

"Let's not get into that one again," said Paul, remembering the stalemate they had arrived at when they'd previously discussed the work of the controversial behaviorist.

"Who would decide," he continued, "and *how* would they decide which research programs should be allowed and which shouldn't? Christ, they'd have to be clairvoyant!"

"They wouldn't!"

"They wouldn't what?"

"Try to decide. Because they couldn't!"

"That was going to be my line." Paul paused for a moment. "I see—or at least I *think* I do," he added doubtfully.

"It's easy! There won't be anything to decide about."

"Are you suggesting throwing the switch on the *whole* operation?"

"Something like that."

"And are you going to be the first to start rubbing sticks together every time you want light or heat? Or refuse antibiotics when you get pneumonia?"

"Now you're just being silly."

"*I'm* being silly?"

"You know you are. I'm talking about man's becoming more *civilized*—in the true sense of the word—not going ape! Our first priority should be learning to live with the technology we have already, not acquiring more. Because, like the Sorcerer's Apprentice, we just *ain't* going to be able to handle it!"

The tape came to an end and for several minutes Paul could hear only the net curtains moving gently in the evening breeze and, from within the bedroom, the sounds of jars being uncapped and capped. He stood up and strolled across to the bookshelves that lined most of the wall between the kitchen and the bedroom doors. He was surprised to see that there appeared to be considerably more books on philosophy than there were on genetics. Books by Dewey, Hume, Kierkegaard, Marcuse, Pascal, Russell, and Sartre. He was turning over the pages of a particularly well printed and bound edition of Rousseau's *Social Contract* when he heard Mary return to the living room. She finished putting on an amber earring and picked up her drink.

"If I'd known about this," he said, holding up the book, "I'd have suggested you to be appointed spiritual adviser to the camp."

She laughed. "You'd have been making a big mistake. I'm as much in the dark now as I've ever been. It's rather like having medical textbooks around the house; you're constantly imagining you've got the symptoms, even though you never actually seem to catch any of the diseases!"

She crossed to the tape recorder. "You know, it's ridiculous," she said. "I've known you all this time and still I don't know what music you like."

116

"It's only ten weeks."

"It seems longer."

"Thanks!"

She covered her mouth with her hand—suddenly aware of what she had said—and laughed. "You *know* I didn't mean it like that. It's just that I've gotten used to the idea that I know you terribly well. Except I keep discovering that there are all sorts of things about you I *don't* know."

Both of them sensed that this had become a conversation which, if unchecked, would lead to a subject they both wished—at least for the moment—to avoid: Paul's marriage. Immediate evasive action was called for, and they both attempted it at the same time.

"Such as my taste in music?" asked Paul.

"Such as your taste in music," echoed Mary, prodding the ice in her glass with her fingertip.

They smiled, each aware of what had happened.

"So what's it going to be?" she asked quietly.

"What I'd most enjoy," he replied, "is whatever *you* most enjoy."

She frowned. "That's a difficult one. There are so many." She looked along the row of cassettes, finally deciding on Albinoni's Adagio for Strings and Organ.

The rich, infinitely sad music melded with the light from the dying sun that was slowly staining the room crimson. "I suppose we'd better do something about dinner," she said.

Paul followed her into the kitchen.

"There's enough electronic gadgetry here to service a medium-sized restaurant," she said, "but do you think I've been able to find a wooden spoon, for instance, or a couple of potholders?" She shook her head sadly. "And what's the point of it all anyway, when just about the only thing the commissary sells is frozen TV dinners! I hope you like omelets."

"Great," said Paul. He made it sound as if he meant it.

"Oh, and there's some wine in the fridge. I don't know what it's like . . ."

McElroy drew the cork from the bottle of Pinot Chardonnay, poured a little into a glass, and tasted it thoughtfully. "It's really very good," he pronounced. "Not unlike a Pouilly-Fuissé."

He filled a second glass and passed it to Mary.

"Perhaps a little more voluptuous than is currently fashionable," she said, gently mocking him.

Paul lit a cigarette and realized that, while they had been talking, it had grown dark. They made coffee and carried it, together with glasses and brandy, across to the couch. Mary switched on the television to watch a late-night newscast and, slipping out of her shoes, curled up on the rug beside him.

The picture that appeared on the screen a moment later was at startling variance with the softly lit room and the still, silent night.

"Meanwhile, in downtown Philadelphia," said the newscaster, "bitter fighting continues between heavily armed members of the Revolutionary Alliance and National Guardsmen—" Mary reached out and switched channels. The voice that was now speaking was almost indistinguishable from the first. "Former Chairman of the Joint Chiefs of Staff, James P. Hinshaw, said in San Clemente, California, today, that the United States was facing what he called 'the bloody specter of Civil War.' Speaking before a—" Mary turned the switch once again. "Hundreds of troops and police stormed into New York's Pan Am Building today to flush out snipers who had brought the city's Grand Central Terminal to a standstill since Monday morning."

"Turn it off," said Paul.

"Let's just see if we can find out what happened in Washington," she said, switching channels.

The picture which appeared was of hundreds of young, bedraggled men and women sheltering from torrential rain under almost illegible, disintegrating placards. On some of them, it was just possible to make out the words GOVERNMENT BY THE PEOPLE MEANS WHAT IT SAYS. "Tonight," said the newscaster, "as an estimated three hundred thousand demonstrators scurried for shelter in storm-swept Washington, violence took an all too rare rain check.

"Early this evening, planes from Andrews Air Force Base took off to seed the clouds massing above the nation's capital with silver iodide crystals. Military rainmaking, first used in Vietnam to reduce trafficability along infiltration routes, has proved an effective and—"

"Thank God for that," she said, switching off the set.

She made herself comfortable against the couch, resting one elbow across Paul's knees.

"Do you really believe that what you and I are doing in here could affect what's happening out there?" she asked, nodding toward the empty television screen. "It's all so unreal here at Detrick. It's almost as though we were living in the eye of a hurricane, too calm somehow, too still. I suppose what I'm saying is that however ingenious the idea of Wild Card might seem, if we'd ever had to push it into the wall of wind surrounding us, it would have been reduced to matchwood and sucked up with the rest of the debris."

Paul caressed the back of her neck. "You make it sound as if the whole thing's been called off."

She turned her head, rubbing her cheek on the back of his hand. "Wishful thinking, I guess," she said.

Paul laughed. "I see Wild Card doing the same job as a sock on the jaw of a guy who's drowning—a guy who, if he's not subdued, will take the lifeguard down with him. And if it stops his struggling long enough for him to be saved . . ."

Mary shrugged, but said nothing.

"You'll tell me when you want me to go?"

"Not yet."

He leaned over and kissed her tenderly on the mouth.

"I was wondering when you were going to do that," she whispered. She wound her arms around his neck, her open mouth seeking his, and pulled him gently down onto the floor beside her.

"I know it sounds silly," Mary said a moment later, "but I think I knew the first time I saw you that I was going to fall in love with you."

"How could you possibly have known that?" Paul asked, gently teasing her.

Mary brushed his lips with the tips of her fingers, studying his face intently. "That's what I kept asking myself. You're beautiful, and clever, and kind—but I've known men before who were all of those things and I didn't behave like an adolescent with them."

"Not even when you *were* an adolescent?"

She laughed. "Especially not when I was an adolescent! I was appallingly proper—you've no idea—such behavior would have been *quite* beneath my dignity."

"Ah ha!"

"And what's that supposed to mean?"

Paul shrugged, as though reluctant to proceed further.

"You're wrong. My feelings for you have nothing to do with a wasted youth—if that's what you're suggesting! And anyway, what about your feelings for me? Or are you going to plead the Fifth Amendment?"

Paul grinned and tapped her on the point of the chin with his fist. "Don't be like that. It's just that I don't know," he said, so seriously that for a moment she was unsure whether he was teasing her or not. "Perhaps, Doctor," he continued, "if I were to describe the symptoms . . . ?"

"Please do so," she replied, miming the action of looking solemnly over the top of a pair of spectacles.

"Well, you see, it's like this," he began. "Ever since I've known you, I've had this strange compulsion to keep staring at you."

"Is that so strange?" she asked, as though deeply offended.

"Perhaps not in itself, but recently I've also been afflicted by a constant and an almost overwhelming desire to touch you."

"And *almost* overwhelming desire?" She kissed him. "I wish you had," she whispered.

"And then there were the dreams."

"Yes, quite so." She was now once more pretending to be a stern but suddenly flustered physician. "Perhaps we should pass over the dreams for the moment. Your appetite—how is your appetite?"

"Ravenous!"

"I didn't mean *that* appetite! Please be serious, young man." She pretended to think deeply. "I'm afraid this will come as something of a shock to you, but the symptoms you describe suggest you are suffering from a serious social disease."

"A serious *social* disease?"

"I'm afraid so, one that is associated with the functions of the heart. Of course, we can't be absolutely sure until we have carried out a thorough *physical* examination and taken specimens."

"And the prognosis?"

"Excellent. There is—I hope—very little chance of your recovering."

"You mean there's no cure?"

She shook her head regretfully. "We can hope to alleviate certain of the symptoms, but I must warn you that if we succeed we will probably accelerate the rate of infection."

McElroy laughed. "Well," he said, "I guess that's a chance I'll just have to take. When do we start treatment?"

Mary took him by the hand and, without another word being spoken, led him into the bedroom.

He undressed and was in bed when she returned, naked, from the bathroom.

"I thought only the patient was supposed to undress," he said.

"Paul, are you awake?" Mary whispered.

"I don't think I am," he murmured.

She lifted herself up on her elbow, her breasts resting on his chest.

"Darling," she said, "what do you think the other guys do about sex? They can't *all* be making it with Charlotte Paxton."

"I don't think any of them are that desperate yet," he said. "Although, come to think about it, she's begun to look pretty damned attractive to me recently."

Mary pinched him hard. "I *hate* you," she said, trying not to laugh.

Paul retaliated by slapping her on the buttocks.

"Ouch!" she cried. "That hurt!"

"But did it turn you on?"

"Like a switch," she said, snuggling up to him.

"Tell me about you and Doug Lawrence. I thought the two of you had something going a while back."

"So did he, until I disillusioned him."

"How many of the other guys have made a pass at you?"

"That would be telling." She began to play with the hairs on his chest. "Anyway, you still haven't answered *my* question."

"Which question was that?"

"You're not listening," she said. "What do the other guys do about sex?"

"Life-size inflatable latex dolls."

"I think we've got a bad connection," she said sleepily. "It sounded like you said 'life-size inflatable latex dolls.' "

"I did!"

"You're kidding!" she said, suddenly wide awake.

"Okay, so I'm kidding." As soon as she seemed to relax again he added, "Mine's a blonde. I tell you, the guys who put this operation together thought of everything!"

Mary sat up in bed.

"And the answer to the next question is 'No,' " he added quickly. "I haven't even opened the package!"

14

At 7:30 p.m. on August 10, Nadelman returned to Detrick, having spent three days in Washington. During that time he had brought the President up to date on the progress of Wild Card, testified before the House Armed Services Committee on the latest ChiCom probe vehicle, advised the Secretary of State on the situation in the Siberian oil and gas fields, and the Cost of Living Council on protein equivalents to meat, and interceded in the nuclear power workers' deadlock—all at the height of one of the hottest summers in living memory. It was a pace that would have sent most men into an early retirement, but Nadelman thrived on it.

After stopping at the administration block to pick up his mail, the proofs of his latest book, and a sheaf of progress reports, he was driven by Barringer to the residential block. Nadelman got out of the car and, leaving Barringer to unload the luggage, hurried inside the building and began opening the triple-locked door to his apartment. Once inside, he undressed quickly. With his two cats trotting alongside him, yowling, he made straight for the shower.

Barringer followed him into the apartment a moment later, dropping the cases just inside the door. Although he had heard that Nadelman never allowed a cleaner inside his apartment, he was unprepared for the squalor confronting him. It was possible to see that the room had once been elegant, and green with house plants. Now it smelled like a zoo and was piled high with books, papers, and scientific apparatus. All but one of the plants had turned brown and died. Disgusted, Barringer turned and left, slamming the door behind him. A cloud of flies rose from the cats' litter box and hovered for a moment before settling.

Ten minutes later, Nadelman padded out of the bathroom, still naked and dripping water on the parquet floor. He cleared a space on his Georgian walnut writing table and began opening and closing the drawers until he found a spoon and two cans of pork and beans. One of the cans he opened for the ravenous cats; the other he began eating himself.

He returned to the desk, opened his attaché case, and pulled out the progress reports he'd collected earlier. On top of the pile was one from Pedlar. He read it through quickly, and picked up a ballpoint pen. Unable to get the ink to flow, he rummaged through the desk drawers until he found another. That, too, had dried out. Cursing, he crossed to where he'd dropped his jacket and took a gold-plated Shaeffer from the inside pocket. Before returning to the report, he made a detour into the kitchen and opened the refrigerator. Back in June, something had gone wrong with the defrosting mechanism, and the interior now looked like an ice cavern. With difficulty, he broke loose a pint carton of ice cream and carried it back to his desk. He sat down and began flicking through Pedlar's report until he found the section head "Aerosol Particle Size." In the margin he scribbled: "Fine, as long as it doesn't get any smaller. We want to hit people at street level, as well as in high-rise apartments." He stamped the report INCINERATE AFTER READING, initialed it, and pushed it to one side.

The next report was from Henry Jerome. He opened it and began reading with little interest. "Happily, we have experienced no difficulties in maintaining adequate supplies via the cover project."

He finished the last of the ice cream and continued reading. "However, I feel it my duty to draw your attention to a laxness among certain members of staff regarding signing-out procedures for items drawn from stock. The accurate registration of quantities is essential . . ." Nadelman stamped the report without finishing it, and threw it to one side. "What the hell does Jerome expect?" he asked himself. "We're dealing with research scientists, not quartermasters."

He opened McElroy's report. The cerebroids, now over four months old, were maturing satisfactorily—cell count, matrix-covering coefficient, and metabolic parameters were all on target. He stamped the report and scrawled "Excellent" across the title page.

Aware that he had begun to feel cold, he padded into the bedroom to put on a dressing gown—his enormous buttocks imprinted with the pattern of the woven-rush seat on which he'd been sitting. He slipped a tape into his cassette deck. It was a recording of humpback whales made years earlier by someone working on biological acoustics. Although Nadelman was tone-deaf, he never tired of listening to the creatures' eerie, curiously musical chirruping and moaning.

For several minutes he stood staring at the Wild Card flow chart pinned to the wall above the cassette deck. They were now past the halfway point, and things had gone better than even he had expected. It was the situation outside that had begun to alarm him—not the bombings and the riots, but the magnitude of the economic crisis now facing the nation. I work my ass off trying to help bail out a sinking ship, he thought bitterly, and those bastards on the International Monetary Fund blast still more holes below the waterline!"

The next report he examined was from Benedict. Pinned to the title page was a card which read: "Dr. Philip Benedict requests the pleasure of the company of Dr. Richard Nadelman at a demonstration to be held in the Flight Testing Facility at 9:30 A.M., August 11. Dress optional. R.S.V.P."

"Arrogant bastard!" he muttered.

15

AT THE AGE OF forty-six, Dr. Philip Benedict was generally acknowledged to be one of the country's leading materials scientists. He had first come to prominence in the early seventies when ecology was still a growth industry, and his novel advances in the field of biodegradable materials—coupled with a highly successful PR exercise run by his full-time press secretary—had brought him an overnight reputation.

He became a familiar face at smart dinner parties, lectured to packed audiences on the college circuit, yet still found time to turn in scientific papers that confirmed his status as a talented researcher. Predictably, his activities were frowned on by some sections of the scientific community and he was labeled an opportunist. But the carping served only to increase his popularity with a public that suspected the science establishment of too close a communion with machinery and too little contact with reality. In the circumstances, it was fortunate for him that they knew nothing of the classified government research he was frequently asked to undertake. Only in certain top-security files was it recorded, for example, that a fragmentation material used in grenade casings—and invisible to X rays—had been developed by him.

Apart from his undoubted skill, the most important asset he had brought to Wild Card was his unrelenting drive: failure was something that happened to other people. In a sense, he had become the project's pacemaker, leading his own team so efficiently that they were now two weeks ahead of schedule.

Benedict waited for his audience to take their seats facing the demonstration area in the Flight Testing Facility, a hangarlike building as big as a football field at the southern end of the maximum-security compound. By nine thirty-five, all the scientists had arrived except Kavanagh, who was on duty in the cerebroid laboratory.

"The craft you're about to see," Benedict began, "is a half-size model. At this stage, of course, the crew of cerebroids are also represented by models. What we've tried to achieve—successfully, we think—is a logically organized, mission-oriented machine built *around* the cerebroids.

"We've given them the appearance of being custom-made space travelers, but that doesn't necessarily put them at the top of the evolutionary tree on their planet. There could be an even higher form of life capable of creating specific varieties of cerebroid for specific tasks. We decided to go for a type particularly suited to reconnaissance duties, totally integrated with the spacecraft, and functioning as an information-processing/decision-making organism."

The basic difficulty his team had faced, he went on to explain, was how to create hardware that was sufficiently different from earthly technology to arouse no suspicion. The solution had been to use Nadelman's "cosmic primes" in such a way that uniquely earth-oriented applications were not duplicated.

"Let me give you an example," he said. "Suppose we'd decided to manufacture an alloy consisting of 68 per cent beryllium and 32 per cent aluminium. In theory, those are okay elements—but not in the proportions I gave. We'd have infringed on Lockheed's patent on the alloy and—much more to the point—raised serious doubts about the authenticity of the craft.

"The prototype you'll be seeing in just a moment doesn't incorporate all the refinements we plan for the full-size ship, but it'll show you our approach. As I said, the actual cerebroids haven't been installed, so the maneuvers you're about to see have all been programed into the spacecraft's central computer."

A low flatbed truck, driven by Weiner, appeared from behind a screen, moved slowly across the demonstration area, and came to a halt ten yards from the group. On the back was the model spacecraft.

Its centerpiece was a geodesic sphere about five feet in diameter, with a surface made up of hundreds of triangular faces that glinted under the fluorescent lights like a cut diamond. Three spokes, each as thick as a man's arm, connected the equator of the sphere to a smooth, circular rim about ten feet in diameter and three feet high. Weiner got down from the driver's seat and, helped by Darrow and Conrad, lifted the craft off the truck. The others were now able to see that the rim had the cross section of an aerofoil. It was as if a narrow, untapered length of aircraft wing had been curved into the shape of a cylinder, then placed around the sphere with the trailing edge of the wing on the ground. Attached to the base of the sphere—and almost hidden by the rim—was a drum-shaped propulsion pack and thrust nozzle.

Benedict moved over to a control console and sat down. "Because of the preprograming," he explained, "all I have to do is transmit the starting instructions, and stand by to override the on-board computer in the event of a failure."

He flicked a sequence of switches on the console. Immediately, the pressure-release valves on the propulsion pack opened and the spacecraft was enveloped in a cloud of gas. With a noise like a small rocket it lifted off, sending a wash of warm air toward the watching scientists. It rose vertically until it was about six feet above ground, then hovered. Attitude jets built into the base of the duct rotated it about its vertical axis until the duct made a shallow angle with the ground, and it began to fly across the hangar. As it approached the front wall, it leveled out, rotated in the opposite direction, and flew back—this time veering off to make a close approach on the wind tunnel at the far end of the building. Again it stopped short of the wall, returned to its takeoff point, and hovered.

"There's a small quartz window in the side of the duct," Benedict explained. "Behind it, an infrared camera is taking a thermograph."

For a few moments he let them study the bizarre coloring of the heat picture, which had been relayed to the overhead cathode-ray-tube display screens. "Okay," he said, "let's move on to the avoidance routine."

Darrow and Weiner, now wearing fireproof coveralls and helmets, began to walk slowly toward the spacecraft. Another CRT screen was pinpointing their positions relative to the craft, and twin electronic counters began blinking up numerical distance coordinates on the control console.

"We've built an ultrasonic scanner into its duct," Benedict explained, "and an avoidance response which it will follow if anything comes within one yard of the scanner. Of course, the spacecraft that is found in L.A. won't need the avoidance response. It won't even have to move under its own steam. But to make sure it looks authentic, we're going to give it all those capabilities."

Darrow was in mid-stride when the spacecraft suddenly rotated into flying attitude and, with a burst of power, shied away from him. He and Weiner moved closer. Each time they penetrated the avoidance zone, the spacecraft backed off with a blast of hot gas. By the time it had been boxed into the right-hand corner of the facility, fifty yards from the console, everyone was craning forward to keep the maneuvering in sight. Darrow entered the spacecraft's territory for the last time; it now had no more space to retreat into. The CRT screen blinked up ZONE VIOLATION: ESCAPE BOOST AND DISPERSAL. A moment later the craft's propulsion pack increased thrust, propelling it to a height of thirty feet.

Suddenly, with a sound like a firecracker exploding, a small metal canister was ejected from the spacecraft's duct. It arced overhead, filling the building with a lavender-scented mist.

"Kills all known household smells!" said Benedict, laughing. Several of the scientists began to cough. "Sorry," he said. "I guess I should have warned you we'd be trying out the virus-dispersal mechanism."

The spacecraft, meanwhile, had entered a glide pattern that brought it back to the takeoff point. It leveled out and made a vertical descent, bumping gently onto the floor. The propulsion pack cut out and the display screens went blank. "That's it. Come and have a closer look," Benedict said, waiting for the others to group around the spacecraft before continuing.

"As I said at the beginning, the production model will differ from the prototype in several respects. For example, the propulsion pack was okay for the demonstration, but it's too Tinkertoy for the ultimate ship. We plan to replace it with a small plasma engine." He nodded to Conrad, who flicked a switch on the control console. The upper hemisphere of the geodesic cabin opened out into three segments, like the petals of a flower, until they rested on the top of the duct.

Inside were three translucent spheres, each containing a model of a brain—but a brain that was larger, even at a half-scale representation, than any that had ever occupied a human skull. Each sphere rested in a molded cavity—Benedict called them flight couches—set into the semirigid foam cabin lining that the team had developed. The spheres were positioned in line with the three spokes and were held in place by restraining collars. The significance of the spokes was now clear. As well as connecting the geodesic cabin to the duct, they also acted as conduits for the mass of wiring that conveyed electrical signals from the sensory apparatus in the duct to the brains.

"The layout is essentially as it will be in the final craft," he said. "The translucent spheres, though,will be replaced by spheres made of the same material as the craft itself, for added strength. The wiring that you see there is conventional metal, and, again, will be replaced by a new material we're in the final stages of processing. It's superconductive, but it consists of strands of *organic* matter . . ."

Benedict saw that they seemed to be following his description.

"Superconducting electrodes will be implanted in each cerebroid," he continued, "and linked to the sensory apparatus in the duct and to the computer. There will also be links between the cerebroids. Effectively, we'll have a closed-loop system. In theory, they could work together as a triple-intelligence unit, interpreting data and relegating routine operations to the computer."

McElroy asked a question about the fluid which held each cerebroid in suspension inside its spherical casing.

"It's under pressure," Benedict replied, "and the best shape for even distribution of the forces in a pressure vessel is a sphere. In fact, we took that as our starting point for the overall symmetry of the craft. Survival depends to a large extent on organization, so we went all out to make these babies as logically organized as possible, on the assumption that the race who sent them must have survived a hell of a lot longer than we have!"

131

"Or seem likely to," Mary Anderson said quietly.

Benedict smiled uncertainly. "What I really like about this arrangement is the implication that the cerebroids can be removed when the hardware becomes obsolete, and transferred to a different type of ship. The biotechnological possibilities of having cerebroid storage banks are tremendous."

Lee Conrad, the team's biomedical expert, took over the commentary, describing how the transducers built into the spacecraft's aerodynamic duct had replaced the human sensory system. Now head of the Department of Biomedical Engineering at Case-Western Reserve University, Conrad provided an interface between living and artificial systems—"translating the subtleties of nature into the kind of language the engineer can understand," as he liked to put it.

"We've also built in three standby circuits *and* a diagnostic logic circuit that traces faults, then calls up replacement parts," he said. "A kind of electronic self-surgery."

Nadelman looked impressed. "I hope the spacecraft's power failure has nothing to do with electronics," he said. "The way you tell it, a crash is out of the question."

Benedict laughed. "He thought of that, too," he said, nodding at Darrow. "We'll leave evidence of an electromagnetic failure, independent of the circuits Lee mentioned.

"Coming back to the question of communications, you've seen that the cerebroids are directly interlinked—implying that information passes from one to the other in the form of electrical pulses."

"To us, it would be ESP," Darrow added, "but to them, there's nothing 'extra' about it. Just their normal means of communication."

"All this," said Lawrence, shaking his head sadly, "and you want me to blow it to pieces?"

"If you've got a couple of counterfeit dollars," Benedict replied patiently, "the best way to pass them is to slip them into the middle of a wad of genuine bills. That's what we're doing—the cerebroids and the plasma engine are the phonies. They'll look right on the night, but they don't work. If the investigators find that everything else was functional, we believe they'll buy them."

"Sure—but how do they satisfy themselves that the genuine gear was in working order?" Lawrence asked. "You want me to reduce this to scrap, don't forget."

"You bet your ass I do!" said Weiner. "As far as I'm concerned, the pieces can't be small enough. I've worked as a consultant on aircraft crash investigations and, believe me, investigative techniques these days are too sophisticated for us to take any chances. The crash guys really know how to put the pieces back together again! They use microscopic, X-ray, electron-diffraction, and fluorescence methods, they look for recrystallization at micropromontories, Neumann banding, parallel banding, spallation, hot-gas washing—you name it!''

"The message is this," said Nadelman. "We have to get this fabrication as near-perfect as we can—and even then, we'll be working closer to the horns than I'd like.''

16

IMMEDIATELY AFTER THE spacecraft demonstration, Lawrence and the three men with whom he would work left for Los Angeles.

At forty-two, Ed Stillman was the oldest of the group. At first sight it was easy to mistake him for a stereotype Hollywood tough guy with maximum action, minimum brain, and B-picture dialogue. In fact, this quiet spoken ex-sergeant in the New York Emergency Service Division was a man of many skills and incisive judgment.

Sam Olsen was an ex-member of the CIA, and an expert in clandestine operations. Tall and lean, his angular, uncompromising features suggested a capacity to both bear and inflict suffering with equal indifference.

Jerry Payne was black and, like Stillman, an ex-cop. He had been with the Los Angeles Police Department for ten years before leaving to join a private security organization.

On arrival in Los Angeles, Stillman, Olsen, and Payne began negotiating the purchase of a bankrupt construction company located a few miles west of Doty Avenue. Meanwhile, Lawrence telephoned Dr.

Ralph Sheldon—a guest at the Statler Hilton. Although the two men had never met before, their brief talk was friendly. "Ralph, it's Ted Hersh," Lawrence began. "I think maybe we've found just the house for you. It's in Hawthorne—13400 Doty Avenue—and they're asking a lot less than your limit. Why don't we meet tomorrow? If you like the feel of it, I can make a start on the survey right away." Lawrence gave him the name and address of the real-estate agent handling the property, and they arranged to meet at the house the following afternoon.

Forty-eight hours later—on August 14—Sheldon placed a deposit on the house, and Lawrence was on his way back to Detrick with the information necessary to complete the next part of his job.

Lawrence was an ex-Special Forces operative and co-author of an Army field manual on booby traps. As far as he was concerned, knocking out a bridge with a sequence detonation of PBX on millisecond delays was child's play compared with this assignment. The objective was essentially the same, but 13400 Doty had first to be rigged to look as though the spacecraft had crashed through the roof and into the cellar before exploding. It was this part of the operation—Lawrence likened it to running a movie backward—that was to test his ingenuity and capacity for meticulous attention to detail.

Ten days after his return to Detrick, he and Benedict began running a series of crash tests, using scale models of the house and spacecraft. Ultrafast cameras, shooting at sixty thousand frames a second, followed the spacecraft as it hit the roof and fell through into the basement. From these studies, they were able to assess the damage that would have been done before the spacecraft exploded.

Lawrence then ran a second series of tests in which the model spacecraft carried an explosive charge.

He discovered, for example, that roof tiling trapped beneath the falling spacecraft in every trial was driven into the ground by the subsequent explosion. For the deception to succeed, it was obvious that the tiles would have to be put in place beneath the craft before it was installed. On the other hand, insulation fabric in the loft was scattered in all directions by the blast, and its placement was not critical.

By the first week of September, Lawrence had selected a crash trajectory and prepared a step-by-step demolition program to simulate

136

the theoretical damage. According to this program, the spacecraft would hit the roof of the house almost vertically, though with slight horizontal velocity. Still in forward flight attitude, it would slice duct first through the loft, the upper floor, and the hallway, coming to rest in the basement. This path, Lawrence calculated, would avoid destroying too many of the main structural supports in the house. When the work was completed, the building would be in a delicate but not dangerous condition, ready for the installation of the spacecraft and the cerebroids.

Lawrence's next job was to evolve a scheme for transporting the spacecraft and cerebroids from Detrick to Los Angeles. However it was to be accomplished, he was resigned to the fact that two shipments would be necessary. Because of its size, the spacecraft would have to be freighted in sections—and trials with a full-size mock-up had shown that it would take him ten days to reassemble it inside the house. The cerebroids could not, therefore, be transported in the same consignment as the spacecraft sections. The brain tissue had to be alive at the moment of detonation, and ten days without the sophisticated life-support equipment available in McElroy's laboratory was a risk no one was prepared to take.

Lawrence decided that there were three possible ways of carrying out the transit operation: by using military vehicles or aircraft; by setting up a bogus freight company; and by using an established carrier.

He rejected the first possibility immediately. He would have to obtain authority for the job, which meant, in effect, involving the President, and the nature and ultimate destination of the consignment would have to be concealed. He'd have to hope that nobody would link such a shipment with the explosion. It was asking too much.

He gave more serious thought to the second scheme, but that, too, presented problems. The most likely route—U.S. 66/Interstate 70 —passed through Indian territory and was considered an indefinite danger zone. On the other hand, if he were to take a southerly route—to bypass the reservations—he knew he'd run the risk of being searched by border patrols checking for arms smuggling from Mexico. To the north the problem was the poor physical condition of the roads and the risk of bad weather.

But what finally tipped the scales against the bogus freight company scheme was the fact that, in spite of the uncertainties of cross-country travel by road, the Interstate Commerce Commission was still function-ing. All the evidence suggested that it would have been impossible to make the journey without, at some stage, being stopped at an ICC checkpoint.

The remaining possibility—smuggling the components in a con-signment being air-freighted by an established carrier—offered the best chance of success. The sheer volume of traffic made it impossible for aircraft to be held on the ground while detailed load examinations were carried out, and airport police tended to take company-authorized cargo manifests on trust. Lawrence knew that they might make a routine inspection, but he was confident that the risk of discovery could be reduced to an acceptable level. The key was careful planning.

17

DR. JOHNSON WAS SITTING in the annex to the cerebroid laboratory, checking through a selection of blue EEG traces. The results were encouraging. Normally, alpha waves are absent from a human EEG before the age of three, with delta waves predominating. But as a result of round-the-clock electrical stimulation, the cerebroids were already showing signs of an adult brain pattern. There was even a suggestion of high-voltage fast waves—which Johnson found intriguing. After all, he reasoned, these beta waves only occurred in the human brain during an alert state, in concentrated problem-solving, for example. Yet what could the cerebroids possibly be "thinking" about? He put the traces to one side and looked at his watch: it was exactly 3 A.M. He stood up, went along the corridor to a door that Kochalski had marked "Hatchery," and went in.

The uncomfortable warmth of the cerebroid laboratory was accentuated by the glow of the infrared lighting, and the air spiced with the smells of a hospital intensive-care unit. Arranged in rows across the room were ten glass tanks, mounted on antivibration trestles and flanked by life-support and monitoring equipment.

Each growth chamber contained a nutrient medium. Waste prod-ucts—ammonia, carbon dioxide, and hydrogen ions—were vented at the base of the tank and circulated by pump to a selective extractor unit. After purification in the extractor, the medium—with its pH and osmotic pressure readjusted—was oxygenated and boosted with fresh nutrients before being recycled to the tank. It was a highly efficient system, sealed to exclude any possibility of contamination, and Johnson was pleased with it; he had collaborated on the design.

He stopped in front of the first tank, occupied by the youngest of the cerebroids, and removed the data log from a clip beside the bank of equipment. He glanced through the latest auto-analyzer figures before stooping to peer through the glass at the nineteen-week-old cerebroid.

It was floating in the center of the tank, a ball of gray tissue twenty inches in diameter, the outer cell layers undulating gently as the nutrient medium circulated. A profusion of insulated organic electrodes deeply embedded in the tissue exited through leakproof seals in the roof of the tank.

A few spots on the surface of the three-dimensional matrix were not yet completely covered by tissue growth, and Johnson could see the honeycomb of polyglycol capillaries that allowed medium to diffuse through to the center. But on the whole, he thought, the growth rate was astonishing. When the seeding had begun, the waffle-grid construction of the matrix had shown through the sparse layers of neuroblasts only too clearly. Now the cells had invaded all the interstices—which substituted for the folds and fissures of the human cortex—and spread over the surface like ivy on a trellis.

He looked again at the data log. The estimated cell count was already higher than that of an adult human brain, yet the density of cells in the cerebroid's matrix was confidently expected to double before termination of development—*and* they were bigger cells.

Johnson straightened and continued down the ranks of floating cerebroids. He inspected each growth chamber thoroughly and had reached the seventh when an alarm sounded—an insistent, high-pitched bleeping from the EEG monitor on tank ten. Not unduly worried, he crossed to the affected cerebroid. With such sensitive equipment, the slightest deviation from preset voltage parameters would trigger the warning signal; it happened frequently. Sometimes it was a temporary electrode displacement caused by turbulence in the medium. Occasionally it was an artifact in the EEG machine. The faults usually cured themselves and he began to look over the system, fully expecting the bleeping to stop in a few seconds.

But the noise continued. He began to move more urgently now, tracing back leads, checking the recirculating pump for malfunctions that might cause turbulence, checking the EEG machine for cross talk between channels. He could discover nothing.

He looked at the trace. The rhythms had slowed dramatically. The amplitude of the waves was decreasing. Then a period of electrical silence followed by a spike cluster . . .

Johnson looked back to the cerebroid. It was irrational, but he half expected to see some physical evidence of what was happening. According to the EEG, the creature was suffering an electrical convulsion; but there was no change in its appearance. Abruptly, the EEG pen traced another spike discharge, then flattened out completely. Johnson stared, an expression of disbelief on his face. He waited. The trace remained isoelectric. Then he turned and hurried across to the telephone. As he waited to be connected with McElroy, he realized that his hands were trembling.

Eight minutes later, McElroy arrived and Johnson led him to the tank containing the dead cerebroid. McElroy listened impassively to his colleague's explanation.

"It just doesn't make sense," Johnson said. He waved toward the data-log sheets. "I've checked the auto-analysis. The nutrient medium pH was on the low side, but that's about all. Cell count was excellent."

McElroy nodded. "Acidosis. What was the pH?"

"Seven point two."

"What about metabolites? Have you checked the bicarb?"

Johnson unclipped the log. "Yes, here it is. The buffer base is down five to fifteen milliequivalents, so the CO_2 partial pressure will be up." He glanced down at the data sheet again. "The chloride's up a little, too."

"Shit!" McElroy said. "We'd better start checking ketones and organic acids." He rubbed his eyes. He was tired and it was an effort to think straight. "How's the pH for the others?" he asked.

Johnson consulted his papers. "All normal except number nine. That's fractionally low, but it doesn't look serious."

"It may get worse tomorrow. Christ, we're going to have to move fast! I want a twenty-four-hour watch on these tanks—especially nine. The first sign of acidosis, let me know. It could be an age-related biochemical lesion. If it is, we're in for a game of ten little Indians!''

Three hours later, McElroy returned to his office completely baffled. He'd taken biopsies of surface and deep tissue from the dead cerebroid, made frozen sections, stained them, examined them under the microscope, even used an electron probe microanalyzer . . . but he was still no closer to diagnosing the cause of death. There *were* lesions—he'd expected that—but nothing specific enough to pin down the trouble. The sophisticated equipment couldn't help him with this one. So he sat down and tackled the problem the traditional way: by going back to first principles.

He made a list of the possible mechanisms of fatality: congenital biochemical lesion; failure of the life-support system; error in the nutrient provision. He dismissed the mechanical failure immediately. The equipment was checked daily and had built-in safety devices. Some form of congenital deficiency was the most dangerous possibility. In just over a week, all nine remaining cerebroids would reach the same age as the one that had died. If the fault *was* inherent, they had no chance of survival. It was ironic, McElroy thought, that his team's manipulative expertise would be powerless against such a tragedy. Transplanting a nucleus with its complete set of genetic instructions was a pushover compared with the needle-in-a-haystack search that would be needed to pinpoint the malfunctioning genes.

He leaned forward at his desk, head in hands, concentrating on what little evidence he had assembled.

Then the phone rang. It was Johnson. ''Nine died a minute ago,'' he said.

''God Almighty! It's happening even faster than I expected. Is eight acidotic?''

''Yes. Same symptoms.''

''So we *have* screwed up the genetic blueprint!''

''It's beginning to look that way. I've got the analyses you asked for. Pyruvate and lactate were way up. I'll call you later with an update on eight.''

McElroy replaced the receiver. He was badly shaken by Johnson's news. It seemed to be all over—and his team was to blame. Christ, he thought, we were so careful. What could have gone wrong? The transplantation? The cell fusion? He began to think back, then realized that he was getting nowhere. It had happened, and it was too late to change.

He looked down at his possible list of causes. There was little point in pressing on with it, he thought, and crumpled up the sheet of paper. He sat quietly for a minute, wondering if he ought to call the rest of the team across to his office. But then his training got the better of him—the others, he decided, would expect him to make a *full* investigation, if only for their own satisfaction. At least, he told himself, the routine of checking the feeding schedules—the last item on his list—would give him time to decide how to break the news to Nadelman.

He turned to the nutrient data, which by now filled several volumes, and began working through the feed-composition analyses for the past 133 days. This had been one of Mary's responsibilities, and, as he expected, all the entries were clear and correct: glucose, essential fatty acids and amino acids as prescribed by the program; each of the vitamins—A, thiamine, nicotinamide, B_6, folic acid, B_{12}—all the details meticulously checked off.

He put aside the schedules and reached for the spectrophotometric graphs.

Every two weeks, as a double check, feeds had been subjected to spectrophotometer analysis. The red-ink curves traced on blue graph paper indicated the concentrations of the various constituents of the nutrient medium. As he expected, the sheets separating the amino acids were correct. The next batch dealt with the fat-soluble vitamins—A, D, E, and K: there was nothing wrong there. Finally, he looked through the water-soluble vitamins—riboflavin, nicotinamide, B_1 and B_6, bicotin . . . ten weekly analyses, each one scrupulously filed and confirming the— McElroy stopped. He looked again at the final sheet. There was no trace for vitamin B_1. He riffled through the earlier graphs; they each showed the presence of B_1. . . But not the last one. He checked the nutrient schedules again: B_1—0.4 milligrams each day. Yet the physical evidence of the spectrophotometer traces proved that the essential vitamin had been omitted from the food for over two weeks.

"Christ," he said aloud. "I don't believe it!"

It was so simple—and yet it had almost escaped his notice. No wonder the cerebroids were dying. Their energy was derived solely from the oxidation of carbohydrates, a metabolic process in which B_1 plays a vital role. That would explain Johnson's comment over the telephone—a high pyruvate and lactate content, he had said. The pieces were falling into place. B_1 deficiency would lead to a buildup of pyruvate and lactate, causing acidosis.

McElroy sat back. How the hell could she make a stupid mistake like that, he thought. It was unbelievable for someone with her training! He reached for the telephone, then stopped abruptly as he realized that there *was* an alternative explanation . . .

18

IT WAS SHORTLY AFTER seven-fifteen when Paul McElroy, breathless from having run up the stairs to Mary's apartment, rang her doorbell.

"Who is it?" he heard her call. Her voice sounded unnaturally loud and he wished now that he had telephoned to say that he was on his way over.

"Paul," he answered.

"It's open. Come on in."

He closed the door quietly behind him and looked around. "I'm in here, darling," she called from the bathroom.

As he entered she pulled aside the shower curtains and leaned out, her eyes closed against the water running down her face, waiting to be kissed. Thinking that he was hesitating to tease her, she opened one eye and grabbed at his belt in a playful attempt to pull him in with her. But Paul stood firm and she lost her balance, falling with a delighted shriek out of the shower and into his arms.

He turned his head away. "Mary, stop it!" he protested, but not emphatically enough to discourage her from attempting to smother his face with kisses. His clothes were now wet. He managed to unwind her arms from around his neck, but she immediately began unbuttoning his shirt.

"Oh, don't be so stuffy," she complained, slipping her hands beneath his shirt to caress his shoulders.

"For Christ's sake, stop it!" he shouted.

The effect on her was instantaneous. Shocked, and suddenly embarrassed by her nakedness, she wrapped herself in a towel and ran past him into the bedroom.

Paul was angry both with himself and with her. What he had to say was hard enough without having to contend with this. He turned off the shower and followed her into the bedroom. She was standing at the window, quite still, with her back to the room.

"May I have a cigarette, please?" she asked, icily polite, as she heard him enter. Her tone convinced Paul that any attempt to console her would be useless. He lit a cigarette and passed it to her. She took it, without thanking him, and inhaled deeply.

"You've discovered," she said flatly.

Paul felt an upsurge of despair. The hope that Mary might, after all, *not* have been implicated in the deaths of the cerebroids had been extinguished.

"Yes," he replied.

"What will happen now?" She seemed no more than mildly curious.

"I don't know."

Somewhere along the corridor a door banged and they waited until the footsteps had receded before continuing.

"Do the others know?" she asked.

He assumed—wrongly—that she was asking if the others knew *what*, not who, had caused the deaths of the somants.

"Not yet," he replied.

She nodded, but make no comment.

"Why did you do it?"

She turned around, her cigarette held awkwardly in front of her. He took the ashtray from the dressing table and passed it to her.

"Because I found out," she replied, as though her answer was self-evident.

146

He waited, expecting her to continue, but her interest seemed now to be concentrated solely on stubbing out the cigarette. For the first time he was able to see how the process of aging would eventually affect her face: the hollows that would appear beneath her prominent cheekbones, the lines that would establish themselves either side of her wide mouth and between her eyebrows. And for the first time he realized the extent to which his love for her was buttressed by compassion.

A gust of wind blew a handful of dead leaves against the window, startling him out of his reverie. "Because you found out what?" he asked, frowning.

She looked up, searching his face for confirmation of the bewilderment apparent in his voice. "About the plan to kill ten thousand people in L.A."

Paul stared blankly back at her. "What the hell are you talking about?"

She let her breath out slowly, at last convinced that he hadn't known, and began speaking rapidly and with renewed confidence—anxious to recruit him as an ally. "Paul, you remember that morning back in April when you got us together to explain your carbon 14 idea? Well, I went to see Nadelman afterward with some crazy idea that I might be able to persuade him not to go on with Wild Card." She smiled at the absurdity of the idea. "I arrived early and overheard him on the phone to Mike Pedlar. They were talking about increasing the cytolytic effects of the virus. Nadelman said, 'How they die is as important as how many die'!"

"So?" said McElroy, still not understanding.

"Paul, don't you see? They're not just going to make ten thousand people sick, they actually want to *kill* them!"

"All right, all right," he said, trying to understand. "Let's take it one step at a time. What *exactly* was it you thought he said?"

"I've already *told* you!" she said impatiently. "And I didn't just *think* I heard him say it. He was asking if your carbon 14 idea changed anything Pedlar was doing. His actual phrase was, 'Does any of this affect what you're doing, not what the others think you're doing?' Then he said, 'You'll have to potentiate the virus's cytolytic properties. How they die is as important as how many die if Wild Card's to succeed'!"

Mary watched him closely, like a poker player displaying what he is convinced will prove to be a winning hand. But like a poker player's, Paul's face remained impassive. "At the briefing," he began cautiously, "Nadelman admitted that it might not be possible to pull off this operation without a few fatalities, right? Okay, now *if* people die, they're the ones who'll get the most thorough investigation—autopsies, the works. It sounds to me as though Nadelman's still worried about the action of the virus on the cells it invades. He wants no cytopathic effects that could lead to the virus being identified by standard matching techniques. *That's* why the method of death is important. And after the rumpus we made at the briefing, are you surprised that he didn't want to go through the whole discussion about fatalities again with all of us present?"

"But he said cytolytic, *not* cytopathic!" she insisted.

Paul shrugged. "After five months, how can you be so sure? Anyway—cytolytic, cytopathic—it's semantics. If there are deaths, I don't see that it really matters if the cells disintegrate completely or simply have their normal morphology distorted. As long as the cause of death is obscured—"

"Okay, okay," she interrupted, "but if he wasn't talking about people when he said 'The destruction over that entire area must be absolute,' what was he talking about?"

"The virus. Virologists *do* talk about the destruction of their organisms, and Nadelman specified that the aerosol mist had to be made harmless after a three-hour exposure to air."

"Paul, you're wrong!" she said, shaking her head vehemently. "You're wrong!"

"Maybe," he said, angry that she had not trusted him enough to tell him about the telephone conversation five months earlier. "But as sure as hell I wouldn't have made the assumptions you have made—or done what you have done—on the basis of such absurdly inconclusive evidence!"

"I'm sorry," she said, suddenly deflated. "I know I should have told you about it before. It's just that I couldn't be sure you weren't in on it too . . . So, okay, maybe I did what I did for the wrong reasons, but I'm still glad I did it. Even if Wild Card were to have succeeded—which I very much doubt—the sociological consequences could well have been appalling."

148

Paul sighed. He knew that if he was to conceal the evidence of Mary's sabotage, and save the eight remaining cerebroids, he had to move fast. There was no time for another debate about the erosion of the integrity of science. "I'm going back to get into some dry clothes. How long will it take you to get over to the lab? I guess what we have to do first is reduce the acidosis—"

"I'm sorry," she said, frowning. "I don't understand . . ."

Paul stared back at her. "The cerebroids," he began uncertainly. "I assume you withheld B_1 from all of them, not just the ones that died during the—"

"But I thought you said they were *all* dead."

Paul shook his head. "Only the two oldest so far." Suddenly, he understood what lay behind Mary's confusion. "You forgot that the accelerated growth rate would lead to a staggering of the effects of B_1 deficiency," he said.

For a moment he thought she was going to faint. He guided her back to the bed and sat her down. He went to fetch a glass of water, and returned to find her sitting as he had left her, ashen and inert. He knelt beside her, trying—without success—to coax her to drink.

"Darling," he said gently, "it'll be all right. I'll tell them you have a migraine." He looked again at his watch. "But I must go *now*," he insisted. "It's our only chance!"

It took him several minutes to find a nightdress among the clothes in the chest of drawers. She neither helped nor tried to prevent him from putting it on her. He tidied the unmade bed as best he could and lifted her into it.

"Darling," he said. "I'll be back just as soon as I can. Promise me you'll stay here until I do. And don't worry," he added. "It's all going to be okay."

For three hours Mary Anderson lay without moving, overwhelmed by feelings of futility and worthlessness, guilt and self-reproach. In order to work against Wild Card she had been required—like a double agent—to work *for* it. But her attempt to destroy it did not, she believed, absolve her from the guilt of having helped create it. Paradoxically, she saw Paul's willingness to go along with Wild Card less as a failure in *him* than as a failure in herself. Was it not *she* who had committed the unpardonable offense of falling in love with someone unworthy of her love? And had *she* not compounded the offense by trying to conceal, from herself, her act of self-betrayal? She felt abandoned in a limitless, endlessly changing maze of dark mirrors.

Paul telephoned her at ten-fifty and again an hour later. On both occasions she told him that although she wanted to remain by herself for the rest of the day, she was feeling better and there was nothing she needed.

Toward noon her depression lifted sufficiently to allow a return of initiative. She dressed and, waiting until she believed everyone would be at lunch, walked across to the laboratory.

It did not take her long to find what she wanted.

"Kill ten thousand people?" Nadelman bellowed at Chesterton. "Of course it's not true! The silly bitch has got the whole thing ass backward!" He turned to glare at Napier. "Perhaps you would now explain why the hell I wasn't told any of this earlier?"

Napier sat hunched on the edge of his desk, his white, short-sleeved shirt stained with sweat where the straps of his shoulder holster had held the fabric tight against his body. He kept Nadelman waiting while he bit off the end of a cigar.

"The decision to bug Anderson's and McElroy's quarters was a routine, belt-and-braces operation," he said wearily. "If we hadn't picked up something other than the sounds of the bed springs being tested to destruction, I was going to call off the surveillance at the end of the week!"

Nadelman was still not satisfied. "Look," Napier continued, "when a couple—any couple—suddenly start making it together like there's no tomorrow, there's always a chance that one of them is going to come up with fancy ideas." He snapped shut the Zippo lighter he had used to light his cigar. "In Watts they'd decide to—I don't know—knock off a gas station. In Beverly Hills maybe they'd start goofing around with life insurance on the guy's wife with the idea of knocking *her* off. At Berkeley it would be plans to defect to the Chinese or overthrow the government." He pulled a face which suggested that after twenty-five years' service with the FBI, nothing would ever again surprise him.

Nadelman removed his spectacles and wiped away the sweat that had condensed on the inside of the lenses. "Okay, okay," he said, "but I'm still not satisfied that your interpretation of what's on that thing is correct." He nodded disdainfully at the tape recorder on the desk beside Napier.

Napier ran his finger around the inside of his shirt collar. He was becoming irritated with Nadelman for what he considered his truculent and stubborn refusal to accept the truth. He looked to Chesterton for support, but the psychiatrist pretended he had not noticed. "For God's sake, Dick," he said, "how many *more* times do you want to hear the fucking thing?" He jabbed the rewind button and allowed the spool to spin for several seconds before stopping it and pressing the play button. The first voice to speak was Mary's. "I'm sorry. I don't understand . . ."

"The cerebroids. I assume you withheld B_1 from all of them, not just the ones that died during the—"

"But I thought you said they were *all* dead."

"Only the two oldest so far. You forgot that the accelerated growth rate would lead to a staggering of the effects of B_1 deficiency."

Napier switched off the machine and stood up. "It's an open-and-shut case," he said, reaching for his jacket. "Perhaps next time you'll take care to see your door's properly shut."

Ignoring him, Nadelman suddenly rounded on Chesterton. "Well, don't just sit there—come up with something!"

Chesterton ran his hand over his carefully brushed white hair. "I could try talking to her," he began, without conviction. Napier's derisive laugh convinced him that there was little point in his enlarging on the proposal.

"Try talking to her, my ass!" said Napier, buttoning his jacket. "She has to go. And I'm going to take a lot of convincing," he added, "that McElroy oughtn't to go with her."

Chesterton nodded his reluctant agreement. "What bothers me, though, is the effect that might have on the morale of their colleagues. It would be bad enough if just *one* of them had to be removed from the camp for"—he searched for the right euphemism—"psychotherapy."

"Bullshit! I'm not talking about removing them for *psychotherapy*!" exclaimed Napier, offended that Chesterton should have thought him capable of such a naive suggestion. "I'm talking about them being removed *period*!"

"Out of the question!" exploded Nadelman, striking the top of his desk with his fist. "McElroy is indispensable!"

Napier shrugged, as though whether McElroy lived or died was of little consequence to him. "Okay," he conceded, "then we just deal with her."

"What is the point," asked Nadelman, somewhat mollified, "of spending God knows how much time and money building a library of psychiatric case histories if, the moment one of our subjects goes sour on us, we can only think in terms of knocking her off?" He turned to glare at Chesterton. "I'm making *you* personally responsible for dealing with Mary Anderson."

Napier shook his head disbelievingly, and started for the door.

"You will examine her tomorrow morning," concluded Nadelman, "diagnose whatever you like—nervous exhaustion due to overwork —but pull her out of the project. What we do with her when all this is over remains to be seen. But until then she is to remain in the compound, and is *not*"—he directed his order at Napier, who was standing, one hand on the doorknob, waiting for him to finish—"I repeat, *not*, to be harmed!"

Mary returned to her apartment at one twenty-five and locked the door behind her. She was now moving slowly but purposefully, her mind focused only on those actions she believed would save her from being buried alive forever under the debris of her rapidly disintegrating personality.

In the kitchen she took out of her handbag a bottle containing twenty-five Nembutal capsules, a syringe, a needle, and a rubber-stoppered bottle of insulin. She inserted the nozzle of the syringe into the head of the needle, filled the syringe with insulin, and put it to one side. It took her several minutes to empty the contents of the Nembutal capsules into a glass of water and drink it. She picked up the syringe, eased the needle into her left forearm just below the elbow, and pushed the plunger.

As she withdrew the needle she felt a massive, orgasmic relief of tension unlike anything she had ever experienced. She dropped the syringe and the insulin bottle into the waste disposer and switched it on for a moment. The Nembutal bottle and the empty gelatine capsules she dropped into the wastebin.

She had just begun to walk back to the bedroom when the floor tilted up and hit her hard on the side of the face.

19

THE DRIVER OF THE ambulance that had carried Mary Anderson on the half-mile journey to the hospital on Chandler Avenue switched off its siren and flashing red light and swung into the emergency-area driveway. Attendants raced over and threw open its doors—brushing McElroy to one side—and lifted out the wheeled stretcher. Waiting on the ramp were the hospital's security guards and a young physician who, McElroy remembered, had treated him for a pulled muscle a month earlier. Together they hurried along behind the stretcher as it was wheeled through the double doors into a long, white-tiled corridor. Somewhere a loudspeaker was repeating the message: "STAT call for Dr. Warren Aubry."

"What happened?" asked the physician.

McElroy handed him several of the empty Nembutal capsules and the glass from which Mary had drunk. Without stopping he tasted the sediment from the bottom of the glass.

"She wasn't feeling well this morning," began McElroy, "and when I went to see her half an hour ago I couldn't get a reply. I found her unconscious on the kitchen floor. Those''—he pointed to the glass and the capsules—''were nearby.''

The physician nodded. ''What I don't get is why she was lying on the *kitchen* floor. Did it look as if she'd collapsed?''

''It did,'' replied McElroy. ''I guess she must have been on her way through to the living room.''

''Had she been drinking?''

''Not as far as I know.''

The physician made no attempt to prevent McElroy from entering the crowded, brightly lit emergency bay. Although they arrived only a few seconds after Mary, she had already been moved from the stretcher to the examination table and two nurses had begun to strip her. The table was flanked by a pair of stainless steel trolleys. One carried trays of surgical instruments. The other, an anesthesia machine, carried three yoked oxygen bottles with their accompanying pressure gauges, vaporizers, and flow meters.

By the time Dr. Aubry, the senior physician, reached the emergency bay, her blood pressure data had been put on a CRT screen, and a technician was connecting electrodes, which had been secured to her chest with micropore tape, to the ECG terminals.

Aubry was a big-boned man in his early fifties who had been assigned, along with several of his colleagues, from the National Security Agency's hospital at Fort Meade, Maryland.

As he swept in through the swing doors he glanced at McElroy. ''Who's this?'' he demanded.

''Her section head,'' replied one of the security guards. ''Dr. McElroy found the patient.''

Aubry threw aside his jacket and was helped by two nurses into a green gown, a mask, and vinyl gloves. Another secured his spectacles to the bridge of his nose with a strip of adhesive tape. There had been no time for him to scrub up and they were still tying the tapes on his gown when he stepped up to the examination table.

''Blood pressure?'' he asked.

''Eighty over forty—falling,'' replied the anesthetist.

Aubry nodded gravely; the circulatory collapse of his patient was severe. ''I'll need to intubate,'' he said.

As he moved to a position level with Mary Anderson's shoulders, two nurses placed a pillow beneath her back to extend and raise her throat. The physician took hold of her head firmly from behind while Aubry, using a laryngoscope, guided a cuffed endotracheal tube into her windpipe. He passed the tube to a nurse, who attached the free end to the anesthesia machine. "Cut-down next, please," he said.

Immediately a nurse cleansed an area of skin midway between the wrist and elbow of Mary Anderson's left arm and a pair of forceps was slapped into Aubry's waiting hand. He leaned forward and, using the forceps, lifted the clean fold of skin. He made a transverse incision, then used a hemostat to expose a section of the collapsed vein. He freed the vein, threaded two loops of nylon under it, and exerted tension on them with artery forceps. He took a new scalpel, made a longitudinal nick in the vein, and inserted a cannula.

"You can connect that up now."

A nurse took one end of the tubing and attached it to a bag of saline suspended on a stand. Aubry stitched in the cannula, packed the skin incision with swabs, and strapped up. Twelve minutes had passed.

Aubry straightened, satisfied that the vital processes of breathing and circulation had been restored. Ascertaining the cause of coma was a secondary consideration. While his brow was being mopped he spoke to a waiting nurse. "Take blood and urine samples, please, and have them analyzed immediately." He turned to the anesthetist. "How's the pressure?"

"A hundred over sixty."

Aubry nodded. "That's better. She's coming back." While the nurse covered Mary Anderson with a blanket, Aubry took an ophthalmoscope from the trolley and examined her optic reflexes. The pupils, he was dismayed to see, remained dilated and fixed. He drew back the blanket covering her legs, lifted her knee, and tapped the patellar tendon with a reflex hammer. Again there was no response. Moving down to her foot, he reversed the hammer and tickled the sole, testing the plantar reflex. But he could detect no response. He turned to his assistant. "Set up an EEG, please." Then he walked over to McElroy.

"When was the last time you saw Dr. Anderson?" he asked. "I mean before you found her unconscious?"

"Early this morning," he replied. "But I'd spoken to her on the telephone since then. The last time was around noon." He waited a moment to see if he was to be questioned further and then asked, "Aren't you going to try gastric lavage?"

Aubry shook his head. "Nembutal's a fast-acting barbiturate —there won't be enough left in her stomach to make it worthwhile."

"What are her chances?"

Aubry looked doubtful. "It's hard to say. She was pretty far gone when you found her, you know. However, she's a strong girl and—" He broke off as the results of the blood test appeared on one of the CRT displays.

"Oh, Christ!" For the first time Aubry appeared agitated. "Change that drip to fifty per cent dextrose, nurse," he shouted, "and fast!"

McElroy knew enough about the displays to realize that, although Mary's circulation was not failing, her brain's nervous activity was dwindling. "What's happened?" he asked.

Aubry turned back to him. "There's no sign of blood glucose. Did she have access to insulin?"

McElroy looked puzzled. "Sure, it's a standard item, but she wouldn't be using any at this stage of our program."

Aubry hurried over to the examination table and lifted the blanket covering Mary's legs. McElroy had noticed earlier that her face and right arm had been bruised; now he saw that her right outer thigh was also bruised. He watched as Aubry took a lens from the instrument table and studied her thighs, then her abdomen, and finally her arms. He fixed on the inside of Mary's left arm, near her elbow. He had found what he'd been looking for: a small needle puncture into the vein.

"I'm getting nothing from the EEG, Dr. Aubry," the anesthetist said, almost apologetically.

"Nothing at all—even on high gain?"

The anesthetist looked back at the screen; the light spot was traveling in a straight line across the green background. He checked with the graph paper rolling trace, then shook his head. "No . . . all activity has ceased. I'm getting a flat record."

Deprived of glucose by the insulin, Mary's brain had died. Aubry would keep the machine running for a while—as a formality—but he knew there was no hope left; his jurisdiction had ended. Suddenly very tired, he pulled off his mask and went across to McElroy. His face, Aubry noticed, was pale but expressionless. The reaction would come later.

"I'm sorry," Aubry said softly. "Very sorry."

20

McElroy had no idea what time it was when he finally left the laboratory that night, only that it was very late. For an hour or more he wandered aimlessly along the dark, empty streets of the maximum-security compound like a sleepwalker, unable to believe what had happened. Could Mary *really* have done such a thing, he asked himself over and over again?

But if she had not intended to kill herself, what had happened? He had been with her to the end, and although he was not a physician, he knew enough to be sure that Aubry and the hospital staff had done all that anyone, anywhere, could have done to save her. Even if they'd found the needle punctures immediately, it would still have been too late.

The hypodermic! What had become of the hypodermic? He stopped, alert for the first time since he'd left the hospital. What, indeed, *had* happened to the hypodermic? Questions suddenly began tumbling, one after the other, into his mind. He had been interrogated by Napier and Chesterton for nearly an hour before being allowed back to the laboratory. But they'd only seemed interested in trying to establish that Mary had worked long hours and had suffered from recurring bouts of depression. Why hadn't they suspected more than a casual connection between Mary's death and that of the cerebroids? And why had there been no suggestion that he, Paul, might have killed her? He knew that *they* knew he and Mary had been lovers; there had seemed little point in trying to hide it. And yet it had never been put to him that they might have quarreled—perhaps about his refusal to leave his wife, anything—and that he'd returned, found her unconscious, and made sure she did not regain consciousness by injecting her with insulin. Why not? Such things happened, and in any other situation he knew he'd have been a prime suspect.

And just what *had* Nadelman meant when he'd said, as McElroy was leaving the security-detail block, "Don't blame yourself for any of this, Paul. Mary was a delightful girl and a brilliant scientist; but on a project like this there's no room for moralistic afterthoughts." At the time he'd thought Nadelman had been talking about the emotional strain of working on Wild Card, and the effect it might have had on her. Now he was not so sure . . .

The seeds of an idea began to germinate; the idea that they—Napier, Chesterton, and Nadelman—had somehow found out about Mary's sabotage and had killed her.

But how had they found out, he asked himself? He had, that very morning, successfully covered all traces of Mary's involvement.

There could only be one explanation, and he cursed himself for not thinking of it before.

He set out for her apartment, determined that if he found what he expected, he would take a terrible revenge on those responsible.

McElroy let himself into Mary's apartment as he had earlier —through the kitchen window. The rooms were cool and silent, and filled with the gray, melancholy light of dawn. Someone had switched off the central heating and the refrigerator, and the clock in the living room had stopped.

For twenty minutes he searched under tables and chairs, behind pictures and curtains, inside lampshades and plant pots—everywhere and in anything that could have concealed a microphone. He found nothing.

162

He collapsed onto the couch, defeated, and closed his aching eyes. There was still a trace of Mary's scent in the air and, all resolve gone, he gave himself up to the ghosts of what had been, and what might have been.

He was somewhere between sleeping and waking, where thoughts turn into dreams and dreams into thoughts, when he heard something move in the bedroom. With a start he turned and stared at the bedroom door.

"Mary?" he called. There was no reply. For several seconds he didn't move, his heart beating like a trip-hammer. Then he heard the sound again. He let his breath out slowly: it was only a central heating pipe contracting.

He got up and was about to leave when his eye was caught by something shiny on the floor near the bedroom door. He crossed over and looked at it; it was a strand of silver wire, not much more than a half inch long and as fine as hair. Recessed into the wall above it was a twin electricity socket. He picked up the wire and rolled it between his fingers. Someone, he guessed, had changed one of the plugs recently and had accidentally cut through the rubber cable sheathing and severed one of the strands of wire beneath. He pulled one of the plugs from its socket and examined it. He was right; the white plastic casing and the brass pins were too clean, too shiny, to be anything other than new.

He looked around him. The plug in his hand was no different from any of the others in the room, but then perhaps they'd *all* been changed?

He crossed swiftly to the bathroom and returned with a nail file. With trembling fingers he unscrewed the plug and lifted off its cover. It was like any other: wires and terminals—and nothing else.

He was about to open another of the plugs when he realized he was wasting his time. He was looking in the wrong apartment. He put the strand of wire back on the floor where he had found it, returned Mary's nail file to the bathroom cabinet, and left.

McElroy arrived back at his own apartment and went straight to the kitchen for a screwdriver. He returned to his sitting room, switched on the radio and pulled out the nearest plug. Pausing for a moment to catch his breath, he unscrewed the cover slowly and carefully, and lifted it off. Inside was what he had expected—a microminiaturized microphone!

The bastards! he thought. The motherfucking bastards!

Mary had been murdered. He was sure of that. He should have realized all along how it would be on an operation like this. How could he have been so stupid? And they had killed her—as they would kill him, or any of the others—just to make things a little tidier, like killing a roach in the kitchen.

His first impulse was to try for vengeance. But what could he do? And what would be the point? An eye for an eye? Would Mary thank him for that?

Escape was out of the question. Even if he managed to evade the guards in the watchtowers overlooking the inner perimeter fence, he would still come up against the dog run, the trip wires, and the strip of mined ground.

By eight-thirty he had thought it through. There was only one thing he could do. Letters and telephone calls would be intercepted as a matter of routine. They would go through everything with a fine-tooth comb. They would find microfilm, detect and break a code—they were experts and he wasn't. But he had to expose Wild Card. At least that would make some sense of Mary's death. He could do that for her.

And he knew how to do it. There *was* a way of blowing the whistle—a foolproof way Napier's men would never dream of, a method they would never be able to detect, a code they could never break—because McElroy was the only man in the world who knew how to do it. The answer lay in the technique he had evolved for encoding information in proteins.

McElroy lit a cigarette and leaned back in his chair. Now he had other problems to solve. Even if he could get out the information in the form of a synthetic learning experience, how was he to get it into a brain where it could become "knowledge"? Injection was out of the question. He would have to come up with some other method of absorption. Digestion was the obvious solution—it shouldn't be too difficult to get the proteins to the right person injected into some innocuous material, like chocolates. But the proteins would almost certainly be broken down by digestive enzymes. And even if they were not, they would have little chance of passing through the blood/brain barrier and reaching the cortex.

He smoked to the end of the cigarette. And another. He knew there was a solution within reach—if only his *own* brain would make the right connections . . .

And then he had it. It was simple. Any protein can be produced from the appropriate DNA template. If he were to synthesize not the memory proteins themselves, but the DNA sequences that coded for them, and if the DNA sequences could be reconstituted with the coat of a brain-specific virus—it would protect the memory sequence from enzymic degradation *and* guarantee that it reached the brain cells. Once there, the DNA would use the cellular machinery to manufacture the memory proteins. He stood up and began to pace the room. That was it. That was the solution.

The next step was to decide the exact content of the memory message—and the person he should get it to. Someone who knew him and would accept a gift from him. Was it too much to hope that he could get it to someone who might even understand how such a mysterious memory might have grown spontaneously in his mind? Someone who would use the kind of technical language that would trigger the memory—like an actor suddenly remembering all of Hamlet's soliloquy after hearing the words "To be or not to be . . ." A colleague, perhaps?

He found his diary and leafed through the pages. On October 22 he had made a note of the next meeting of the American Biochemical Society. As retiring vice-president he would have been expected to attend and present a paper. The new vice-president was a good friend—Angela Hubner. What more natural than to send her a gift, to apologize for his absence, and to wish her luck in her term of office. Nothing extravagant—a simple box of chocolates . . .

He realized that it was far too risky to send out only one box of chocolates. Apart from anything else, the mails were chaotic. It was becoming almost a matter of course to send duplicates of important letters. He would therefore send chocolates not only to Angie, but to the other three women members of the ABS executive. Even if all four of them were dieting, at least one would surely offer the chocolates to friends—hopefully, friends with a scientific background. With each box, he would send a note of regret that he was unable to attend, and of thanks for their cooperation in the past year. Inside the chocolates would be another message:

presidential plot based detrick to fabricate extraterrestrial spacecraft and crew of organotypic cerebroid cultures in closed-loop system low c-14 cosmic ray bombardment artificially ages assembly faked spacecraft crash and virus dispersal scheduled los angeles december 3 but installation 13400 doty avenue thanksgiving.

It would take an army to invade Detrick, but a cop on the beat could get into the Los Angeles house.

The surface of the desk was covered with a square of linen gauze. On it stood four boxes of Whitman's Samplers and four racks, each containing twenty-four ampules; a high-pressure syringe and individually packed microneedles; a scalpel and tweezers; adhesive and a bottle of organic solvent.

McElroy pulled on a pair of medical gloves and picked up the first box of chocolates. Using the scalpel, he lifted one end flap of the cellophane outer wrapping and loosened it. The irregularly applied layer of adhesive separated easily. He peeled back the other flaps, then tilted the box, allowing it to slide through the opening. He put the cellophane to one side, lifted the lid of the box, and removed the packing slip and corrugated-paper blanket, and took out the top tray. Then he lifted off the second blanket and removed the lower tray.

After experimenting with a trial box, he had decided that he would inject the memory molecules through one of the air bubbles that form during manufacture in the base of each chocolate.

He stripped the sterile covering off the first microneedle and fitted it to the syringe. He unstoppered an ampule, filled the syringe, and eased the needle into the chocolate.

When he had injected the twenty-four chocolates in the first box, he replaced the trays and internal packing and closed the lid. Using a gauze pad, he applied organic solvent to the patches of dry adhesive on the cellophane covering and wiped the surface clean. Then he slid the box back into the cellophane, guiding the wrapping over the corners of the box with tweezers. It was the most difficult part of the operation. After resealing the flap with a new layer of adhesive, he began on the second box.

Fifty minutes later, four boxes of chocolates contained details of Wild Card.

21

On October 12, McElroy mailed the chocolates.

The same day, in a downtown Los Angeles office, two attorneys —one representing the vendor of 13400 Doty Avenue, the other representing Dr. Ralph Sheldon—met to complete a transaction. A cashier's check was exchanged and Sheldon became the owner of a house that would, in seven weeks, be a ruin.

The following day, Jaycee Construction—the company set up a month earlier by Stillman, Payne, and Olsen—landed its first big job: the conversion and redecoration of 13400 Doty Avenue. They began loading their truck, a battered ex-Army vehicle with a canvas-covered rear section, and, early the next morning, set out for Doty Avenue.

Number 13400 turned out to be at the Hawthorne end of the avenue, about three miles north of the old El Camino College site. It occupied a corner lot and was one of the larger properties in the area—a rambling, two-story building with a clapboard frontage, a pitched roof, and dormer windows. Cotoneaster bushes, Martha Washington geraniums, lilies, and a pyracantha crowded the path leading to the porch. To the right of the path, parked outside a recently built brick garage, was a blue Volkswagen minibus.

Lawrence and a slightly built, middle-aged man dressed in the

167

casual style of a student were waiting in the garden. While Payne and Olsen began to unload scaffolding from the back of the truck, Stillman stepped over the fence and shook hands with Lawrence.

"Dr. Sheldon," said Lawrence, turning to the other man. "Meet Jack Chieszkowski. Jack runs Jaycee Construction."

"Okay," said Sheldon, after they had spent ten minutes examining the exterior of the house, "I'll leave you guys to get on with it."

As soon as he had driven off, Lawrence unlocked the front door and went inside with Stillman. The porch opened onto a wide hall that ran down the center of the building. To the left of the hall was a sitting room and, beyond that, a library; to the right was a dining room. The stairs were roughly halfway along the hall; a door to their left closed off the rear of the house and led down to the cellar. Behind the door were the remainder of the hall, a ground-floor washroom, and, to the right, a kitchen. A door from the kitchen led directly into the garage. The upper floor was divided into four bedrooms and two bathrooms. At the back of the house, a patio overlooked a large garden planted with mature Monterey pines and bordered by tall hedges. A small greenhouse stood against the rear boundary fence.

"What about utilities?" asked Stillman, opening a well-worn carpenter's bag that Payne had brought into the hall. He took out two gleaming submachine guns and began checking the firing mechanism.

Lawrence bent down and squinted at the door lock. "We've gotta get this changed before the end of the day," he said. "Utilities? Gas and electricity were connected Friday; water not until later today."

Stillman swore. He would have to remain behind to guard the house that night, and had planned to sleep during the afternoon.

"It's okay, you can sleep upstairs," said Lawrence, straightening up. "Or better still, in the garden. That way it'll never occur to the neighbors to think you're anything but a workman!"

During the first two weeks, work went ahead on the foundations, cellar, and ground floor, and a crater was excavated for the spacecraft to rest in. Compression tests carried out on a sample of the surface concrete in the cellar had shown it to be capable of withstanding a force of 8,000 pounds per square inch. By the time the spacecraft had fallen to this level, it would have been robbed of much of its velocity and, according to calculations, would create a crater eleven and four tenths inches deep.

The third and fourth weeks were taken up with work on the bedroom, and the wall of the kitchen below. No detail was too small to escape Lawrence's attention. Special hammer drill attachments, shaped like a section of the spacecraft's duct and made of the same material, were used to punch through the woodwork, leaving a characteristic "footprint." If it was possible, Lawrence had reasoned, for forensic experts to classify a blunt instrument by the shape of the indentation it left in a shattered skull, then the investigative team would be able to apply a similar technique to the debris left behind after the explosion.

Meanwhile, restructuring of the house was proceeding in parallel with its demolition. It had been agreed that if the debris were to consist *only* of the original materials in the house, suspicions would be raised immediately. So while Lawrence, Payne, and Stillman continued with the demolition, Olsen converted the two bedrooms and the bathroom on the right of the upstairs floor into one master suite, and applied fresh plaster and several coats of paint.

Sheldon returned to the house three times during this period. On the first occasion he took a brief look at the work being done in the master bedroom, and pottered about in the garden for an hour. During his subsequent visits, he repaired a faulty latch on the front gate, made an amateurish job of repainting the fence, and got himself invited in for coffee by his next-door neighbor.

On November 15, Benedict began packing the spacecraft's component parts, ready for transit to the West Coast. All of the crates bore the markings of Consolidated Engineering Inc.—a long-established and respectable machine-tool manufacturer in Pennsylvania—and were sealed with metal bands and large-gauge wire staples.

The following day the crates were loaded into two freight containers that had been painted in the same company's livery, and put on the back of an articulated trailer. Finally, a Plymouth sedan, painted and equipped to look like a police car, was driven up a ramp into a second trailer, secured, and hitched to the back of the trailer containing the spacecraft.

At 11:40 P.M. Stillman and Olsen arrived from Los Angeles. They spent an hour talking with Napier, changed into State Trooper's uniforms—over which they wore white coveralls—and drove the rig to a turnoff three miles from where Highway 40 joins U.S. 70.

At 2:15 A.M. Napier saw what they had gone to meet. "Right on the button," he said to Stillman, putting away the light-intensifying glasses he'd been using. He switched on the car's rotating red light, drove out into the middle of the road, and stopped.

With a hiss of air brakes, the big diesel with the words CONSOLIDATED ENGINEERING INC. painted on its side came to a standstill ten yards in front of the police car. The driver leaned out of the cab window and called, "What's up, Mac?"

Napier and Stillman strolled over to the cab, one on either side.

"Out!" said Napier. He shined his flashlight at the driver's partner. "You, too, buddy!"

The driver started to protest, but stopped when he saw Napier's hand drop onto his holster. Reluctantly, he and his partner opened their doors and climbed down.

"Okay," said Napier, "you know the routine."

Slowly, the driver turned to face the cab and leaned forward, his feet apart, and his hands held above his head. Napier kicked the man's feet farther apart, lifted the papers and cargo manifest from his white coverall, and began examining them. "It's the Jaycee consignment, all right," he called across to Stillman.

The driver looked over his shoulder, just in time to see Napier pocket the papers he'd taken from him. "What the fuck's going on here?" he asked.

"Turn around," said Napier.

The man did as he was ordered, screwing up his eyes against the glare from the flashlight.

Napier chuckled. "You've just been hijacked, fella," he said. "That's what the fuck's going on here!"

The driver began to turn his head away from the glare. Without warning, Napier's right hand came scything up at him, his palm flattened and fingers extended in a classic atemi blow. The edge of his hand struck the driver at the base of his nose, crushing the septal cartilage and delivering a massive shock to his nervous system. He was dead before he hit the ground.

His partner was dispatched a moment later with equal economy by Stillman.

Napier threw away the cigar he'd been chewing, and looked at his watch. "Okay," he called across to Stillman. "Let's move it."

After locking the bodies in the trunk of the police car, Napier returned to the hijacked rig and—followed by Stillman—drove to where Olsen was waiting with the rig containing the spacecraft.

Moving rapidly and silently, the two men coupled the trailer to the rear of the hijacked rig and ran out the ramps. Stillman drove the police car back into the trailer, secured it, and locked the doors.

There were now only two things to be done to the rig containing the spacecraft. While Stillman exchanged license plates, Olsen sorted out six of the metal stencils he had brought with him, and slotted them into a frame in the order CE1469—the hijacked rig's fleet number. Holding the frame against the door of the rig containing the spacecraft, he applied a burst of quick-drying paint from an aerosol.

Taking care not to smudge Olsen's lettering, Stillman and Napier—once again wearing white coveralls—climbed into the cab and started the engine. "See you back in Detrick," Napier shouted as he pulled out onto the highway that would take him to Baltimore's Friendship Airport.

Napier joined the long line of carriers waiting to enter the freight terminal at 3:55 A.M., arriving at the papers check twenty minutes later. The Consolidated Engineering cargo manifest was accepted without query, and they were quickly marshaled through to the security section. In the distance, Napier could see the apron and four of the waiting fat-bellied 747 freighters.

Airport police checked the cab and chassis for concealed arms, looked with little interest at the containers, and passed the rig along to the loading bay. There, the containers were winched off, weighed, and transferred to a hydraulic loading platform. The platform was driven up to the nose of one of the 747s, and the containers started their short journey into the plane's belly.

By 6 A.M. Stillman and Napier were back at Fort Detrick. Parked outside the Flight Testing Facility was the hijacked rig. The containers with the machine tools ordered three weeks earlier by Jaycee Construction had been winched off and were inside the facility, along with the trailer containing the fake police car, waiting to be melted down.

On his return to Detrick, Olsen had transferred the two bodies into the trunk of an unmarked sedan—together with a land mine—and was waiting for his colleagues' return. "How'd it go?" he asked, switching on the engine.

Napier gave him a thumbs-up sign. "It should be well on the way by now," he replied.

Napier and Stillman replaced the license plates on the hijacked rig and followed Olsen back to where they had commandeered it earlier. By the time they arrived, he had set up the mine—a type frequently used by terrorists—and was waiting by the roadside, ready to connect up the pressure-sensitive detonators.

Napier parked next to the sedan and, with Stillman's help, lifted the bodies into the cab and replaced their papers in their coveralls. The sky to the east had begun to lighten, and they worked rapidly.

The next part was up to Stillman: Napier would have been slower and was far too bulky. He climbed into the cab and, half sitting in the lap of the dead driver, started the engine. With some difficulty, he drove out onto the highway and flashed the headlights.

A hundred yards away, Olsen began connecting the pressure-sensitive pads to the mine he'd buried under the inside lane of the highway. When he had finished, he flashed his torch and Stillman moved the rig forward on hand throttle, turned and lined up with the pads.

Twenty yards short of the mine, Stillman dropped clear of the rig and ran for as long as he dared before throwing himself flat on the ground. Even then he was showered with debris when the mine exploded a second later.

At 7 A.M. Pacific Standard Time, the 747 freighter carrying the spacecraft landed at Los Angeles International Airport. The containers were collected and taken to Jaycee Construction, arriving at nine. An hour later the crates had been fork-lifted into a storage shed and the delivery note signed.

Five hours later Stillman and Olsen arrived back in Los Angeles to continue working on the house. They had been away exactly twenty-four hours.

Over the next ten days, the spacecraft was transported a few sections at a time in the Jaycee truck to 13400 Doty. Using a small winch to maneuver the components into position, and a laser to bond them together, Lawrence's team pressed on with the assembly.

In the early morning hours of December 2, Paul McElroy and Philip Benedict began preparing three cerebroids for their journey from Detrick, following an identical procedure for each of the creatures.

McElroy had already reduced the temperature of the nutrient medium to decrease the cerebroid's rate of metabolism, and removed the EEG monitor electrodes. Now, he separated two of the leads from the depth electrodes used for stimulation of the cerebroid and connected them to its miniature life-support pack. He gathered the remaining electrodes into four bundles, attaching each to one side of an end plate of organic superconductor. The major part of the cerebroid's electrical activity was now concentrated into these four sensory end plates. He released the gas-tight seal on the tank, removed the lid, then lifted the cerebroid—with life-support pack attached—into the lower hemisphere of its metal shell. The hemisphere was already partially filled with cold nutrient medium.

Benedict took over and slotted the four end plates into notches in the rim of the hemisphere. He placed the upper hemisphere, with its matching notches, on top, and bonded the completed sphere. The end plates could still be seen around the equator of the sphere, but they formed leakproof seals, and did not affect the overall structural integrity of the shell. The end plates were, in effect, the junction boxes that would enable Lawrence to "plug" the final assembly together, achieving the closed loop that Benedict had described at the demonstration.

The final stage was to force more nutrient medium into the shell, through a small inlet in the top of the sphere. Benedict watched the pump pressure gauges until he was sure that the cerebroid was completely immersed in medium, then sealed the inlet hole.

Throughout the maneuvering procedures, neither man had touched the cerebroids directly, using instead a telechiric manipulator.

Still at the controls of the manipulator, Benedict lifted the first cerebroid and buried it in protective foam inside a lightweight metal container. He sealed the container and placed it inside a yellow packing case bearing the galleon motif of the Mayflower World-wide Moving Service. The container fitted the case perfectly, leaving a clear space —thirty inches deep—above it.

By 6:30 A.M. the third cerebroid had been packed. Wearing gloves, Benedict and McElroy filled the spaces at the top of the crates with books. Finally, they stapled the lids and stuck "Load First" labels onto each of the crates. By the time they were loaded in a Mayflower container, they would be hidden by 2800 cubic feet of furniture. Two members of the security detail put the crates into an unmarked truck and, at seven, Napier took them to Sheldon's house in Georgetown. From there they would be air-freighted to Los Angeles together with Sheldon's domestic effects.

The project now had less than twenty-four hours to run before the explosion.

The weather in L.A. was still a clammy seventy degrees. For the past week, an anticyclone had remained stationary over the West Coast, gradually intensifying, and the high pressure was expected to persist for several more days. A layer of warm air had formed over the city and hung there like a lid. Beneath it, tons of pollutants were simmering in the heat; even at night there was little relief. The conditions were ideal for the explosion. The viral agent would be confined close to ground level, where it would be most effective.

The sweating Mayflower crew whose trailer backed up to 13400 Doty at four that afternoon quickly made it obvious that the sooner this job was over the happier they would be. "How's it to be placed, Doc?" asked the crew chief.

Lawrence shrugged. "I guess it'll have to be the front rooms downstairs and the hallway. You can lay the carpets in the sitting room and library—they're okay—then just pile the rest in on top."

The crew chief looked surprised. "Everything?"

Lawrence shook his head sadly. "The fucking contractors aren't through yet. Would you believe it? *Three* weeks over their schedule!"

Unloading went quickly. By five o'clock the last three crates were being trolleyed into the house. While the quilted pads in which the crates had been wrapped were being removed and returned to the trailer, Lawrence signed Sheldon's name on the delivery note. Five minutes later the Mayflower rig had left.

Lawrence walked past the crates and unlocked the door at the side of the staircase.

Five feet away, dwarfing him and dominating the shell of the house, was the spacecraft. It was resting on its side in an almost vertical position. The hall floor in front of him was completely destroyed, as if the duct had smashed through it to the cellar. The spherical cabin had been displaced downward by the "crash impact," tearing the upper spoke away from the duct to expose the honeycomb strengthening material inside. The two lower spokes had crumpled and now supported the cabin at ground level. Six feet below, the bottom edge of the duct was embedded in the floor of the cellar; the opposite edge jutted up to the loft. Although the cabin had retained its structural integrity, the duct had been distorted to a rough oval shape. The outer surface was deeply scored and torn and, despite the powerful spots mounted in the library, loft, and kitchen, the craft appeared dull, the result of a heavy coating of dust.

The remains of the building reflected the chaos that Lawrence had so carefully designed. Beyond the left-hand edge of the duct, the library wall had been reduced to rubble—bricks, plaster, and splintered shelving spilling across the floor. To the right, the kitchen wall was now no more than a stub. The sink unit and fitted cupboards were demolished, buried beneath masonry and heavy timbers. The ground-floor washroom, concealed behind the cabin of the spacecraft, had escaped with minor damage. The door had been wrenched off its hinges and punched inward against the toilet bowl.

The spacecraft's path during the hypothetical crash was clearly defined by the gaping holes in the floor and ceiling of the bedroom above. The bathroom, too, had been badly damaged; twisted piping and a fractured water tank were visible through the breach. Roof rafters, obviously struck from above, now hung downward around the spacecraft, pinning it in position.

Lawrence edged forward through the ankle-deep layer of debris to stand at the foot of a lightweight extension ladder that reached up to the loft. "Ed! Jerry!" he called.

There was a shuffling noise from above, a few flakes of plaster spun down to the hall, and Stillman's face appeared. At the same time, Payne looked over the rim of the hole in the bedroom floor. "Ed, come on down and give me a hand with this loading," Lawrence called. "Jerry, when you're through in the bedroom, would you bring in the books?"

Stillman pulled on a coverall and a pair of gloves and began to remove the layers of books that concealed the cerebroids.

Carefully, Lawrence and Stillman lifted the first of the metal containers out of its packing case, opened it, and stripped away the upper layer of protective foam. Lawrence switched on a grab. With its electric motor humming softly, he guided the manipulative arm toward the cerebroid, lowering the padded grip until it circled the creature's mid-section and locked on. Slowly, the grab lifted the cerebroid clear of the foam. With the pitch control he rotated the cerebroid into a horizontal attitude, its base toward the spacecraft. The telescopic arm now extended gradually toward the cabin, Lawrence using vernier controls to make fine adjustments to the position. This part of the procedure was painfully slow, and Lawrence withdrew the arm twice before he was completely satisfied that the cerebroid was properly docked in the flight couch. "Right on the nose," Stillman said. Another signal from the transmitter and the cerebroid was locked firmly in place by the restraining collar. It was, as Lawrence had said during a practice session at Detrick, like the reverse of delivering a baby with forceps. By the time the last cerebroid had been installed, Lawrence had been controlling the grab for more than an hour. He was already perspiring heavily from the intense concentration that the procedure demanded—but the really tricky part was still to come: closing the loop. The "cables" of super-conductive organic fiber from the sensory gear in the duct and from the computer had to be attached to the cerebroids' end plates, then the cerebroids themselves had to be interlinked.

"You take the first hour, give me a rest," Lawrence said to Stillman as they exchanged the padded grip for a "finger" attachment, capable of ultrafine manipulations. "And don't break the fucking things!"

Meanwhile, the other men were repacking the crates and clearing away the equipment used during the construction of the spacecraft. From the truck, they brought in several stacks of books, mainly scientific, and purchased over the past few weeks from a number of booksellers in the Los Angeles area. These books now filled the crates in which the cerebroids had traveled.

At nine o'clock, Lawrence completed the final attachment, and Stillman transmitted a signal to close the geodesic cabin. The grab, spots, manipulative attachments, and metal cases that had protected the cerebroids in transit were then taken out to the truck. Finally, debris, retained for the purpose, was distributed over the now sealed spacecraft.

Shortly afterward Olsen and Payne drove away, leaving Lawrence and Stillman to set up the explosive device.

Earlier in the project, Lawrence and Weiner had spent many hours discussing the techniques used by airline-crash investigators. One fact had emerged very clearly: the giveaway in all sabotage cases was the presence in the wreckage of materials alien to those used in the construction of the aircraft.

For the deception to succeed, the explosion of the spacecraft would have to stem from sources occurring naturally within the structure—the high-test peroxide tanks supplying the attitude-control jets, and the fuel in its main tanks. The problem then became one of finding some method of detonating the fuel—and the answer had lain in the craft's navigational subsystem. Benedict had built a laser gyroscope into the system. It was exceptionally accurate and, unlike a conventional gyro, could function well under high accelerative forces. Basically, it consisted of two laser beams traveling in a closed loop through pathways drilled in a solid block of quartz. If the quartz were to be damaged—in a crash, for example—the highly concentrated beams of energy would "escape," and would have more than enough power to pierce the peroxide tanks, causing an immediate and serious explosion. But even this would be minor compared to the massive blast that would follow when the main tanks were affected. In the jargon of explosives experts, the laser gyro was to function as detonator, the peroxide as booster, and the fuel as bursting charge.

At midnight, after making a thorough check of the virus-dispersal mechanisms, Lawrence and Stillman went down to the cellar. It was only at this level that the "damage" sustained by the spacecraft could be fully appreciated. Impact with the floor had caused the duct to split open like a pea pod, exposing the electronics apparatus, the gyro, and the attitude-control system. Evidence of the crash poked out from the edges of the crater beneath the duct—the tangled remains of a television aerial, shattered roof tiles and battens, felt and insulation material. There was even a pigeon, its wing caught in electrical cable.

He focused his flashlight on the quartz block. The hairline fracture at one corner of the prismatic system was almost invisible to the eye, but it was from this point that the laser beam would escape. Lawrence and Stillman now had two tasks remaining: alignment of the fracture with the peroxide and main tanks; and setting the on-board computer to activate the laser gyro, an operation that could be done remotely, using the transmitter.

By one A.M. on December 3, they had finished. They left the house through the kitchen, going directly into the garage. Silently, they pushed the minibus fifty yards along the deserted avenue before starting the engine, then drove to the airport.

In two hours' time 13400 Doty Avenue would be on its way to becoming the most widely known address in the world.

22

DOUGLAS WALLCROFT PEERED into the smog and dipped the Pontiac's headlights.

The five *Countdown* specials he had come to the West Coast to make were, he thanked God, finished at last. To be called "California: A Cold Wind in Eden," the programs set out to examine the causes of the state's decline from being the richest in the Union to an economic wasteland. Wallcroft should have returned to New York with the rest of his team at 11 P.M., but he had stayed overnight with a girl he had picked up at a party. Before taking off in his secretary's rented Pontiac, he had asked her to check his luggage at Los Angeles International and arrange for his ticket to be switched to an early-morning flight.

He drummed his fingers impatiently on the steering wheel as he waited for the traffic signals to change at the intersection of Redondo Beach and Crenshaw. It would not be many minutes now, he estimated, before he would strike the San Diego Freeway.

The traffic signals changed and he moved forward. He was in the middle of the intersection when the smog to the north glowed for an instant; seconds later the car was buffeted by a pressure wave that set the keys in the ignition rattling. He braked, switched off the engine, and lowered the window. Somewhere in the distance a patrol car turned on its siren. Then a second and a third. Christ, he thought, something big must have gone up to have rated an APB!

It was then that he saw headlights piercing the smog to his right. He turned the ignition switch; the instrumentation lights dimmed. He tried again. This time the starter turned, but the engine failed to catch.

The distance between his car and what he could now see was a massive truck was closing fast.

He began hammering furiously on the horn. The truck was less than ten yards away when the driver suddenly vomited against the windshield and lurched forward, the top of his head smearing the glass as he slipped out of sight beneath the dash. A second later the truck struck the rear corner of Wallcroft's car with a deafening crash and sent it spinning across the intersection. The double doors at the back of the truck flew open, showering the road with crates of oranges.

The truck rumbled across Redondo Beach Boulevard, mounted the sidewalk, and demolished a car-accessory store before coming to a standstill only inches from the line of gas pumps on the forecourt of a filling station.

Wallcroft unfastened his seatbelt and shoulder harness and got out. All he could hear now was the sound of settling masonry and a hissing from the truck's punctured radiator and hydraulics system.

He had begun to pick his way through the oranges toward the truck when he heard another vehicle approaching from behind. He turned. Floundering toward him out of the smog, from the same direction as the truck, was a driverless sedan. Painted on the hood was a head entwined with snakes. The sides of the car—a 1971 Cadillac mounted on high-riders—were decorated with an acid head's vision of the Garden of Eden. Trailing alongside was what appeared to be a floor mat.

As the car drew level with him, the passenger door swung open, releasing the button that switched on the interior light. Lying across the front seat was a young girl. What he had taken to be a floor mat was the body of the girl's companion. Trapped by his legs, the man—if it was a man—had been dragged along the road until his face and shoulders had become a bloody pulp of skin, hair, and tattered silver lamé.

180

The Cadillac drifted slowly to the left, hit a fire hydrant, and stalled. Wallcroft ran across and opened the passenger door. The girl was lying, quite still, in a fetal position, her eyes open. Like the truck driver, she had vomited—but with a violence that had caused her to hemorrhage.

Unable to find any trace of a pulse, Wallcroft returned to the Pontiac and switched on the engine. It started immediately.

He had begun to drive north along Crenshaw—intending to return to his girl friend's apartment and telephone for help—when he saw the flashing red lights of two patrol cars in his rear-view mirror. He pulled over and stopped. The patrol cars came screeching to a standstill, boxing in the Pontiac. Wallcroft had begun to open his window when a sergeant—a man with a barrel chest and a face like a small-bore target—got out of the car in front of him. "Hands on the roof and feet apart, Buddy!"

As the sergeant frisked Wallcroft, the driver of the patrol car behind him began asking, over the car's radio telephone, for verification that an ambulance had been sent to Redondo Beach and Crenshaw. "How do you like this, Sarge?" he shouted. "We run our asses ragged getting here and the guys back at headquarters decide to take a coffee break!"

"Just keep trying," replied the sergeant, as he walked around to examine the contents of the wallet in front of the Pontiac's headlights.

A police helicopter swept overhead, illuminating the intersection with its searchlight. Wallcroft glanced over his shoulder and saw that the driver of the second patrol car was now standing on the sidewalk, a telephone pressed to his ear. Above the thumping of the helicopter engine, he heard him shout, "Hold it a minute!" The patrolman waited until the noise had reduced in intensity and called across to the first patrol car. "Hey, Doc, headquarters wants to talk to you!" There was no reply.

The sergeant returned Wallcroft's wallet. "Don't tell me that sonofabitch has fallen asleep again!" he said. He returned his pistol to its holster and walked slowly back to shake someone slumped on the rear seat of his car.

The man who eventually unfolded himself onto the sidewalk was as long-legged and uncoordinated as a newborn foal. He was dressed in white sneakers and slacks—but no socks—and a white trenchcoat with sleeves that stopped several inches above his prominent wristbones.

He ambled over to the second patrol car and took the telephone being waved impatiently at him. He cradled the instrument in the hollow of his shoulder. "Dr. Landstrom, Harbor General Hospital." His voice was sonorous and relaxed; his accent Bostonian. He placed the large Gladstone bag he was carrying on the driver's seat and, while he listened, fumbled with both hands in his coat pockets. The search produced an empty Gauloises pack, which he held up for the patrolman to see before screwing it into a ball and tossing it over his shoulder. The patrolman sighed and produced a pack of Marlboros. Landstrom grinned, tucked one of the crumpled cigarettes into the corner of his mouth, and mimed the action of striking a match. "You want me to"—he paused to light the cigarette from the match the patrolman held in his cupped hands—"perform an autopsy *here*—on the street?" Landstrom and the police officers exchanged incredulous glances.

"Now just hold it a minute!" he shouted after trying several times to interrupt the voice on the telephone. "This is a matter for the county coroner. I have no authority to—"

The voice interrupted him again, more loudly than before. "Okay, okay," Landstrom replied wearily, "I'll do it—but not until I get the order from the horse's mouth, not its ass."

He held up the telephone disdainfully, as though the instrument itself had offended him in some way. "How do you like those guys?" he asked indignantly.

As if in answer to his question the phone came alive again, this time with a voice that was slow and heavy with authority. "Jesus Mary!" Landstrom covered the telephone with his hand and looked up, as though about to speak to the police officers, but changed his mind. "As quickly as I can, Mr. Mayor."

Landstrom stared at the police officers. "Christ almighty! No wonder the poor bastard I was talking to first didn't know which end was up any more . . . Disaster Control have just put out that we've been hit with a CBW weapon of some sort—and if they've got it right"—Landstrom waved the telephone in the direction of the wrecked vehicles—"that's what knocked off those guys!"

Wallcroft suddenly realized just how close he had been to death. *If* he hadn't left the girl's apartment when he did . . . *If* he hadn't lost his way and driven south out of the danger zone . . . *If* he hadn't been overtaken by the police and prevented from heading north again . . .

"You okay, fella?" The doctor was looking at him with professional interest.

Wallcroft nodded.

"Great!" said Landstrom. "Because I'm going to need your help."

"Well," said Landstrom, stroking the top of his head, "it's no good sitting around here hoping for the Seventh Cavalry to arrive."

The two patrol cars had left several minutes earlier, assigned by the dispatcher to evacuation duty somewhere to the west.

Landstrom licked his finger and held it up to check the wind direction. "Okay, fella," he said, handing Wallcroft his bag, "let's get it over with before the wind changes and starts blowing the crap back over us."

While they searched for a room to work in, Landstrom explained that he had been ordered to take the autopsy specimens to the Health Center at North Figueroa Street.

"But why not whole bodies?" Wallcroft asked.

"That much I *do* understand," replied Landstrom. "They don't have room for them. But I guess the real answer is they've been caught with their pants down—the textbooks say that once it's known that a CBW agent has been used it's the responsibility of specialized clinicians—not bums like me—to collect suspected material. They're even supposed to inoculate growth media during the ride back to the lab."

After pushing bells and pounding doors for ten minutes, they decided that the district was either no longer inhabited or the people living there were keeping well out of the way.

"So," said Landstrom, rubbing his hands together, "we'll have to do it the hard way. Is this yours?" he asked, pointing a flashlight at the Pontiac. Wallcroft nodded. "Okay," said Landstrom, "then we'd better use the psychedelic Caddy."

Landstrom disentangled the driver's legs from the seat belt and pulled the body clear of the vehicle. Together they lifted the girl into the back.

Landstrom wiped the blood from the driver's seat with a box of tissues he found in the glove compartment, and got into the car. He switched on the engine, sent the car careening back with full lock, and braked.

Wallcroft, watching from the sidewalk, suddenly realized what the doctor was about to do. "Are you out of your mind?" he shouted.

Landstrom began winding up the window. "What am I supposed to do, fella? Wait for a Supreme Court ruling?"

Landstrom drove the car hard against the metal grill covering the window of a nearby liquor store, tearing it clear of its mountings. He reversed to the middle of the road, revved the engine, and drove the car into the metal grille again. The front fender shot it forward and, at last, the sheet of plate glass and the hundreds of bottles behind exploded under the impact. Landstrom was thrown forward by the rapid deceleration, then bounced to the ceiling as the wheels passed over the metal window casement. He braked, but too late to prevent the car from ramming the counter. The bolts holding it to the floor sheared off and the entire structure was pushed violently against the bottle-filled shelves behind. The windshield frosted over and both tires on Landstrom's side of the car blew out.

"Welcome to L.A.'s first drive-in pathology lab!" he said as Wallcroft clambered over the debris to rejoin him.

Landstrom kicked the car door open and went in search of a light switch. "That explains why there were no alarm bells," he called out, after a couple of minutes. "The power's been disconnected!"

Landstrom decided that the small office at the back of the store best suited his needs and, handing Wallcroft the flashlight to hold, began clearing the desk.

When he had finished, he covered the desk with a plastic sheet, then laid out a selection of surgical instruments, screw-capped specimen bottles, and cotton gauze. Wallcroft's job, he explained, would be to hold the flashlight steady and "not throw up, or at least not over me!"

Landstrom slipped his rings and wristwatch into his trouser pockets and took off his trenchcoat. Under it, strapped to his bare chest, he wore a shoulder holster containing a Colt .45 automatic. While he washed his hands with an antiseptic solution, he explained why he was armed. "The practice of medicine has become a high-risk occupation in this city. And I don't mean just for the patient! A white ambulance crew were damned near lynched a few blocks from here. They'd answered a ten-twenty involving a white hit-and-run driver and a little black kid. While they were having the shit beaten out of them by the kid's parents and their buddies, she bled to death in the gutter." Landstrom shook his

184

head sadly and opened a pack containing a disposable paper face mask, a gown, and a pair of latex gloves. "In L.A. alone, there have been ten or so cases of medics being rolled by junkies since Thanksgiving. It's gotten to be so bad that they are talking about passing a city ordinance prohibiting medics from carrying morphine on accident calls."

He transferred his pistol from its holster to the hip pocket of his trousers and began sliding the sleeves of the surgical gown over his outstretched arms, taking care to touch only the inside of the garment. He tied the neck and waist strings securely and, with Wallcroft's help, lifted the body of the girl on to the table.

"Okay," he said, "here we go!" He first cut through the hem of the girl's skirt and, the scissors still in his hand, tore the dress open to the neck. The body beneath was young and naked except for a tiny pair of black panties.

He broke open a packet of scalpels and rotated the girl's left forearm to expose the inner wrist.

"I guess we'd better make sure she really *is* dead; all I need is to get hit with a malpractice suit before I've even finished my internship."

The blood which seeped out from her severed radial artery was dark and sluggish. "Good," said Landstrom, and began closing the incision with a length of adhesive strapping. When he had finished he picked up a scalpel and took up a position directly behind the girl's head. "Behind me with the light," he ordered. Following the center parting, Landstrom drew the blade along the girl's scalp, from a point just below the hairline to the crown of her head. He leaned forward and, using both hands, took a tight grip on the long, fair hair either side of the incision. There was a sound like tearing calico and suddenly the whole of the vault of the girl's skull was exposed. Wallcroft, his teeth clenched, turned away. Landstrom straightened up and breathed out. "Okay, relax," he said. "From now on everything's going to be an anticlimax."

Landstrom worked silently and swiftly. It took him six minutes to saw through the skull and take tissue from the medulla, midbrain, and temporal-lobe cortex. He removed the whole of the girl's trachea and, using an osteotome to break through into the thoracic cavity, took specimens from the superior and middle lobes of her left lung.

"How are you bearing up?" he asked as he finished sealing the bottles containing lung tissue. Without waiting for a reply he picked up the scissors, cut through the girl's panties at the hips, and bared her belly. He swabbed the skin between her ribs and pubis—and to the left of her navel—with formaldehyde, and tore the wrapping off a new scalpel. With one stroke he cut through the sheaf of muscles lying over the left lumbar region of the abdomen; the peritoneum, however, he severed slowly, careful not to penetrate the large intestine lying underneath. Using a pair of dressing forceps, he dried off the cavity with a gauze mop before gently separating out a length of descending colon. He tied off a three-inch segment, complaining that Wallcroft was not holding the flashlight steady, and cut carefully through the tissue compressed between the double ligatures at either end of the specimen. Using a pair of tissue forceps he transferred it from the abdominal cavity to the waiting container.

"That wasn't so bad, was it?" he asked, wiping his hands on the girl's dress.

Wallcroft carefully placed the flashlight on the table, so that its beam was reflected back from the ceiling, and walked swiftly past Landstrom to the wash basin.

While Wallcroft was vomiting, Landstrom began closing the incisions in the mutilated body with metal wound clips.

Wallcroft had just begun to grope for a handkerchief when he heard Landstrom exclaim, in a voice that was almost awestruck, "Jesus H. Christ!" He looked over his shoulder and saw that the doctor was staring down at the body, a wound probe in one hand, the flashlight in the other. Wallcroft straightened up and walked cautiously back to the table.

The wound clips with which Landstrom had attempted to close the thoracic cavity had not held, but the body looked much as it had a few minutes earlier.

"I don't get it . . . I *do not* get it," muttered Landstrom, as he touched something inside the chest with the probe. "This just *can't* be happening!"

Wallcroft leaned forward and suddenly saw what was causing Landstrom so much consternation. The exposed lung, which less than fifteen minutes before had been firm and pink, had turned into a pulpy gray mass.

The doctor turned, stupefied, to Wallcroft. "Okay, I'm going nuts," he said, "but this chick is *decomposing!*"

186

23

AT 9 A.M. EASTERN STANDARD Time, December 4, two hours after the explosion, Nadelman received a call from the President. "It's looking good, Dick. Preliminary reports indicate a death toll within a few hundred of your projected figure . . ."

Authorization to broadcast the first news report of the incident was given by Los Angeles Disaster Control at seven-fifty Pacific Standard Time. "During the early hours of this morning, a device containing poison gas exploded in the southwestern area of the Los Angeles Basin," it stated. "Although a number of persons in the immediate vicinity have died as a result, the danger is now past." The news flash, which was broadcast simultaneously by all of the city's television and radio stations, was followed by a brief message from the mayor. He expressed his "deep and profound regret at the tragic loss of life" and ended with an appeal at Angelenos to treat that day "as they would any other day, and to go about their business in a routine and orderly fashion."

For several hours it looked as though the deliberately bland, low-key approach had worked. But with the heat came an acceleration in the rate of putrefaction, and with the putrefaction came the stench, unidentifiable to most people but awakening in them a strange and primitive dread. For five miles downwind of the disaster area people began to cover their noses and mouths with handkerchiefs sprinkled with disinfectant before venturing on to the streets. With the stench came the flies; and with the flies came the rumors.

At first the rumors were not unreasonable. The deaths, it was suggested, had not been caused by poison gas but by disease-infected insects.

But as the story spread it mutated, becoming increasingly bizarre with each telling. Sanitary squads working near the scene of the explosion were, it was said, being overcome and suffocated by swarms of flies. The flies were soon thought to be depositing their larvae in the living, as well as the dead, to reemerge—within hours—as mature insects through pustules on the bodies of their hosts. A teen-age boy with a boil on his neck was soaked with gasoline and burned alive by a frightened crowd in Watts. A number of people, believing that they had become hosts for the larvae, drank disinfectant and died agonizing deaths.

The President, it was said, was under pressure to authorize "the surgical removal of the entire city and all of its inhabitants in an attempt to contain the plague." The exceptionally low cloud ceiling and the fact that fifteen hundred airplanes take off and land at Los Angeles International Airport each day created the perfect conditions for such a rumor to proliferate. Already, many believed, a bomber armed with a termonuclear device was flying a holding pattern above the city while the President agonized over the terrible decision he was being asked to take.

By eleven-thirty it was apparent that large numbers of people were moving out of the city, aware that the official line on what had happened was, at best, grossly understated. Others began to besiege hospitals and Health Department bureaus demanding inoculation or the treatment of symptoms which were, in the main, entirely psychosomatic in origin.

At five past noon the governor telephoned Mayor Mansio and insisted that he call a press conference within the hour. "Just give them the facts, Frank, the facts! For God's sake, they'll sound like Little Red Riding Hood compared to the stories that're coming out of your city right now!''

Wallcroft had returned to the Beverly Wilshire suite he had vacated the previous day.

His first problem had been to locate his production team. Most of them had taken off as soon as they arrived in New York to catch up on leave that was due them. While Wallcroft had been on one telephone, a girl from the hotel's secretarial pool had been on another trying to book seats on a plane to bring as many of them as could be found back to Los Angeles. It had proved to be nearly impossible: although Wallcroft had been on to the story well ahead of his competitors, everything that could fly had already been grabbed to transport newsmen from the East to the West Coast. His own network, he was told, had sent men to Kennedy International Airport with instructions to offer passengers booked on Los Angeles flights anything up to four times the fare in return for their tickets. Two had been obtained in this way, but the problem had only finally been solved when the President of the network had volunteered his own executive jet for the job.

Wallcroft arrived at the massive tinted-glass and concrete Health Center half an hour before the mayor's press briefing was due to begin. In any other circumstances he would have refused to attend anything designated either a briefing or a backgrounder. But on this occasion he was confident that his fellow journalists would be unanimous in their determination to drive a truck through any attempt to limit what could be reported.

Security had been tightened a great deal since his early-morning visit with Landstrom. Now, he was asked to produce his press card three times before he had even reached the desk signposted ALL SHIELDS AND ID'S MUST BE SHOWN ALL GUNS MUST BE CHECKED—the first time to get through the police lines holding back the vast crowd assembled on the forecourt, the second to be allowed through the ranks of National Guardsmen standing with bayonets fixed at the top of the steps leading up to the building, and the third to pass the security guards in the foyer. A taped message, recorded in English and

Spanish, was being relayed over the public-address system at two-minute intervals, reassuring the crowd outside that the danger had now passed and that "no emergency measures are indicated."

Wallcroft found the crew who had been assigned to him, and together they rode up in the elevator to join the two hundred reporters, photographers, and television cameramen who were milling around in the press suite.

As usual at such gatherings, all the telephones were being used —many of them by reporters who were making private long-distance calls at the city's expense. All the rooms were thick with smoke and all the ashtrays full; discarded coffee cartons, carrying the slogan KEEP L.A. CLEAN, were everywhere. The large briefing room was filled with rows of folding chairs—most of them reserved by hats, coats, or notebooks. The chairs faced a low dais on which stood a long, reproduction American Chippendale table and matching chairs. In the middle of the table was a cluster of microphones, their cables trailing back along the floor to the recording equipment at the end of the room. Immediately behind the equipment was another dais, several feet higher than the one at the front, where shirtsleeved electricians and cameramen moved around, surefooted as cats, in a jungle of cables, grips, lamps, film, and television cameras.

Behind the table, flanked by the California state flag and the Stars and Stripes, hung a large map of Los Angeles dotted with blue and green markers. Recessed into the wall above it was a line of clocks showing Eastern, Central, Mountain, Pacific, and Greenwich Mean Time. Three easels to the right of the table held more maps of Los Angeles.

As the minute hands of the clocks moved toward the hour, the reporters began to take their seats. On the hour precisely, a door to the left of the camera dais opened and Mayor Frank Mansio, followed by his entourage, walked briskly into the room. The reporters rose and remained standing until the mayoral party had taken their places behind the table. Immediately the TV lights were switched on and a crowd of press photographers rushed forward, jostling for position and angle.

Mansio was a stocky, dynamic man of Neapolitan ancestry who looked—and, cynics were fond of suggesting, on occasions acted—like an enforcer for the Mafia. His brusque manner and conservative appearance suggested that he took pride in a simple, no-nonsense approach to life and its unending problems. He was the only man at the table who was not wearing full, color-television makeup.

He spent a minute or so conferring with his colleagues before getting to his feet. While he went rapidly through the preliminaries—thanking his audience for attending and for their patience and cooperation earlier in the day—he put on a pair of horn-rimmed spectacles and checked to see that his notes were in order.

"Okay," he said, looking up, "we all know why we're here, so I'll waste no time coming to the point. The first call reporting an explosion in the vicinity of Zela Davis Park was logged at three-ten this morning. Eight other calls reporting a similar event in the same area came in between three-twelve and three-sixteen. Five patrol cars—two attached to the Wilshire Division and three to the Southwest Division —responded to the call to investigate and assist between three-eighteen and three-twenty, and units of the Los Angeles City Fire Department and Ambulance Service were dispatched to the scene of the incident at or about that time."

Mayor Mansio turned to the map behind him and pointed to nine green flags that formed an inner perimeter to the large cross which had been drawn in red ink over Doty Avenue.

"The Communications Center lost radio contact with the vehicles shortly after they passed these points . . ." The mayor glanced down at his notes before turning back to face his audience. For almost a minute the only sound in the room was the whirl of film cameras and the squeak of an oil-starved tape recorder at the back of the room.

"The Communications Center then"—the mayor, in trouble with his notes again, paused for a whispered consultation with the white-haired police commissioner—"this was at three twenty-seven—advised all mobile units within a two-mile radius of Doty Avenue to halt and await further orders." He pointed to an outer perimeter of blue flags. "These indicate the disposition of units at three twenty-seven."

Mayor Mansio filled a tumbler with water and drank. "At three-thirty," he continued, "an ASTRO helicopter was dispatched to investigate the area in question, and at three forty-eight reported the first sighting of stalled and crashed vehicles at El Segundo and Hawthorne.

"Headquarters immediately ordered the units at the holding points to withdraw but an acknowledgment was received from only one of these units—an Emergency Service detail from the Orange County Sheriff's Office. Radio contact was lost with this car at three fifty-two."

The mayor walked across to the maps pinned to the easels. Above each was a slip of paper: the first read 3:27; the second 3:48; the third 3:52.

"These fatalities," he continued, "enabled headquarters to make the first assessment of the rate of dispersal of the toxic agent, and the communities threatened. At three fifty-eight Commissioner Kuleshow mobilized all emergency services available to the city and ordered the evacuation of the area west of a line from Inglewood Boulevard to the coast, and bordered by Imperial Boulevard to the north and Manhattan Boulevard to the south." He placed the flat of his hand on the area lying immediately in front of a rectangular shaded area that had been drawn in red ink on the third map. "During a two-hour period from approximately four-fifteen to six-fifteen, twenty-five thousand men, women, and children were evacuated from the path of the agent. To reduce the risk of panic and to facilitate the speedy and orderly withdrawal of persons residing in the threatened communities, a news blackout was requested from four o'clock to seven-fifty local time."

The mayor put his notes down for a moment while he wiped his hands on a handkerchief.

"The first victim," he continued, "was recovered at four-twenty, and under provisions set out in the State Health and Safety Code, tissue samples were obtained and brought to this building, where a clinical diagnosis was made by a team led by the Health Officer of the county, Dr. Peter Kamekura.

"Dr. Kamekura's findings, which were later confirmed by post mortem examinations carried out by other Health Department teams, indicated that the prime cause of death was due to inhalation, or the absorption through mucous membrane, of aerobic particles of one to five microns consisting of as yet unidentified microagents.

"The toxic action involved inhibiting the formation of—" he paused.

The Japanese-American sitting next to him came swiftly to his rescue. "Acetylcholinesterase," he said.

The mayor nodded, and began again. "The toxic action involved inhibiting the formation of that chemical at nerve endings, leading to muscular fibrillation, respiratory paralysis, and cardiac arrest. Although highly toxic, the agent—which is now inactive—possessed a negative infectivity.''

He looked around the room uneasily. "In other words, if you inhaled it you'd be dead, and if you're *not* dead there's no longer any risk.''

He pushed his spectacles tight against the bridge of his nose and turned back to his notes. "The final death toll,'' he continued quietly, "is expected to be in excess of ten thousand persons.''

Many of the reporters either did not hear or could not believe what they had heard, and the room erupted with demands that he repeat what he had just said.

He sipped from the tumbler and read the line again, this time almost defiantly. Someone at the back of the room shouted: "But your office has been suggesting all morning that the casualties were *minimal!*''

"Federal, military, and state investigative teams,'' continued the mayor, as though he had not heard, "are at this time examining a single-family dwelling on Doty Avenue which was the scene of an explosion during the early hours of this morning.''

He put down his notes and slipped his spectacles back into the breast pocket of his jacket.

"If you have any questions,'' he added lamely, "we will do our best to answer them.''

The mayor froze midway between standing and sitting, as every reporter in the room simultaneously rose to his feet and began shouting.

It took Lester Bohm, an overweight, asthmatic man who was Public Information Officer for the Health Department, several minutes to restore order.

"Gentlemen, gentlemen!'' he implored, above the uproar. "Please, gentlemen, *one* at a time.''

For ten minutes reporters competed with one another to belabor Mayor Mansio with questions, heavy with sarcasm and implied criticism, concerning his administration's decision to withhold the truth of what had happened for so long. His defense, to which he clung doggedly, was that the full extent of the disaster had become clear only during the past hour.

Three reporters rose to their feet and began speaking at the same time. Bohm pointed to a thin man wearing a tartan jacket. "This gentleman was first!"

"Samuel Felfe, CBS News. I'd like to ask about the decision to evacuate persons west of a line from Inglewood Avenue. Looking at those maps," Felfe nodded his head in the direction of the easels, "it seems to me that many thousands of additional lives might have been saved if the Police Department had started work even ten blocks *east* of the line chosen."

The commissioner rose to his feet, but the mayor, anxious both to demonstrate that he was unshaken by the previous exchange and to head off further criticism of his administration, was the first to speak. "I would just like to say that the Police and Fire Departments of this city acted with courage beyond the call of duty. Were it not for their valor and resourcefulness the death toll would be in excess of thirty-five thousand."

Commissioner Kuleshow, his eyes downcast in the manner of a man too modest to accept such fulsome praise, however well deserved, waited several seconds after the mayor had finished speaking before looking up. "The fact is, Mr. Felfe," he said quietly, "that we just couldn't be sure that the westerly drift would maintain a constant speed—"

Felfe sprang to his feet. "No, I agree! It could have gone more *slowly* than estimated."

"Or *faster!*" Kuleshow snapped back.

"But were the officers assigned to evacuation duty not equipped with respirators?"demanded Felfe.

Bohm cut in ahead of the police commissioner. "That must be your last question, Mr. Felfe. There are a lot of other people here and these gentlemen"—he smiled thinly at the men alongside him—"have very little time available, as I am sure you all appreciate."

The commissioner had taken advantage of the interruption to have a whispered exchange with the Army Chemical Corps officer sitting next to him. He straightened up and returned his attention to the reporter. "Many of the personnel assigned to evacuation duty were equipped with respirators," he continued, "but not all of them. And in any event, at that time we could not be certain that respirators would afford sufficient protection."

An elderly woman with blue-rinsed hair stood up. "But surely, Commissioner, the United States has been at risk—"

"Will you kindly state your name, madam," demanded Bohm.

"Sue Cabell," she replied tartly, *"San Francisco Chronicle*. I was saying, before I was interrupted, that surely this country has been at risk from enemy missiles armed with CBW warheads since nineteen-fifty, or thereabouts?"

"What is your question, madam?" Bohm was now having considerable difficulty with his breathing.

"My question, sir, is why such a contingency was not taken account of in the city's civil-defense program."

Bohm drew a mouthful of air through his rapidly narrowing bronchial tubes and turned to the puzzled commissioner. "I think the lady's question relates to your answer to Mr. Felfe's question concerning the availability of respirators." He paused to consider if his remark had made any sense. "However," he added, "I'm not sure whether any of this has much relevance."

"I think it might have considerable relevance!"

Bohm turned and glared at the young man standing in the middle of the room.

"Gilpatrick, *Los Angeles Times*. Why was no CBW detection and warning system in operation at the—"

"That's classified information!" snapped Bohm, between inhalations from an ephedrine nebulizer. "As you know perfectly well, Mr. Gilpatrick."

Gilpatrick remained on his feet, waiting for the roar of protest to subside. "Were there no CB suits available?" he asked. "Or is that information also classified?"

"There were, sir," replied Kuleshow, "But the logistics of the operation was such that we could not avail ourselves of them in sufficient quantities and *still* clear a densely populated area in the time available."

Where were the bodies to be buried? What was the Department of Health doing about the smell and the flies? Why would the Police Department not identify the house in which the explosion had occurred? Why had overflights of the area been prohibited? For twenty-five minutes questions were fielded, caught, ducked.

The officials were showing signs of nervousness and strain. Wallcroft had played a waiting game, letting the other reporters wear them down. Now, his attention was solely on the information officer. He waited until the man had glanced at his wristwatch for the third time and had placed the palms of his hands on the table ready to push himself upright and bring the briefing to an end. Wallcroft beat him to the draw by a split second.

"Douglas Wallcroft, *Countdown*."

Throughout the room reporters replaced coats and hats beneath their seats, reopened notebooks, or checked that they had sufficient magnetic tape for what was to come.

"I would like to ask a question of Colonel Michener." The Army Chemical Corps officer replaced his cap on the table and sat down, listening attentively. "Colonel Michener, there's been a lot of talk here today about how easy it would be for a subversive group to manufacture a CBW agent. It's been suggested that any competent chemist could, for example, synthesize nerve gases. Now tell me, Colonel"—Wallcroft's tone was that of one man of the world to another—"just how easy *would* it be to manufacture the kind of agent used to kill ten thousand people this morning?"

Michener rose slowly to his feet. He was a tall, well-built man in his early fifties with an intelligent, kindly face. His short, iron-gray hair and olive-green uniform were impeccably cut and brushed. His campaign ribbons showed him to be a veteran of Korea and Vietnam. Michener straightened his tunic and leaned forward in a confident but friendly manner, supporting himself on the table with the tips of his fingers.

"As you'll appreciate, Mr. Wallcroft, it is difficult for me to answer that question, since we've not yet identified the agent." Michener's smile suggested he believed that Wallcroft would understand his predicament. "However, I'd think that it would *not* be easy—"

"Would *not* be easy?"

"That is what I said." ·

"You'd need—what—well-equipped laboratories, well-trained men?"

"I would think so."

"Such as the Army Chemical Corps possesses?"

Michener smiled patiently, as though dealing with a difficult but not very bright child.

"Let me remind you, Mr. Wallcroft, that the United States has been subject to a moratorium on the development and production of CBW weapons since nineteen seventy-one."

"Do you mean by that, Colonel, that the Army has stopped *all* work in this field, including the production of antitoxins for protecting its own men against an enemy who has, perhaps, not observed such a moratorium?"

Michener smiled sadly. "To answer that question fully, Mr. Wallcroft, I'd have to divulge classified information."

"Just answer yes or no," said Wallcroft, as though offering him an easy way out.

"Well . . . if you insist on a yes-or-no answer . . ." Michener looked disappointed, as though Wallcroft had, in some mysterious way, let the side down. "The Army would be failing in its duty if it were not to, shall we say, keep abreast of developments in the field of CBW technology—"

"And to do that, isn't it necessary to work with a variety of pathogens," Wallcroft raised his voice slightly to discourage Michener from interrupting, "no matter on *how* small a scale?"

"Well . . . in general terms I suppose the answer would have to be yes—"

"And isn't it true that one ounce—I repeat—one ounce of type A botulinum would be sufficient to kill sixty million people?"

"Mr. Wallcroft!" snapped Mansio. "This is a press conference, *not* a trial!"

"I've been trying to establish three points, Mr. Mayor," said Wallcroft. "The first is that a toxin of the type used today *could* only be manufactured by an organization possessing *immense* technical facilities—like those available to the Army Chemical Corps.

"The second is that in spite of the Army's much-publicized moratorium, it has continued to work with a variety of pathogens for the purpose of 'keeping abreast of developments in the field of CBW technology.'

"The third is that the amounts of toxin needed to produce an unimaginable death toll can, in certain instances, be concealed in the pocket of"—Wallcroft hesitated, as though not able quite to think of an appropriate garment—"an Army uniform, for example!"

24

FOR A WEEK PRIOR to the spacecraft crash the Wild Card team had been without television. A terrorist's land mine, they had been told, had blown up a section of the road beneath which lay the TV cable into Detrick. Without newspapers and still unable to listen to the radio due to interference from the electronics shop, they had—like practical jokers denied the opportunity of seeing the outcome of their joke—demanded that something be done to enable them to watch the newscasts immediately following the crash.

Late on Sunday evening, two of Napier's men arrived with a TV aerial which they erected on the roof of the recreation center early the following morning.

By 6 A.M. the common room was full, with everyone gathered around the television set waiting anxiously for the first newscast of the day. The picture quality was even worse than they had been led to expect, but, more disappointing still, there was no story about what had happened in Los Angeles.

Drinking coffee and eating doughnuts, they watched a program of cartoons—some laughing loudly, others not at all—until just before seven, when Kochalski switched to CBS News. The first story was about the start of a nationally organized strike of prisoners, demanding better conditions in America's overcrowded jails. It was followed by the latest news of the deepening dollar crisis, and then a story about a cop defusing a bomb inside a tanker containing six thousand gallons of gasoline. During the second commercial break the picture began to flicker, then disappeared, the program continuing in sound only.

There was a roar of protest and Kochalski leaped up and began fiddling with the controls. The screen remained blank. "For Chrissake, Cy," he called, "get off your ass and over here with a screwdriver!"

Darrow pushed his way through to the front of the crowd and struck the top of the set hard with his fist. A flurry of multicolored snowflakes appeared on the screen, but no picture. Kochalski groaned. "I could have done *that* myself!" he said scathingly.

Kochalski and Darrow, now joined by Benedict and Weiner, had begun arguing about what had caused the loss of picture when Charlotte Paxton, who was sitting nearest the set, suddenly turned up the volume. "Listen!" she called.

"An outbreak of what is believed to be a strain of Asian flu has brought much of downtown Los Angeles to a standstill this morning," the newscaster was saying. "Although not thought to be serious, the city's public-health authorities have advised all Angelenos not employed in essential services to remain at home until the strain has been identified and vaccine made available.

"Meanwhile in the nation's capital, Attorney General Pines has admitted to discussing the terms of a proposed truce with intermediaries acting for the terrorist organization Revolutionary Alliance. The meeting, which took place in Irvington, New York, last August, is said to have—"

"How do you like that?" cried Benedict, badly ruffled. "My boys work their asses off, and the hardware doesn't even rate a mention!"

Nadelman leaned across and put his hand reassuringly on Benedict's shoulder. "Relax," he said, as the picture returned to the screen. "It'll be at least a week before anything leaks out about your part of the operation."

Most of the team reassembled at noon to watch the next big news show of the day, *Panorama*. The main story was about an uprising of three thousand armed members of the American Indian Movement on the Oglala Sioux Pine Ridge Reservation. Almost the entire program was taken up with coverage of the uprising, much of it live, and it ended without any mention of the Los Angeles epidemic.

During the afternoon the scheduled programs were interrupted with news flashes about what was happening on the reservation, and by six o'clock the story was still getting saturation coverage on all of the evening news shows, including *Countdown*.

At six-fifteen Nadelman returned to the common room and turned down the sound on the television set. "Dr. Paxton, gentlemen," he said. "May I have your attention, please. I have just finished talking to the President and he has asked me to convey his thanks and warmest congratulations. The first phase of Wild Card has been an unqualified success! Indeed, it has gone off better than even I had dared hope. There's a lot of aspirin being taken by a lot of people in Los Angeles at this moment, but so far not one single death has been attributed to the effects of the virus! The media have not yet established a connection between the explosion in Doty Avenue and the epidemic—which, incidentally, is receiving wide coverage on the West Coast—but the authorities most certainly have! The LAPD realized they were out of their depth by nine A.M. Los Angeles time and called in the FBI. And I have just heard that the FBI have asked for assistance from NASA!"

Nadelman spent several minutes answering questions, then excused himself, saying he had work to do, and left for his house in Chevy Chase.

By 10 P. M. the last of the scientists—jubilant if a little frustrated that *their* story should have been eclipsed by the Indian uprising—left the smoke-filled common room. As soon as he was alone, Napier picked up a telephone and called Joe Mizushima in the basement of the security-detail block. The previous Monday, Mizushima, a one-time employee in the electronics section of the CIA, had cut the TV cable into the maximum-security compound and video-taped all of that day's programs. Into it he had spliced Thursday's newscasts and flashes and Friday's weather forecasts; the item about the Los Angeles epidemic, which the scientists had heard but not seen, he himself had recorded. That morning the videotapes had been tapped into the cable and transmitted to the set in the common room. Totally cut off from the outside world, the scientists had had no way of knowing that the programs they had been watching were a composite of what viewers outside had seen days earlier.

"Okay, Joe," said Napier, rubbing his aching eyes. "Let's wrap it up for tonight."

"Thank God for that," replied Mizushima. "I was beginning to think they'd want to watch the late late show. What about tomorrow?"

Napier yawned and began loosening his tie. "As planned. We tell them the cable's been repaired, and get rid of the aerial. When we make like the cable's bust again, I've a hunch it should be just *before* the ABC News story about the start of the Green Berets trial, not after. Some bastard might just remember it was slated for *last* Tuesday, not tomorrow."

"Will do," said Mizushima. "But, say, what happens if they ask for the aerial to be put back up again?"

"The way they were bellyaching about the lousy picture they thought they were getting *with* the aerial, I don't think they will. But if they do," Napier paused to bite the end off a cigar, "you and Sam get clumsy and break the darn thing! Right? Anyway, they won't want to sit around on their butts watching TV with all they've got to do if they're to be out of here by the end of the week."

"How did it go today, anyway?" Mizushima asked.

Napier struck a match on the underside of his chair and lit his cigar. "Like a dream. But, brother, I sure as hell wouldn't like to be in Nadelman's shoes when he tells them what's *really* happened!"

Mizushima laughed. "I've heard of news manipulation," he said, "but this is Orwellian!"

"Orwellian?"

"George Orwell. The guy who wrote *Nineteen Eighty-Four*."

Napier grunted. "I'm a Harold Robbins man myself," he said, and put down the telephone.

25

WHEN WALLCROFT WON HIS first Pulitzer Prize, his colleagues had presented him with a framed pastiche of a nineteenth-century sampler embroidered with Lord Northcliffe's maxim *News is what somebody, somewhere, doesn't want printed*. And in the case of the L.A. story Wallcroft was convinced that the somebody would turn out to be the United States Army. The fact that he had failed to uncover actual *evidence* to support his hypothesis in no way deterred him from using it as the underlying theme of *Countdown*.

By two P.M. on December 4, the program to be broadcast that evening had a shape and much of it was already in the can. It was, admittedly, little more than a sketchy history of the development and application of chemical and biological weaponry—illustrated with engravings, old newsreel clips and photographs, and a few filmed interviews. Starting with the Carthaginian general who, in 200 B.C., had won a battle by tricking his enemy into drinking wine spiked with mandragora, the program would move rapidly through the centuries. His Research

Bureau had unearthed the fact that in 1155 the Emperor Barbarossa had taken Tortuna by poisoning its water supply with decomposing bodies; that in 1763 Sir Jeffrey Amherst, commander in chief of the British Forces in America, had waged biological warfare against the Indians by sending them smallpox-infected blankets, and that during the First World War gases had caused more than a million casualties. Mention was to be made of the use of mustard gas by the Italians against the Abyssinians in 1936 and, a year later, by the Japanese against the Chinese. The program would float along, on a cushion of electronic music, through the discovery of nerve gases in 1937 and their development during and following World War II, and would end with the uses made of chemical agents in Vietnam and the closing of Fort Detrick as a CBW research center. Film editors were busy cutting back-to-camera interviews with a Weatherman and a member of the Ku Klux Klan which went some way toward ridiculing the theory that one of their organizations had been responsible.

To give the program some feeling of immediacy—and to avail himself of any last-minute news breaks—Wallcroft intended opening live in front of the mass graves being dug in the Mojave Desert. But even the footage which had just come in—about the goings-on at the Army Combat Development Command Outpost just up the coast from L.A.—wasn't going to turn what he regarded as a pig's ear of a program into a silk purse. With only four and a half hours to go before the start of transmission, Wallcroft found himself conducting his afternoon news conference in a state of depressed agitation.

He hurled an empty coffee carton across the room at the wastepaper basket in the corner—hitting it seemed to lighten his mood—swung his legs off the desk, stretched, and began massaging the back of his neck. "Okay," he said hopefully, "let's go through it all again!"

The people in the room with him stirred, but without any show of enthusiasm.

"We know that this morning's press conference was a lot of crap. Okay, the Weatherpeople and the Klan have been fooling around with CBW weapons since nineteen-sixty. Big deal! So why have they never used them before? And why—if it *was* them—would they choose Doty Avenue, for Chrissake? If it had been Watts I might have believed it. But Doty Avenue!"

He turned to the head of his Research Bureau, a hard-faced Englishwoman of indeterminate age. Wallcroft knew that her staff hated her and that even the reporters she serviced so efficiently and unstintingly regarded her as something of a pain in the ass. But the inescapable fact was that she was better at her job than anyone else in the business.

"Miss Rattenbury. Are we any nearer discovering who actually owned the house?" he asked.

"I'm afraid not," she replied. "One of my girls was talking earlier to a police officer who knows the area well. He remembers that a lot of work was done to the house a few weeks back."

"What kind of work?" asked Wallcroft, annoyed that he had not been told sooner.

Miss Rattenbury shrugged her shoulders and began tapping tobacco from a Bull Durham sack into an ancient cigarette machine.

"Decorating, plumbing . . . he didn't seem too sure. But he does remember men in overalls coming and going for quite a few weeks."

"Coming and going with what?" demanded Russell Gorman. Wallcroft regarded Gorman—an ex-sports writer from New York with a head shaved smooth as a billiard ball—and Miss Rattenbury as an equally matched pair, although their fighting styles were very different. Gorman was a slugger with a good left-hand punch, Miss Rattenbury more a poisoner.

She made him wait for his answer while she lit her cigarette with a kitchen match. "Planks, ladders," she waved her hand impatiently. "What you would expect decorators and plumbers to be coming and going with!"

"If they were coming and going with planks and ladders," growled Gorman, "they must've brought them in a truck. And the truck would have had the name of the contracting company painted on its sides."

"That may well be so, Mr. Gorman." She looked disdainfully at the assignments editor. "But the officer my girl talked to doesn't remember it. Mr. Smith, Miss Bundy, and myself have telephoned every contractor and interior decorating company listed in the Los Angeles classified directory. None of them report carrying out any work in Doty Avenue during the past year."

Gorman tried to conceal his embarrassment by busying himself with relighting the stub of his cigar.

"Have we managed to trace the next of kin of any of the people who lived in the street?" Wallcroft directed his question at Gorman, like a lifebuoy to a drowning man.

"Some," he replied, squinting through the cloud of acrid smoke in front of his face. "But they haven't come up with anything we can use."

Wallcroft was about to speak when a telephone rang. It was answered by Gorman's secretary. The girl listened for a moment, said "Okay" and turned to her boss, the telephone held to her chest.

"It's Mike ringing from Pasadena. He says he's got something on the Doty house."

"Let me talk to him." Gorman eased past his seated colleagues and took the telephone. "Mike, it's Russ. What've you got?" He listened, responding only with an occasional grunt. "Okay, stay with it. And for Christ's sake, don't let anyone else get to them."

The chattering, which had started with Gorman's being called to the telephone, petered out as everyone switched his attention to what he was saying.

"Pay them if you have to . . . Give the address to Jackie and I'll get a crew straight over there."

Gorman, now very excited, handed the telephone back to his secretary and turned to Wallcroft. "Mike has just run to earth the daughter of the people who lived next door to 13400 Doty—"

There was a ripple of reaction from everyone in the room except Miss Rattenbury.

"And she's dug out a letter her mother wrote to her on the twenty-third of September last. Apparently the party bought the house earlier this year and moved to L.A. from Washington about eight weeks ago!"

Gorman looked around the room to make sure that he had the undivided attention of his audience; the only eyes he avoided were Miss Rattenbury's.

"But get this! The guy was an assistant professor at USC. In the *Microbiology* Department, for Chrissake!"

Wallcroft felt the heat from the late-afternoon sun move around from the back of his neck to his face as the helicopter banked and began to slide toward the ochre-colored desert below.

206

Ahead and to his left, looking no bigger than toys, were several dozen vehicles—bulldozers, trucks, and portable generators—dotted in and around three enormous rectangular pits. To the east were more trucks and a great many cars parked beside the ribbon of road which stretched away into the distance. Between the road and the graves was the outside-broadcast caravan—its roof covered with the network's logo—which would transmit the opening, live portion of that evening's edition of *Countdown*.

By 6:59 P. M. the desert was rapidly losing its heat to the darkening sky and Wallcroft was glad of the thick turtlenecked sweater he had borrowed from one of the crew. Behind him, clusters of spotlights mounted on pylons cut through the swirling dust and diesel smoke on to the bulldozers moving the last of the earth dumped at the edges of the communal graves.

Wallcroft was still being briefed when his director announced, over the caravan speaker, "Two minutes, D.W. And we're still getting glare off his hard hat! Will one of you guys fix it, for Chrissake!"

A makeup girl dashed into the pool of light illuminating Wallcroft and killed the highlight on his yellow helmet with an antiglare aerosol spray.

His team had achieved something approaching a miracle during the past three hours. They had discovered that the owner of 13400 Doty Avenue was named Ralph Sheldon, white, single, and in his late thirties or early forties; that he had had a Ph.D. in biology from Princeton, where he had been active in left-wing student politics; that he had freaked out for a year after graduating—nobody knew where—but had returned to work for NASA. He had stayed with them for two years but his contract had not been renewed for security reasons. Sheldon had apparently made something of a song and dance about it at the time, but the only people who showed interest were the underground press, and even they had dropped it in the face of the apathy which had greeted their tepid revelations. He had bummed around for a while—again nobody seemed to know where—before getting himself a job with the Division of Microbiology at the Food and Drug Administration in Washington. After five years, he had left them to take up his present post at USC at the start of the fall semester, had reported sick two days before the explosion, and had not been heard of since.

Wallcroft watched out of the corner of his eye as the program titles ended and an artist's impression of Sheldon appeared on the tiny monitor. He cleared his throat and, as the red transmission light came on, began to speak.

26

WALLCROFT HAD PUSHED HIMSELF and his reporters and re-searchers to the limit on the Los Angeles story, with the result that his ratings for the past week were two and a half million up on his previous all-time high.

The day following his revelation that the house on Doty Avenue was owned by Ralph Sheldon, a federal warrant had been issued charging Sheldon with unlawful interstate flight to avoid prosecution for murder. Thirty-six hours later he had been arrested in a Chicago supermarket. The bruises and lacerations on his face—sustained, it was claimed by the Chicago police, while resisting arrest—had provided Wallcroft with another scoop. By then, he had accumulated a considerable amount of information about Sheldon and had bought up all the prime sources—his parents, his brother, and his closest friends and colleagues going back well over twenty years. This had enabled him to put together an edition of *Countdown* which showed not only that it was entirely out of charac-ter for Sheldon to have been armed and to have violently resisted arrest, but that he would have been physically incapable of doing so. It had been what Wallcroft called "an exercise in tough, old-fashioned, foot-in-the-door journalism."

But the scoop of his life was to walk up to Wallcroft—on the day following his revelation—and shake him by the hand.

"Good afternoon," the man said, in a light Bostonian accent, "it's very good of you to see me at such short notice."

Wallcroft glanced down at the form the man had been asked to fill out in the lobby. "Dr. *Bum*-berg, is this?" he asked, peering at the small, compact handwriting.

The man smiled sympathetically. *"Blom*-berg; Irving Blomberg."

"I'm sorry, Dr. Blomberg." Wallcroft glanced up and smiled before looking again at the note one of his researchers had clipped to the form. It read: "This guy says he's an astrophysicist from Goddard—claims to have something big on the L.A. story. Will not tell me what it is or where it came from. I think he *thinks* he's doing a Danny Ellsberg! Doesn't seem like a nut, but keep the engine running for a fast getaway in case I'm wrong! Pat."

Wallcroft looked up. Blomberg appeared to be the archetypal exurbanite: the evening club car to Scarsdale was full of them. Medium height and build, neither young nor old, rich nor poor, he certainly didn't look like Wallcroft's idea of a scientist. A Wall Street broker, perhaps? He decided not. There was something about Blomberg's lean face, alert eyes and shock of graying hair which suggested a man with a creative aptitude; a copy chief or a creative director in one of the more conservative Madison Avenue advertising agencies was nearer the mark. Wallcroft had not intended to invite him to sit down until he found out whether or not he had anything useful to say. But Blomberg's composure was so impressive that he not only took his topcoat and motioned him toward the easy chairs near the bar, but put himself into hock for ten minutes by offering him a cigarette.

Blomberg placed his attaché case on the floor beside him and took a gold lighter from the vest pocket of his gray flannel suit. He lit Wallcroft's cigarette, then his own, and settled back confidently.

"As the young lady who talked to me earlier has no doubt informed you," he began, "I am an astrophysicist employed by the Goddard Space Flight Center. You no doubt also know that we at Goddard are

210

involved—in the main—with theoretical research into celestial mechanics."

Blomberg studied the tip of his cigarette for a moment as though observing some abnormal, but only mildly interesting, phenomenon. "Nine days ago," he continued, carefully tapping the ash from his cigarette into an ashtray, "I was—to my utter amazement—asked to join the investigative team which has been evaluating the physical evidence accumulated from the Los Angeles disaster site. I use the word 'amazement' advisedly—my immediate reaction was to assume that they had simply got the wrong Blomberg! After all, the work I am engaged in at Goddard is"—he hesitated, unsure of the phrase which would best convey the infinite, and unworldly, nature of his job—"pretty way-out. However, it *was* me they wanted. I immediately left—totally nonplussed—for Los Angeles. But I was ill prepared for what I was to be confronted with on my arrival!"

Blomberg bent down and picked up the attaché case. "I realize that what I am about to do," he said, snapping open the locks, "is likely to have grave consequences for myself and my family. However, my conscience will not—it seems—permit me any other course of action." He smiled sadly, as though wishing to apologize for any embarrassment his remark might have caused.

Blomberg opened the lid and sat looking into the case's red leather-lined interior for a moment. Wallcroft did nothing, reluctant to make any move which might upset the delicate balance of the relationship between himself and the other man.

Blomberg looked up. "I should, in all fairness, Mr. Wallcroft, warn you that I have no authority to invite you to read the documents I am about to hand you, and that if you ever make this information public you may be considered in breach of national security."

Wallcroft smiled. "If they are half as good as your buildup, Dr. Blomberg," he said, "it'll be a risk I'm more than happy to take!"

He took the large, buff-colored file Blomberg handed him, but did not open it immediately. "Let me ask you something," he said. "Why are you doing this?"

Blomberg looked surprised, almost offended. "I thought I'd explained . . .?"

Wallcroft interrupted: "No, I don't believe you have, Dr. Blom-berg."

Blomberg hesitated. "I think," he replied at last, "that it was charging Ralph . . ." he paused, not quite able to remember the surname.

"Sheldon?" said Wallcroft.

"Thank you. It was the charging of Ralph Sheldon that was the catalyst. I'm not sure what I would have done had that not happened. But making a pawn of that unfortunate man in one of the most monstrous —and I can assure you, that is not too vivid a word—*monstrous* conspiracies ever to have been perpetrated is, as far as I am concerned, an unpardonable offense!"

Wallcroft began to speed-read the fifty-two pages of Xeroxed documents. The first batch consisted mainly of memoranda revealing little more than that a great deal of wrangling had taken place between the Los Angeles police, the FBI, and other government agencies about responsibility for conducting the investigation. But the real mind-bender was the twenty-four-page secret-sensitive memorandum of an NSC special action group meeting that had been held in the White House on the previous Wednesday. Although it was heavy with officialese and contained a great deal of technical language that Wallcroft did not understand, there was no escaping the nub of the matter under discussion. The investigative team, it seemed, had come up with the theory that an "extraterrestrial craft" had flown in low over L.A. to avoid radar detection, developed power failure, and dropped on 13400 Doty Avenue!

The spokesman for the investigative team had been given a very rough ride, particularly by the head of the CIA and certain members of the Joint Chiefs of Staff, but the validity of their claim that the debris was "at least not of human origin" had finally been accepted. The meeting, chaired by the President's chief scientific adviser, had ended with the passing of what Wallcroft—and Blomberg—agreed was a very sinister resolution. "Since it would not, at this time, be in the National interest to make this committee's findings a matter for public debate," it read, "there is no alternative but to rely on a more conventional rationalization to account for the event." The meeting had been adjourned, Wallcroft noticed, at six-fifteen—less than three hours before Ralph Sheldon had been picked up and beaten in Chicago.

Wallcroft got up and strode across to his intercom. With the edge of his hand he pushed down all the top row of switches. "I want you all in here at the double," he shouted. "Something very big has just broken!"

The President switched off the TV set in the Yellow Oval Room as the captions began to roll at the end of *Countdown*.

"Well," he said, smiling, "Wallcroft has taken that one hook, line, and sinker!"

Nadelman took off his spectacles, yawned, and rubbed his eyes with his knuckles. "I'm not surprised. Sheldon and Blomberg have done a pretty remarkable job. What happens to them now?"

The President turned, reached over the back of the Louis XVI-style couch and opened the humidor on the table behind. He took a gold cigar cutter from the pocket of his cardigan and, after removing the band, carefully pierced the long Havana. "No problem," he replied, moistening the end with his lips. "They've both been working undercover since they graduated." He struck a match and rotated the end of the cigar slowly in the flame. "One of the last things Hoover did before he died was plant sleepers in key industries." The President chuckled. "The old bastard called it 'Keeping his finger on the pulse'!" He drew on the cigar and tossed the match into the grate. "Sheldon could do quite well out of it financially," he continued, "if he gets himself a smart-assed lawyer to act for him against the Chicago police.

"As for Blomberg"—the President shrugged—"he's got a tough couple of years ahead of him. We'll have to go through the motions of bringing him to trial, I guess, but in view of what's on the agenda it shouldn't be too hard to finally lose the whole thing between the radiator and the wall of the Justice Department."

Nadelman smiled. "Just how much *do* they know?" he asked.

"Remarkably little," replied the President, his eyes still fixed on the TV screen. "Certainly not a total picture. Remember, these guys are professionals—it's part of their job *not* to see more than they have to. So, okay, Sheldon's assignment was to apply for a post at USC—and that's one of the *easiest* things to fix—buy a house and get to know the neighbors! He had to stand still for a whipping—but these guys are trained to ride out a lot worse than that! And Blomberg's story to Wallcroft was true in all respects but one—he didn't *take* the file—he was given it!''

The President smiled. ''Well,'' he said, turning to pick up the telephone, ''I guess I'd better start raising hell about who let the saucer story out of the bag.''

''Before you do,'' said Nadelman, ''there's something you'd better know. The guys at Detrick were never told we'd be using a lethal virus—except for Zelinski and Pedlar, of course.''

Stunned, the President slowly and clumsily replaced the telephone and turned to stare at Nadelman. ''They *what?*'' he demanded.

Nadelman, his face as round and pale and impassive as the moon, stared back at him. ''They were never told we'd be using a lethal virus,'' he said flatly. ''What was the point? There was nothing to be *gained* from their knowing, and—if they'd objected to this aspect of the project—everything to lose.

''However, this does mean that we'll have to start making plans to feed them into the shredder, along with everything else. And for that I'm going to need your help!''

27

His PREDECESSOR IN THE nineteen-sixties, John F. Kennedy, had thirteen days to decide how to confront the U.S.S.R. over the installation of Soviet missile and bomber bases in Cuba. Now the President, history would record, had barely thirteen hours to decide how to confront a crisis of even greater import.

The sudden unavailability of high officials immediately following Wallcroft's disclosures, the summoning overnight of congressional leaders, and the announcement, made at the beginning of the following morning's press briefing, that the President had obtained network time that evening for what was described as "a speech of the highest national urgency" left no one in doubt that the administration had been caught attempting to suppress evidence—if not of an extraterrestrial threat, at least of something pretty damned big.

But what caused the reporters assembled in the White House press center to gasp with amazement was the announcement that Douglas Wallcroft was leaving *Countdown* to become director of communications for the executive branch.

An embarrassed press secretary—unsure just where this left him on the executive totem pole—explained that the President had made the appointment "believing that it was now more vital than ever to the functioning of a free and responsible press that the administration's public-information apparatus should be headed by a working journalist known personally to, and widely respected by, the media."

As the questions began to fly, Wallcroft—who had flown overnight to Washington in an Air Force jet—was about to sit down to breakfast with the President and his chief of staff.

"It's good to see you again," said the President, shaking Wallcroft warmly by the hand. "In welcoming you onto the federal payroll, I won't try to pretend that there haven't been times when you've been one hell of a pain in the administration's ass!

"But as a communicator, you're the best in the business. And with the kind of communications problem I've had dropped into my lap —boy, am I going to need your help!"

While his valet poured coffee, the President passed Wallcroft a draft of the speech he would deliver later that day. "See how this strikes you," he said. "Sixteen guys have been working on it all night, and *I* think it reads like sixteen guys have been working on it all night. When we're through here, Bob will fix you up with an office and anything you want—and we'll meet again at noon. Now, let me try to fill you in on what we know and don't know . . ."

At eleven fifty-five Wallcroft, escorted by a young Air Force colonel, took the elevator to the basement of the West Wing of the White House and stepped through the airlock into the Situation Room.

He swallowed to equalize the pressure within his ears with the slight overpressure in the room, and looked around. Although he knew the room had been enlarged and extensively altered since Nixon's presidency, he had not expected it to look quite so much like a cross between a planetarium and Mission Control, Houston. Spotlights—looking no bigger than stars—shone down from a black, domed roof on to five semicircular rows of consoles facing an enormous glassine screen. Projected onto the screen was a map of the continental United States covered with phosphorescent blips, each marked with an alphanumeric tag. Seated at the consoles were a score or more men, some staring at what looked like television monitors, others talking quietly into telephones. Women hurried silently up and down the aisles between the consoles carrying signals and sheets of computer printout. The air was cool and dry and smelled faintly of shellac; the atmosphere was one of controlled nervous tension.

The President, Nadelman, and an Air Force general were standing on a platform in front of the screen. The President caught sight of Wallcroft and waved him over. "Come and listen to this," he called, in a voice robbed of its familiar resonance by the sound-absorbent material that lined the room.

"I was explaining to the President and Dr. Nadelman," the general said to Wallcroft, after they had been introduced, "that what we have on the board right now are unidentified-flying-object sightings logged since seven-thirty last night, Eastern Standard Time . . ."

"An hour after our friend here," said the President, nodding at Wallcroft, "pulled the rug from under us!"

"The thing to remember," continued the general, smiling uncertainly, "is that these sightings come only from trained observers —pilots, air traffic controllers, astronomers, and so on."

Nadelman frowned. "You mean this isn't *all?*" he asked.

The general shook his head and began tapping out instructions on a nearby keyboard. Immediately, the blips blossomed to form an almost solid field of light from the East to the West Coast.

"That," he replied, "is what we get if we display the total number of reports received from *all* sources. Almost as many as Air Force Intelligence has logged during the past *thirty* years!"

"Christ!" said the President, glancing up at the panel of status lights above the screen. "Now I see why you're on Condition Yellow."

The general called up a message from a nearby hard-copy unit and handed it to the President. "We got this flash at four A.M.," he said. "Radar units at Dulles and Washington Center reported a positive UFO contact west of the Capitol. An interceptor was scrambled to the coordinates radar gave us, and at four-oh-seven the pilot confirmed radar lock-on to the bogey, closing fast. It was dark, of course, but he advised Air Traffic that there was no sign of tailpipe flame, navigation, or anticollision lights. *Nothing!* Yet according to radar, there was a UFO at three hundred feet, making approximately fifty knots.

"The plane went in without further radio contact, both blips disappeared, and we lost a pilot with five thousand hours under his belt."

The President passed the message to Nadelman. "Have you been able to check the wreckage yet?" he asked the general.

"We're still collecting fragments, but our preliminary investigations show no evidence of its having been shot down or in a collision."

"So how do you explain the radar contacts?"

The general shrugged. "I can't. We do still get bugs in the hardware from time to time, and a radar operator always has a lot of anomalous propagation to contend with, but—"

"What the hell's anomalous propagation?" asked the President.

"We call them angels. Unwanted signals—satellites, radio frequency interference, balloons, meteors—even birds and insect clouds—all can and frequently do show up on radar. But an experienced operator—an air-traffic controller for example—learns to ignore them and concentrate on the aircraft he's working. He has to. He wouldn't hold his job down for long if he was forever calling his watch supervisor across to look at angels."

"If I understand the general correctly," said Nadelman, turning to the President, "he's suggesting that radar operators have suddenly begun to trust their equipment rather more than their intuition."

"But that doesn't explain how a five-thousand-hour man gets himself killed if all he's chasing is a skein of geese."

The general looked doubtful. "It *has* happened," he said. "If it was a skein of geese, and he flew into them, it would be like being hit by a burst of cannon fire."

"But there is no evidence he *did*," said Nadelman.

The general thought for a moment. "Pilot disorientation?" he offered, with little conviction.

Nadelman shook his head. "A *five-thousand-hour* man?"

"I know," said the general, his face grave. "It doesn't make sense . . ."

Nadelman took off his spectacles and began polishing them vigorously. The others watched intently, as though expecting him to produce a genie which would illuminate the problem in one blinding, inspired flash. He inspected the lenses against the light from the screen before putting them back on again, blinked, and turned, smiling, to the general. "What we are now faced with, I would suggest, is the probability that much of the anomalous propagation witnessed by radar operators in the past was not as benign as they chose to believe."

The President looked puzzled. "Let me get this straight—what you're saying is that until we uncovered hard evidence of extraterrestrial overflights, they just weren't giving a goddamn?"

Nadelman blew his nose loudly. "That's perhaps a little hard, Mr. President. As I see it, it's roughly analogous to say, Manson's discovery that malaria is carried by the mosquito—a creature which, until eighteen ninety-four, was seen as little more than a nuisance."

The President shook his head. "Christ!" he said to Wallcroft, looking across at the array of clocks above the airlock. "We'd better come to grips with the problem of how the hell I'm going to get all of this over to the boondocks!"

The office into which the President led Wallcroft overlooked the main floor of the Situation Room. It contained a long conference table surrounded by chairs, the center one flanked by the presidential flag and the Stars and Stripes. The President took off his jacket and sat down. "Okay," he said, putting his feet on the table and leaning back, "let's see where you're at."

Wallcroft withdrew two sets of papers from the folder he was carrying, and handed one to the President. "The top copy is the original draft, the other my amended version," he explained.

The President began reading and, without looking up, pushed back the chair next to him with his foot. "Sit down," he said, with a trace of impatience. "And take off your jacket if you want to." He glanced through the huge glass window that overlooked the main floor. "Down there it's cool enough for a topcoat. Up here you could grow orchids."

He read quickly through Wallcroft's version of his speech, turned back to the beginning, and began reading aloud. "It was with a profound sense of shock and deep sorrow that I learned of the tragic event which occurred in Los Angeles last December third." He looked up at Wallcroft. "That's a much better opening. By the way, you can smoke if you want to . . ."

Wallcroft reached instinctively for his jacket pocket, then stopped. "Thank you, but I'm trying to give them up."

The President smiled, and turned back to his speech. "You've picked a great time to do *that!* Tell me, why have you moved the astronomers and biologists bit ahead of my summary of the investigator's report?"

"You were coming to the point a shade too quickly, Mr. President. They'll be expecting you to knock down the story of an extraterrestrial threat, not confirm it. It calls for fine judgment, I know, but if you pitch it to them too quickly you run a very real risk of blowing their minds."

The President nodded thoughtfully. "Fine," he said at last. "Provided I can change it to read, 'Astronomers and biologists have long accepted the probability that, within the immeasurable depths of space, there exist other life-bearing planets than our own.' Okay?"

Wallcroft nodded, and penciled in the change on his copy. "Paragraph six, section eight worried me a little," he said.

The President suddenly got up and opened the door, holding it ajar with a chair. "I'm going to have to get them to do something about the goddamn air conditioning in this room," he said testily. "Go ahead, Mr. Wallcroft, I'm with you."

"Paragraph six, section eight. It seemed to me, Mr. President, a little early in the ball game to start talking about friendship and understanding. Whoever, or whatever it was that zapped L.A., killed close to ten thousand people, and what your audience is going to be looking for is reassurance that there isn't going to be a repeat performance someplace else. I would therefore suggest you go straight into the stuff about ordering the Strategic Air Command—"

"Good point, Mr. Wallcroft. Let's do that."

Wallcroft turned over a page. "The section dealing with civil-defense procedures, shelter programs, and so forth, is fine as it stands. And so is the section about communicating our peaceful intentions to whatever's out there . . . It was just coming up a bit too early before."

"This line about trying to raise them on the fourteen-twenty-megacycle wave band . . . Do you think anyone'll know what the hell I'm talking about?"

"It doesn't matter—it *sounds* impressive. But I'm not so sure about paragraph fifteen—'This country has passed through a difficult—even perilous—period in its history.' Have you got it?"

The President grunted. "What's the problem?" he asked.

220

"It's—I don't know—a shade admonitory in tone."

"I mean it to be!"

"Okay. But would you buy this: 'We stand today on the threshold of a new chapter in the history, not only of this country, but of this planet'?"

"Can you stand on the threshold of a new *chapter*?"

Wallcroft smiled. "Okay, let's make it '*start* of a new chapter in the history, not only of this country, but of this planet.' Then you go on to say, 'And if we are to meet the challenge—and the opportunity—which confronts each and every one of us, we must rediscover that sense of national unity . . .' and so forth."

"Good!"

"That way you frame the Roosevelt quote more effectively."

The President made a face. "I'm not sure I want to use it."

" 'We have nothing to fear but fear itself.' It's a *great* curtain line in this context," said Wallcroft.

"It would be if it were mine."

"That's why it's good. It'll remind them of other crises faced and overcome."

"Maybe." The President didn't sound convinced. "What still worries me is whether or not we'll seem to be on top of the problem."

"I've got an idea on that one," said Wallcroft. He bent down, framing the President's face with his outstretched hands, and began backing slowly away. "You finish speaking—right?—and the camera pulls slowly back until we see that on one side of your desk there's an enormous blowup of—I don't know—the Milky Way, and on the other a mechanical model of the solar system.

"And we cut away—not to the front of the White House, but to a shot of the telescope at Mount Palomar!"

The President stood up and began putting on his jacket. "I like it," he said, "provided you don't intend replacing the national anthem with the title music from *2001*!"

28

NADELMAN TOOK THE WATCHMAKER'S glass from his eye and cleared a space for his black leather attaché case on the brightly lit bench at which he'd been working. He was at last ready to begin packing for his trip, with the rest of the Wild Card team, to the Virgin Islands.

He looked up as the first of several chiming clocks in the workshop of his house in Chevy Chase began to sound the hour. It was four A.M., more or less. He reckoned that it would probably take him the best part of an hour to do what had to be done, and with a car coming at seven-thirty to drive him to Andrews Air Force Base it hardly seemed worth going to bed. He got up and filled a mug with coffee from a pot he was keeping hot on an electric furnace. For several minutes he stood, the steaming mug cradled in his hands, thinking back to when he was a boy. Night after night, he'd waited until the rest of the house was sleeping, got out of bed, and crept back to this same room to work until it was almost dawn. He smiled as he remembered some of the things he'd built then: the working model of a motor torpedo boat that had blown a hole in the side of a bath; the radio-controlled robot that had received visitors at the front door—until one of his mother's friends had nearly died of fright.

During the past forty-eight hours—the best he could remember since those days long ago—he had once again experienced the same deep sense of satisfaction at having built something with his own hands. Only this time it had not been a motor torpedo boat, or a robot, but a bomb. A bomb that would destroy all of the people who had worked alongside him at Detrick during the past eight months. The people who knew everything there was to know about Wild Card, and had now to be disposed of in the interests of absolute security.

He put the mug down as the other clocks began to chime, and returned to the bench. In front of the attaché case, surrounded by a gleaming array of tools and instruments, lay the bomb. He opened the lid of the case. It was filled with a thick block of polystyrene into which he'd cut four irregularly shaped holes. He picked up the first of the bomb's components—a power pack and master time switch—and eased it gently into place in the polystyrene block. He'd had no difficulty obtaining the metal box of RDX that went next to it; Benedict had employed a technique known as explosive forming to shape the more complex of the spacecraft sections and had—to the despair of Henry Jerome—been very lax in logging the amounts used. Next to the explosive went an accelerometer and cutoff switch. Among the contingencies he'd had to plan for was one in which the pilot was forced to make a premature landing as a result of the aircraft's developing mechanical trouble. Nadelman would not be on board to disarm the bomb, and if the aircraft blew up on the ground—or, indeed, anywhere except over deep water—he knew it would not take the accident investigators long to discover what had happened and who was responsible. However, if the aircraft were to be turned back, the accelerometer would sense the duration and intensity of the decelerative forces generated during landing, activate the cutoff switch, and disarm the bomb. The case—a type commonly used by government officials for carrying top-secret documents—would be triple-locked and had Nadelman's initials stamped on it, so all he would have to do in such a situation was simply await its return and dismantle it.

He picked up the last component to go into the case, handling it almost reverentially. For with this single piece of equipment he had, he

224

believed, found a way of utilizing the death of his colleagues to further the work they had done during the last eight months of their lives. It was a miniature radar transmitter. Just before the bomb exploded, it would send out a signal that Air Traffic Control would interpret as an echo from an unidentified flying object which had suddenly appeared alongside the aircraft carrying the Wild Card team. Shortly afterward a tiny spool of magnetic tape would begin to revolve, transmitting a message—apparently from the pilot—saying that he was being buzzed and was taking evasive action in an attempt to avoid a collision.

The concept had been simple and ingenious, and Nadelman had realized it by refusing to be overawed by the immense technical problems it posed. Radar, he had told himself, was kid stuff. A revolving transmitting antenna sends out a pulse which, when it encounters an object, is reflected back like an echo to the antenna. The antenna is linked to a cathode-ray scope, the screen of which is bombarded by a stream of electrons that move in a straight line from its center to its edge and back again. As well as traveling to and from the center, the stream of electrons—called a sweep—also revolves like the second hand of a watch. An echo reflected back to the antenna strengthens the flow of electrons long enough to cause a phosphorescent blip to appear on the screen.

Because the sweep rotates once every ten seconds, and because it takes seventy seconds for the afterglow of a blip to disappear, an Air Traffic Control radar operator can chart the speed, altitude, distance, and compass bearing of every plane flying in the area covered by his station's antenna.

The device Nadelman had so lovingly built was primed to respond to the ground station's radar pulse one minute before the bomb exploded. Microseconds after first receiving a pulse, it would send out its own pulse. By then, the stream of electrons would be fractionally nearer the edge of the scope than when they had recorded the normal echo from the aircraft. The appearance of a *second* blip on the same radial line as the blip caused by the aircraft's return would suggest that something else had flown, at a very high speed, into the airspace between sweeps. The time lag between the aircraft's return and the false return would then begin to decrease, causing the distance between the blips to decrease until they were finally superimposed. To Air Traffic Control, it would

225

appear that the "something else" had collided with the aircraft carrying the Wild Card team. At that moment the bomb would explode.

Unable to resist the temptation of listening to the recording once more, he connected the reproducing head of the tiny tape deck to an amplifier, the amplifier to a loudspeaker, and switched on. An alarmed voice began talking over a crackle of static: "Coastal Radar. SAM Zero Five. I have an unidentified flying object at five o'clock my level. Range ten miles, closing left to right—and fast. It looks metallic . . . an enormous disc with some sort of—Am taking evasive action—My God, it's going to hit us!"

By five-twenty Nadelman had wired up the components, gotten the latest ETD from Andrews Tower, and made the final settings on the master time switch. He closed the lid of the case and locked it. It was done. He got up from the bench, stretched, and crossed to the window, pulling aside the blind. The sky was beginning to lighten and he was relieved to see that the snow which had been forecast the previous evening had not fallen. He turned back into the room, humming to himself, and opened the furnace door. All that now remained for him to do was destroy the various structural plans, navigation maps, and aircraft-sabotage reports he'd worked from, change, feed himself and the cats, and wait for the car.

At Andrews Air Force Base, the plane assigned to the Wild Card Team—a blue and white Boeing Advanced 737 of the 89th Military Airlift Wing—still swarmed with engineers and ground crew as Nadelman climbed up the icy air stair to the forward passenger door.

The duty office had at first been reluctant to allow him on board ahead of the other passengers, but had finally given way in the face of Nadelman's insistence that he had work of national importance, which he needed to start on immediately.

One of the two stewardesses assigned to the flight was taking delivery of food from the catering bus when Nadelman arrived and interrupted her. She hurried him through a lounge furnished with sofas and tables into the main passenger cabin. As he had expected, it contained six rows of rearward-facing triple seats on either side of an aisle. Through the open bulkhead door ahead of him he could see the long conference table and chairs which occupied the remainder of the passenger space.

226

"This'll do fine," he murmured, dropping his attaché case and an armful of papers on the first seat to his right—a seat that placed him directly over the starboard wing-fuselage joint. Although he was careful to make it appear as though his choice of seat had been random, he had picked it with great deliberation. When in the air, the wing-fuselage joint would be subjected to enormous stress—more than any other part of the aircraft—and it was only by having the bomb explode here that he could be absolutely certain of the aircraft's breaking up.

As soon as the stewardess left, he slipped the document case out of sight beneath his seat, covered his knees with the blanket she'd given him and settled back to await the President's message recalling him to the White House.

By eight A.M. the passenger cabin was full. As Nadelman had expected, even the more reserved members of the team were in high spirits at the prospect of being disbanded after what they had been told would be a not too arduous acclimatization course. Several times he had been convinced that someone was about to sit next to him, but in the end even the boldest had been repelled by his obvious unwillingness to remove the papers scattered across the two unoccupied seats next to him.

At eight-ten the passenger door was sealed and the lights dimmed for an instant as each engine was ignited and warmed up. Nadelman turned from the papers he'd been annotating and glanced out of the window. Beyond the trailing edge of the Boeing's wing he could see exhaust gases shimmering across the rime-covered apron. Then, with a slight buildup of power, the aircraft began to roll gently away from the terminal building. An orchestral version of "White Christmas" being played over the P.A. stopped abruptly, and a stewardess began welcoming the passengers on board.

Nadelman glanced anxiously at his watch: the President's message recalling him was now five minutes overdue. He knew that if it came *after* they were airborne, he'd have to take the attaché case off the plane with him; there was nothing he could do to prevent the fail-safe mechanism from disarming the bomb during landing. And then they would be back to square one. It would give rise to too many suspicions if they were to attempt a similar subterfuge on the return trip from the Islands. His anger and frustration gave way to fear as an alarming

227

thought occurred to him; supposing the recall *never* came? It was a possibility that had never before entered his mind. It wasn't his immediate safety that worried him. If he were not to be recalled, he knew that all he would have to do was pretend he'd been taken ill and the aircraft would be bound to land to let him off. But what had begun to make him sweat was the realization that if it *was* the President's intention to get rid of him along with the others, all he would achieve by bluffing his way off the aircraft was a stay of execution.

"Are you feeling okay?"

Startled, he turned and found that Napier had moved to the seat next to him. For a moment he didn't know how to react. "I'm not sure," he muttered, his mind racing.

Napier nodded sympathetically, and began fastening his seat belt. "You've been working too hard," he said. "A couple of weeks in the sun'll do us all good."

Nadelman turned back to the window, cursing the President for having put him in such a predicament. Time was running out fast—they were now at the end of the taxiway and the plane was being brought around to its holding point, at right angles to the runway.

He felt Napier nudge his arm. He turned back and saw that he was being offered a silver hip flask. "Go on," said Napier, smiling. "Take a slug. You'll feel a whole lot better."

Nadelman shook his head.

"Go on!" Napier insisted, thrusting the flask forward. "It won't kill you, for God's sake!"

Reluctantly, and only to give himself time to think, Nadelman took the flask and put it cautiously to his lips. Relieved to discover that it contained brandy, and not whiskey, as he'd expected, he took a long pull. To his surprise, he began to feel better immediately. He tried to return the flask but Napier waved it away. "Finish it," he said. "If I have any more I won't need a plane to get me where we're going!"

Nadelman drank again from the flask and turned back to the window. They were now on the runway and lined up.

The only logical thing to do in the circumstances, he decided, was to assume that the message recalling him had fouled up somewhere along the line, and get off the plane immediately. If the assumption was correct, the operation would proceed more or less as planned; if it were not he would be in no worse a position than if he remained on the plane.

228

He began unfastening his seat belt. "I think I'm going to have to ask them to let me off," he said, turning to Napier. "I'm beginning to feel pretty rough." He reached up and was about to press the bell for the stewardess when Napier grabbed his wrist. "Relax," he said softly. "Just relax. It's only pretakeoff nerves. You know something? I get 'em myself. I'm not kidding! Just relax—the worst part's nearly over."

Nadelman tried to break Napier's hold, but he seemed to have lost his strength and his powers of coordination. It was almost as though he were drunk. And yet he knew he couldn't be; the flask had been less than a quarter full when Napier had given it to him. He turned, intending to order Napier to let go of his arm, but instead found himself giggling. He tried to get up, but his legs seemed to have gone to sleep. Grinning inanely, he turned back to the window. The whine of the jets deepened to a full-throated roar, and the wing below him began buffeting as though impatient to be airborne. Suddenly the brakes were released and the plane bucked forward down the runway. White high-intensity lights raced past the window and, across the airfield, a rotating identification beacon dissolved into a red blur and slipped out of sight behind the wing. His eyelids had begun to feel heavy; he tried to keep them open to watch the passing kaleidoscope of lights, but couldn't.

By the time the aircraft's undercarriage had come to rest in the wheel bays beneath the passenger cabin, Nadelman was in a deep, dreamless sleep.

Napier screwed the cap back onto his flask and slipped it into his jacket pocket. The President had sure as hell been right, he decided, as he began loosening Nadelman's collar and tie: flying *really* scares the crap out of the poor bastard! Now that he thought about it, most of Nadelman's trips out of Detrick had been made by road, at a time when it would have been a lot safer—and quicker—to have taken the chopper. He smiled as he remembered how the President had told him of his hunch that Nadelman might try to duck out of the trip. "Frank," he'd said, "this acclimatization course you're all going on might look like a bit of a clambake, but believe me, it's an essential part of the operation. And I don't want it screwed as a result of Dick turning up late—or not turning up at all. Short of shooting an anesthetic dart into his ass as he's climbing the boarding ramp, is there any way of making sure that having got him to the goddamn airport, he gets on the plane and stays on it?"

Napier turned to the window for a last glimpse of the Potomac as the

229

Boeing climbed away to the south. The "No Smoking Fasten Seat Belts" sign went out and he took a cigar from his pocket and bit off the end. Nadelman might wake up with a bit of a hangover, he thought, as he moved back to his seat on the other side of the aisle, but by the time the chloral hydrate he'd put in the brandy had worn off, the worst of the trip would be over . . .

At 09.22 Special Air Mission Zero Five was 350 miles southeast of Andrews, cruising at 420 knots. The cloud layer was at last breaking up and, thirty-three thousand feet below, Major Norman Karlovac could see turquoise water shading into a deeper blue where the North Atlantic Basin began.

A small man with thinning sand-colored hair and a pale complexion, Karlovac was the antithesis of the popular image of an aircraft captain. Yet he was qualified on eight types of jets and had more than nine thousand flying hours to his credit.

In ten minutes they would reach Bass Intersection. Bass was no more than a grid reference on aeronautical charts, but for aircrews it had a special significance: it was a compulsory reporting point. At Bass, Karlovac's co-pilot, Lieutenant Eugene Dozier, would advise Air Traffic Control of SAM Zero Five's position and Karlovac would turn the aircraft onto a magnetic bearing of 164 degrees. They would then be on an airway known as Whiskey Route, which would lead them via reporting points Scotch, Irish, Bourbon, Corn, and Rye into the jurisdiction of San Juan Center. And if stewardess Egan's description of the state of some of the passengers was accurate, he thought as he handed her his empty breakfast tray, they couldn't be flying a more aptly named route.

Patti Egan closed the flight-deck door and returned to the galley. As she did so the second stewardess—Karen Rowland—returned with a pile of empty passenger trays. "Why did the fat guy in thirty-six tell you to hide those?" she asked, nodding at a pile of the *Washington Post* carrying the headline: PRESIDENT TO REVEAL DEATH CITY FINDINGS TONIGHT.

Patti Egan shrugged. "He said a lot of the passengers had lost relatives in L.A. But you'd never know it the way they're whooping it up back there!"

By 09.24 the poker game in the lounge had become very noisy.

230

Kochalski, ahead of the game by twenty-five hundred dollars in spite of having drunk the best part of a bottle of bourbon, had just produced his second royal flush. Weiner, egged on by Johnson, was complaining loudly that since the predicted frequency of royals was one in 649,740 hands, how the hell could Kochalski have gotten that lucky twice in a row? Benedict's interest had moved from the cards in front of him to a view of Karen Rowland's thigh as she knelt—on her way to Nadelman with a tray of Danish pastries and coffee—to pick up a discarded copy of the *Journal of Molecular Biology* from the cabin floor.

In the conference cabin, Payne looked up from checking the security duty roster as Zelinski shuffled past on his way to the aft toilets. It was the fourth time he'd had to get up since they'd become airborne, and he found himself wondering, again, whether he should try to persuade Nadelman to allow him to stay on in America for his now long overdue prostatectomy, or wait until he was safely back in Paraguay.

Payne, unlike Napier, Stillman, Olsen, and Mizushima, had decided to exercise his option to retire from the Service rather than accept promotion. He planned to spend a year traveling around Europe before moving to San Francisco to set up a private investigation agency with part of his Presidential Contingency Fund bonus. He would have liked to give up work completely, but had not so far figured out a way of explaining to his wife and family how he'd suddenly become rich at the age of thirty-five.

McElroy was sitting alone at the end of the table, drinking heavily and worrying. He knew that the message-encoded chocolates had reached their destinations because of the polite but puzzled thank-you notes he had received from the four women. Why then hadn't they worked? Wouldn't at least *one* of the women have eaten at least *one* of the chocolates? That was all that was needed for them to discover what had been happening at Detrick. Or had all four been dieting? But then wouldn't they have given the chocolates to someone else?

McElroy refilled his glass. The irony was painfully obvious to him. Suppose he had succeeded, and Wild Card had been stopped. An angry mob, aware of the conspiracy, might have lynched him. If the President had been impeached, he would have gone down too, and never worked again. Yet because he had failed, he could continue his research with all the benefit he believed it would bring to mankind. He could revolutionize teaching, remove the drudgery from learning. It was work, he believed, that would win him a Nobel Prize.

In the main cabin only thirteen seats were now occupied. Chesterton had laid aside his leather-bound copy of Trollope's *Phineas Redux,* and was worrying about whether two weeks would be long enough to prepare his colleagues for the questioning they would be subjected to on their return home.

Kavanagh had moved from the seat next to Chesterton to sit with Mizushima, and was demonstrating the moves of a Queen's Pawn Nimzovich Defense on his traveling chess set. Neither had ever really believed they would become rich as a result of their work on Wild Card, and now they weren't quite sure what to do about it.

Darrow was dozing in the hot sun that streamed through the cabin window, fantasizing about the electronic house he planned to build for himself at Big Sur, and the girls he'd seduce in it.

Next to him, Pedlar was engaged in mental arithmetic. As a hedge against inflation, he had insisted on receiving half of his payment in kind; one kilogram of uncut heroin. Mixed with lactose, it would, he estimated, be enough for twenty thousand fixes. And at the current street-level price of fifty dollars a fix . . .! He settled back, feeling very pleased with himself.

Behind him, Henry Jerome was wondering how to react to Charlotte Paxton's highly detailed account of a bizarre sexual adventure she claimed to have had two years earlier while on a vacation in the Virgin Islands. Her plans for the future did not extend beyond getting laid at the earliest possible opportunity, even if it meant her having to pay for it, while Jerome wanted nothing more than to get back to the world of split-levels and power mowers, the PTA, and the Rotary Club—the world he believed he'd helped to preserve as a result of his participation in Wild Card.

Conrad was asleep, dreaming erotic dreams in which he gamboled naked with the two stewardesses in a swimming pool, filled not with water but with crisp new dollar bills.

Napier had been joined by Stillman. Olsen, and Lawrence, and had begun arguing about the relative merits of the Winchester 71 and the Marlin 336 deluxe for shooting heavy game in tight cover.

Karen Rowland stopped beside Nadelman, not sure whether she should wake him. She glanced at her watch, saw that it was coming up to nine-thirty, and decided she would. "Dr. Nadelman!" she called. He stirred and his eyelids began to flicker.

"I'd let him sleep it off," said Napier from across the aisle.

She turned, laughing. "It's like that, is it?" she replied, stepping into the space beside Nadelman to let Patti Egan pass with a tray of bottles and glasses.

As she did so the timing mechanism activated the radar transmitter in the attaché case beneath Nadelman's seat

By the time she had turned back to Nadelman, his eyes were open and he was looking around, puzzled.

"Good morning!" she said brightly, and began to lower a small folding table in front of him. "You've woken up just in time for—" But she didn't finish the sentence. With a wild swing, Nadelman smashed the table and tray away from him, soaking the front of her white blouse with coffee, and began groping frantically between his feet for the attaché case.

As Patti Egan turned to see what had happened, the taped message that SAM Zero Five was being buzzed by an unidentified flying object came to an end and the bomb detonated.

With an ear-shattering roar the case disintegrated, punching a jagged hole, thirty feet in diameter, in the aluminum-alloy fuselage.

Nadelman blew apart like watermelon, splattering the white leatherette walls and ceiling with blood, tissue, and fecal matter. Fragments of what had once been his seat support ripped through the cabin at velocities exceeding those of a bullet, cutting down Zelinski and Patti Egan. Karen Rowland, her hair and the front of her blouse and skirt charred by the flash, died instantly; Napier, Stillman, Olsen, and Lawrence a moment later from massive lung damage caused by the shock wave.

Immediately, the cabin decompressed. From either end of the aircraft an almost solid tide of debris—clothing, hand luggage, trays, bottles and glasses, bulkhead and toilet doors—converged on the gaping hole and was sucked into the near-vacuum outside. With it went Lieutenant Dozier, still clutching the flight-deck door he'd been about to open when the bomb exploded, together with Zelinski and the bodies

233

of Karen Rowland and the three security men. Although bleeding profusely, Patti Egan managed to save herself from being swept away with the others by clinging on to the seat supports on either side of the aisle.

Then as abruptly as it had begun, the decompression spent itself. The cabin, which in less than a minute had been picked clean by the near-hurricane-force wind, filled with fog as the air temperature fell below the dewpoint. Suddenly it was forty-eight degrees below zero —cold as a Siberian winter.

Hundreds of hours spent in flight simulators had conditioned Karlovac to respond instinctively and immediately to such a crisis. Disregarding the screams coming from the passenger cabin, he flung aside his headset and put on an oxygen mask, made sure the cabin masks had been released by throwing the passenger oxygen override switch, turned on the "No Smoking Fasten Seat Belts" sign, scanned an array of instruments and warning lights for indications of systems malfunctions, silenced the altitude horn that had started to blare as soon as the pressure differential began falling, and, because his mask contained no earphones, switched on a standby speaker in the cockpit roof.

If Dozier had been there, Karlovac would have sent him aft to check on the damage. As it was, he had no way of knowing that the explosion had buckled one of the three forged main frames supporting the passenger cabin, fractured the front wing-box spar at the root, and sheared off many of the retaining bolts. All he *did* know was that he had to get the plane down into warmer, less rarefied air as quickly as possible if he was to prevent everyone on board from being overcome by the intense cold.

As he was pulling the throttles back to idle, a voice—barely discernible above the roar of wind and engines—began talking over the standby speaker. "SAM Zero Five, this is Coastal Radar," it said. "Your message received. We still have you in radar contact. Do you read?"

Because Karlovac knew that the plane's collision avoidance system would warn him of conflicting traffic during his descent, he had decided to wait until the immediate danger of hypothermia—and anoxia for the passengers not on oxygen—had passed before alerting Air Traffic Control. So, he wondered, how in the name of God had they found out he was in trouble?

He moved the speed-brake lever to Flight Detent, and felt the wings begin to buffet as the flaps rose up into the air stream. He was now approaching the moment of supreme crisis: if the rate of descent he had set was too rapid in relation to the amount of damage which had been done to the aircraft, or the maneuvering loads too great, it would only be a question of minutes before it began breaking up.

"SAM Zero Five, Coastal. Do you read? Squawk Mayday if you read us. Squawk Mayday if you read us . . ." The voice from Air Traffic Control had begun speaking again, but all of Karlovac's attention was concentrated on getting the aircraft to a lower altitude and in one piece. He pressed the auto-pilot-disengage button and began a descending turn to starboard.

At twenty-eight thousand feet, Karlovac rolled the plane out of the turn but continued the dive. The starboard wing-fuselage joint was now under intolerable stress. Suddenly, with a report like an enormously amplified rifle shot, the joint cracked and the wing swung upward. The outboard section—from wingtip to engine mounting—broke away, rupturing the number two integral fuel tank. Twenty thousand gallons of aviation gasoline vaporized, mingled with the engine's high-temperature exhaust gases, and exploded with a thump that rocked the aircraft. The inboard section of wing swung up, slammed against the fuselage, and came away—taking with it the starboard horizontal stabilizer.

The flight deck immediately became a bedlam of lights, bells, and horns. Not even at the hands of the most sadistic simulator operator had Karlovac been subjected to so many simultaneous systems failures. Fuel and pneumatic systems, flight controls, hydraulics, electrics—all were registering damage. And with no starboard wing—and therefore no starboard lift—the aircraft began to roll. One moment the sea was below him, the next moment above him. And as the rate of rotation, and the speed of descent increased, the sea and the sky began to turn from a brilliant blue to gray and he felt his limbs becoming heavy as lead.

At fifteen thousand feet the crippled Boeing began to disintegrate. First the port wing sheared off and was flung, in a great arc, clear of the fuselage. Then the fuselage itself broke in half on a level with the bomb-damaged mainframe, scattering bodies like peas from a pod.

Below, a flock of sea birds wheeled away to the south as wreckage began plummeting into the sea, throwing up tall white columns of spray. For nearly five minutes, over an area three miles wide, wreckage continued to rain down out of the sky. Then, as suddenly as it had begun, the commotion was over; the last column of spray fell back onto the oily sea and the bubbles ceased rising.

Ten minutes later, sharks—at first frightened away by the impact of the wreckage on the water—returned to forage among the bobbing seat cushions and the empty yellow life rafts for what remained of the Wild Card team.

29

THE FIRST LADY, STILL clutching the bouquet of red roses presented to her at Los Angeles International Airport, leaned across the President to look out of the helicopter window.

"Darling! I can't believe it! There're even *more* people here than there were at the airport!"

The President closed his internal security adviser's status report and began buttoning the cuffs of his shirt. His decision to go ahead with Wild Card was, he believed, completely vindicated by what he'd read in the report. Even the prospect of what lay ahead did not dampen the glow of satisfaction he felt.

There had been a handful of demonstrations in cities with large hippie communities—demanding that the extraterrestrials, when they arrived, should be met with flowers, not guns—but rioting, protest marches, strikes and sit-ins had petered out completely.

The President made a quick calculation: even *if* he'd been able to contain the casualty figures at their fall average, by this time next year as many people would have been killed in riots as had been killed by the virus. And that was to discount the tens of thousands who would have been injured and maimed.

Everywhere were signs of renewed life. Even the number of unemployed had begun to fall as a nationwide shelter and respirator program got under way. Most gratifying of all, the Dow-Jones Index had at last begun to show that there was still a pulse, however faint, in the nation's economy.

He put on his sunglasses and turned to the window, looking down through the web of high-tension wires at the muddle of shabby stores and filling-stations, red-roofed stucco houses, blighted palm trees, and peeling advertising billboards. "Well," he said to the First Lady, "it sure as hell isn't Williamsburg!"

She smiled, still craning forward, and put her hand reassuringly on his arm. "In a hundred years it'll have acquired a folksy charm," she said. "And in a thousand years they'll rate it one of the wonders of the world!"

The idea of preserving an area around Doty Avenue as it had been on the night of the disaster had seemed to him a good one when it had first been suggested by the director of the Smithsonian Institution's National Museum of Man. But the fact that he'd be expected to attend the inauguration ceremonies had not occurred to the President until it was too late. The money had been raised and the required legislation rushed through in double-quick time, and an army of archeologists had descended to take an inventory of every artifact on the thousand-acre site. Everything was to be handled and catalogued as though it had come from the Treasure Chamber of Tutankhamen—Sears, Roebuck furniture, filling-station calendars, worn-out shoes and clothes, empty beer cans and Coke bottles—nothing was too insignificant or battered to be thrown away. Even aerosol slogans and obscene graffiti were to be preserved as though they were Renaissance frescoes.

Guided by a landing signal officer, the helicopter came gently to rest on the helipad in the grounds of El Camino College. The President, anxious to have a disagreeable task over and done with, unfastened his seat belt and began putting on his jacket. He stood up, but, realizing that his wife would be worried about the rotor wash mussing her hair, waited until the blades had spun to a standstill before guiding her out onto the steps alongside.

238

Immediately, a scarlet-uniformed Marine band struck up "Hail to the Chief" and a roar of greeting rose from the vast crowd behind the chain-link fence bordering Redondo Beach Boulevard.

The heat and the noise hit the President and First Lady like a shock wave. For a moment neither knew how to react. Both had dressed somberly and both wore black armbands, expecting the occasion to be solemn and uncompromisingly formal. The President had even decided to carry a hat, something he would never normally have done, as an additional mark of respect.

He felt his wife tug at his sleeve. "What do we *do?*" she said.

"I guess it's a when-in-Rome situation," he replied, tossing his hat back inside the helicopter.

For several minutes they remained at the top of the steps, waving and smiling at the wildly cheering, flag-waving crowd, before descending to greet the welcoming committee.

The noise was now deafening, and the President had to shout to make himself heard as he shook hands with Mayor Mansio. "I said," he yelled, his mouth close to the mayor's ear, "that I'm deeply sorry that my first visit as President to your fine city should have been occasioned by such an overwhelming tragedy!"

The reception line broke up. But instead of crossing to the waiting motorcade, the President and First Lady, surrounded by scores of television cameramen and photographers, began walking toward the chain-link fence.

The crowd became delirious. For several minutes the two of them strolled in front of the fence, smiling and saying "Hello," "Good to see you," just out of reach of the forest of waving hands. The head of the Secret Service detail, afraid that the fence would give way under the press of bodies, pleaded with the President to come away.

"Just a couple of minutes more, Hank," he muttered. "Just a couple of minutes more . . ."

Here it was still easy for him to believe he had been right to allow Wild Card; in there—on the killing ground—the President knew it would be a different matter.

Reluctantly, he turned and followed the First Lady across to the motorcade, taking his place beside her in the rear of the black Lincoln Continental.

One hundred thousand people had been allowed inside the national-monument site. They were divided into two groups. The next of kin of the victims had been seated in front of the ruins of the house on Doty Avenue, facing the platform from which the President was to speak. The other group—by far the larger—was restricted to either side at a five-hundred-yard-long section of Crenshaw Avenue, now renamed the Avenue of the Galaxies, that ran north from the intersection at Redondo Beach Boulevard. They would have to content themselves with a glimpse of the President as he drove by and a relay of the ceremony over the public-address system.

A jubilant roar engulfed the motorcade as it swung out of the grounds of El Camino College and began its journey along the Avenue of the Galaxies. Overhead, the flags of the United Nations floated at half mast against a flawless cerulean sky, one row on either side of the long, straight avenue.

The President stood up and, with his arms held above his head, began waving. Suddenly, a bagful of paper rose petals, thrown by someone in the crowd, burst on the roadway in front of the lead car. It was followed by another, and then another; soon the air was red with the swirling petals. Within minutes the President, his motorcycle escort, and everyone in the slow-moving, open Lincoln looked as though they had been splattered with blood.

The President had asked that victims of terrorist attacks should be allowed in front of the police lines either side of the avenue. Although he'd wanted them to be able to see him safely and easily, he was even more anxious to see *them*. These people, with their broken bodies, were to be the emotional base camps that would help sustain him through the ordeal ahead. They *proved* that Wild Card had been necessary.

He stopped the motorcade and got out. Accompanied by the First Lady and two Secret Service agents, he crossed the avenue to shake the remaining hand of a pretty ten-year-old girl in a wheelchair, who told him she was learning to use her artificial legs "real well." He moved on to talk to a National Guardsman who'd been paralyzed by a sniper's bullet, and then to a small boy who'd been burned by napalm.

Still he showed no sign of returning to the Lincoln. The police officers in the lead car looked anxiously at their watches and began to wonder whether he intended walking all the way to Doty Avenue.

240

Amazed, they watched an elderly woman, tears streaming down her face, get up from her wheelchair and hug the President. It was, as one of them said, getting more like Jesus' entry into Jerusalem every minute.

Thirty-five minutes behind schedule, the motorcade finally came to a halt alongside the tiered platform on Doty Avenue. The whole assembly came to their feet and began to clap. Preceded by the First Lady, the President mounted the steps and began shaking hands with a glittering array of dignitaries. All three branches of government were represented, as well as the Joint Chiefs of Staff, the directors and trustees of the Smithsonian Institution, and the ambassadors of each of the member countries of the United Nations.

The President took his seat and the applause died away. During the speeches that followed, he never once allowed his eye to be caught by any member of the audience; neither did he look at the ruins of the house behind them.

And then, at last, it was his turn. He stood up and crossed to the podium that bore the blue-and-gold presidential seal. The applause was tumultuous. He gripped the edges of the podium and waited; still the applause continued. He held up his hands as though to say "enough," but instead of diminishing, it rose to a new crescendo. My God! he thought. Why don't they stop? That they were so fervently applauding the man who'd murdered their fathers and their mothers, their sons and their daughters, their brothers and their sisters, was a burden he'd not expected to be called upon to bear. He felt himself beginning to panic. It was as if, by compounding his own act of desecration, they were deliberately calling down the wrath of God upon his head.

The applause was at last beginning to fade, and soon it was replaced by a silence so total that it seemed to him that he could hear his own heart beating.

He looked up from the neat pile of yellow cards on which his speech had been typed, out across the thicket of microphones ranged in front of him, and began to speak.

"When American astronauts . . . first set foot . . . upon a world outside our own . . . they carried with them a message for posterity . . . 'We came in peace for all mankind' . . . in peace for all mankind . . . for all mankind . . . mankind." In spite of the heat, he

241

suddenly felt himself grow cold. His words, relayed through scores of loudspeakers, were being flung contemptuously back at him from the walls of the empty buildings.

The President turned to the last of the yellow cards. It'll soon be over, he thought. In half an hour—three quarters at the most—I'll have gotten to hell out of here.

He brushed back a lock of brown hair from his forehead and looked up. "We must never forget," he said, "that we are but one species . . . occupying one planet . . . of one solar system . . . within the immeasurable and infinitely mysterious depths of space.

"We must regard ourselves as a young species . . . with much to learn . . . and much to atone for in the courts of history.

"Above all . . . we must adopt a cosmic consciousness . . . and work toward a community of space.

"For there lies our destiny . . . in a Universe of Nations."

He left the podium and walked briskly across the platform and down the steps to where an aide was waiting with a wreath of laurel leaves as big as a truck tire. He took it in both hands and began slowly, alone and in total silence, to walk a path through the crowds toward the memorial stone that had been erected at the scene of the spacecraft crash.

By the time he'd arrived his arms were trembling from the strain of carrying the enormous wreath. He laid it gently against the rough-hewn block of granite, promising himself that as soon as he got back to Washington he'd kick the asses of his chiefs of protocol for not having specified something lighter.

As he straightened up, he felt a cool breeze blow past his face. He blinked; there was something in his eye. He blinked again, but it only made it worse. His hand was halfway up to his face when a squad of Marines, stationed on the opposite side of the ruins, fired the first volley of a twenty-one-gun salute. Somewhere a bugler began playing taps. He let his arm drop back to his side and came to attention. His eyes began to water and, a moment later, the first tear brimmed over and began to trickle down his cheek.

By the time honors had been sounded, both of the President's cheeks were stained with tears, and the watching television cameras had been holding him in a relentlessly tight close-up for two minutes.

30

BY FOUR-THIRTY A.M. ON THE twenty-first of December the temperature at Fort Detrick had dropped five degrees below freezing. A north wind, carrying with it the first snow flurries of the winter, slipped unnoticed through the electrified fence and the razor wire to explore the dark and now deserted laboratories.

Bill Barringer, the last man inside the maximum-security area, was hurrying to clear out his office before leaving. He felt unwell soon after he got up that morning, and now his throat was sore, his head ached, and he felt cold in spite of the heavy topcoat he was wearing and the electric heaters with which he had surrounded himself. He took the last handful of papers from his last file and began feeding them into a shredder. That's all I need, he thought as he watched the thin strips of paper stream out of the machine—a dose of flu for Christmas!

He looked around him. The office had been stripped as clean as if an army of soldier ants had passed through it. All he had to do now, before leaving, was check to see that the other officers attached to the mail-censoring detail had cleared their desks as thoroughly as he had his.

He switched off the shredder and the heater, picked up his suitcases, and crossed to the door. Before turning off the lights, he looked around once more to reassure himself that he'd left nothing behind. In a way, he was sorry to be leaving. As assignments went, it had not been at all bad. He'd never really managed to get to the bottom of what the hell they'd all been up to, although his own hunch was that it had been something to do with developing a laser bomb.

Not that he cared much one way or the other. He'd worked reasonable hours, lived on the fat of the land in luxurious quarters, and hadn't been shot at once. And he had, during the past eight months, made more money than during the same number of years working as a cop.

His only regret was that the assignment had prevented him from spending any time with his daughter. If only he had, he told himself, or if her mother had still been alive to keep an eye on her, maybe she wouldn't have gone off the rails quite so badly.

A biochemistry student at Kent State, Susan Barringer had been arrested during a demonstration at the beginning of the fall semester and charged with destruction of government property and inciting to riot. He'd had to pull a lot of strings to get the charges against her dropped, and had been hurt and puzzled when he later discovered that in spite of all his efforts she was still active in the student protest movement.

Kids! he thought indignantly, closing the door behind him.

The office next to his was large and contained six scarred wooden desks, a few bits and pieces of conventional office equipment, and a row of khaki filing cabinets. It took him fifteen minutes to work his way through the cabinets and five of the desks. So far he had found nothing more incriminating than a roll of Scotch tape, a dried-out Bic pen, a half-empty box of Kleenex, a few postage stamps, and a week-old copy of the *Washington Post* carrying the story of the shooting down, by an unidentified flying object, of the plane carrying the Wild Card team.

He used some of the Kleenex to blow his nose and moved on to the sixth and last desk. He began his search, as he had with the other desks, by opening the top drawer of the left-hand pedestal. It was empty. So were the second and the third. The top drawer of the right-hand pedestal was also empty, but the second contained an open packet of carbon paper. The top sheet had been used. He held it up to the light and saw that it had been used to make a duplicate of a memo from one of his men to Henry Jerome, complaining about the time it had taken to get the department's microscope repaired. Scarlet with anger, he stomped across the room and began feeding the entire packet of carbon paper into the shredder.

When he had finished, he returned to the desk, grabbed the handle of the bottom drawer, and pulled. It moved an inch, then stuck fast, and he heard something heavy slide across the bottom of the drawer. "Shit!" he exclaimed, his breath condensing in the cold air, and looked around for something to force open the drawer.

Mounted on the wall near him was a large reel of brown wrapping paper. He lifted it off its supports and pulled out the heavy wooden spindle. Using the spindle as a lever, he managed to open the drawer a further two inches. He knelt down, pushed back his sleeve, and eased his hand inside. His fingers touched something smooth and rectangular. He pulled it forward and peered in; it was a large box of Whitman's Samplers.

He pushed back his hat and frowned. "What the hell was one of my boys doing with *chocolates?*" he asked himself. Whiskey he could have understood, but chocolates? Using both hands, he carefully lifted the box out through the gap and put it on top of the desk. Suddenly the answer came to him: it was one of four boxes McElroy had mailed a couple of weeks after his girl friend had taken an overdose! At the time, he remembered, Napier had been taking no chances with McElroy, and had him send out for four identical boxes, rewrap them with McElroy's letters, and mail them. A couple of McElroy's boxes had been broken up and examined minutely. He remembered that the report which had come to him a few days later had been negative. No rolls of microfilm or secret messages had been found—in fact, nothing to suggest the chocolates had been tampered with in any way.

He stood up and stared at the unopened, cellophane-wrapped box. An idea had occurred to him; Whitman's Samplers used to be his daughter's favorite chocolates . . .

He pulled an envelope from his pocket, tore it open, and took out a Christmas card and a money order for a hundred dollars. Working as quickly as his freezing fingers would allow, he ripped a length of paper from the reel and wrapped the card and the money order together with the chocolates. He sealed the package with some of the Scotch tape and

245

addressed it, first on one side and then on the other, weighed it, and stuck on three of the stamps he had found.

"Even if she doesn't like them any more," he told himself, "at least it'll show I haven't forgotten." He smiled. "Anyway, there's nothing in Chairman Mao's Little Red Book that says her antiestablishment buddies can't eat chocolates!"

Pleased with his little joke, he picked up his suitcase, switched off the lights, and left to look for a mailbox.

Acknowledgments

BY THE TIME we came together in April 1971, *Wild Card* was in draft outline—Raymond Hawkey having been persuaded by Len Deighton to think about writing a novel, and by Eric Clark (an authority on matters of governmental machinations and security) that the plot was by no means as preposterous as it seemed prior to Watergate.

Having begun the detailed work, we were fortunate in that Len Deighton and Eric Clark continued to advise us with extraordinary skill and generosity, as did Dr. Elizabeth F. Lobl and John Knowler, whose merciless yet brilliantly incisive critique of our first draft we will never forget.

During our research trip to the United States, we were grateful for the guidance of Daniel S. Greenberg, editor and publisher of *Science and Government Report*, and for the opportunity of spending time on assignments with Gabe Pressman of ABC News, New York. William C. Jordan, president of Continental Investigative Agency and a former lieutenant of detectives, patiently explained the police system of his city, and Dr. Carl R. Merril of the National Institute of Mental Health, Bethesda, generously spent time with us in his laboratory, demonstrating techniques and discussing theoretical approaches.

Dr. Panayotis Phililithis of the Institute of Urology proved an invaluable source of information and devoted many hours to refining the scientific details as well as suggesting several of the techniques we describe.

Dr. L. M. Franks, head of the Pathology Department at the Imperial Cancer Research Fund; Dr. Bruce MacGillivray, clinical neurophysiologist and head of the EEG Department at the Royal Free Hospital; Dr. Bernard Hyne, research registrar at the Middlesex Hospital; and Mrs. Moore, M.P.S., were no less kind in giving of their time to discuss particular medical aspects of the story.

For expert advice on the "hardware," we are indebted to Bob Golding of the Department of Flight, Cranfield Institute of Technology, whose knowledge of electronics and ingenuity in solving the problems we raised were inexhaustible. Brian Hockenhull, of the Department of Materials at the same institution, assisted us with the background data to the spacecraft demonstration, and Arthur Bingham, a controller at Ringway Airport, gave us the benefit of his radar experience and pilot's lore.

Captains Miller and Johnson of Britannia Airways described for us the intricacies of the Boeing 737's safety procedures, and Mr. Robert Sceats of the Civil Aviation Authority was good enough to track down a number of aircraft accident reports.

Finally, we wish to acknowledge the unfailing support of Sheila Bingham, who must know every word of the book as intimately as its authors, and who suggested a number of invaluable additions to the scientific content.

To all these people we offer our sincere thanks, as we do to those who —because of the sensitive nature of their jobs—cannot be thanked publicly. If we have made mistakes, the fault rests entirely with us.

London, 1973   Raymond Hawkey
                                                                 Roger Bingham